THESE SEXY HUNKS ARE LARGER THAN LIFE,
HARD BODIES WHO ARE

Playing Easy to Get

From *New York Times* bestselling author *Sherrilyn Kenyon* comes "Turn Up the Heat," the story of an average woman who wins the vacation of a lifetime—a trip to Sex Camp. But what Allison George gets is a race for her life with none other than an ex-Mafia hit man who is now being sought by his prior employer. Vince Cappelleti knew the island was a risky proposition, but he'd run out of options. Now the only thing he wants in his sights is Allison, but in order to have a future with her, he must first deal with his past.

Jaid Black's sizzling hot "Hunter's Oath" sends grief-stricken Sofia Rowley to the Arctic Circle, where her brother, a U.S. Army officer, was lost in a deadly helicopter crash. She's about to take a shocking journey into a secret underground world where Viking bride-hunters auction off their bounty . . . and where a strapping warrior vows to make this beautiful Outsider *his*.

Possession and passion entwine in *Kresley Cole*'s sultry story, "The Warlord Wants Forever." Nikolai Wroth, a ruthless vampire warlord, searches for his Bride—the one woman who can render him truly alive. When his fevered chase leads to Myst the Coveted, a Valkyrie seductress who craves only freedom, a battle of domination and desire begins. Will the power of her seductive wiles overcome his strength? Or will she surrender and experience the deliciously agonizing lust that Nikolai has endured waiting for his one and only Bride?

OTHER EROTICA ANTHOLOGIES FROM POCKET BOOKS

Big Guns Out of Uniform
Four Degrees of Heat
Tie Me Up, Tie Me Down
Kiss the Year Goodbye

Playing
EASY TO GET

SHERRILYN KENYON

JAID BLACK

KRESLEY COLE

POCKET BOOKS

New York • London • Toronto • Sydney

POCKET BOOKS, a division of Simon & Schuster, Inc.
1230 Avenue of the Americas, New York, NY 10020

Library of Congress Cataloging-in-Publication Data is available

ISBN-13: 978–1–4165–1087–1
ISBN-10:   1–4165–1087–7

This Pocket Books trade paperback edition February 2006

10 9 8 7 6 5 4 3 2 1

Manufactured in the United States of America

For information regarding special discounts for bulk purchases,
please contact Simon & Schuster Special Sales at 1–800–456–6798 or
business@simonandschuster.com.

CONTENTS

Turn Up the Heat

SHERRILYN KENYON

PROLOGUE

*V*ince Cappelleti had dodged the bullet. Literally. It had cut so close to his head that he'd felt the wind burn all the way down to his DNA.

Luckily, he possessed reflexes that made lightning look slow—something he could thank Uncle Sam and a childhood spent on the New York City streets for. Not to mention that he'd always been able to think quickly and move his ass when he had to.

And tonight he'd had to.

Now there was nowhere to hide where they wouldn't find him. No one he could turn to for fear of betrayal or of them dying because of him.

Vince was alone. Then again, he'd been that way most of his life.

He didn't dare go to the authorities—they would only get him killed even faster than taking his chances on the street. Their brand of protection was a joke and all they would do is get in his way and cause a lot more innocent people to die.

He didn't dare leave the city by car, bus or plane. If he left a trail of any sort, they would find him.

If he breathed wrong, they would find him.

Basically, he was screwed, and not in the good way.

Vince let out a long, tired breath as he leaned against the brick wall and loosened his grip on the .45 that had once again saved his life.

He'd slipped into the dark alley and escaped the hit men who were hot on his ass. But they would be back. Sooner or later, they would discover his trick and double back to find him.

He heard a car approaching.

His heart racing, Vince raised his weapon, ready to do whatever he had to do to survive this night.

The hiss of rain and the drone of the engine echoed in his ears. It was moving slowly, methodically . . . looking for him, most likely.

He aimed for the opening of the alley, lining up for his shot.

Then he saw the black stretch limo that gleamed in the rain. In this neighborhood, it could be only one person. He smirked at the thought.

So Gino Martelli had come himself. He was honored. It wasn't often Gino got his hands dirty anymore.

Fine. Let them have this out then. It was time he and Gino set things right between them.

Just as Vince was ready to open fire, the door opened.

Instead of gunshots, he heard a low, deep command. "Get in."

It took a full ten seconds to register the voice. It was one he hadn't heard in a long time, and it wasn't Gino's.

Vince glanced around to make sure no one could see him, then he dodged into the car and slammed the door shut behind him.

Soaking wet from the rain, he threw himself into the long seat that curved around behind where the driver was on the other side of the raised partition.

"You planning on shooting me?" Z asked.

Vince glanced down to the gun in his hand. He flipped the safety on and then straightened up in the seat to face the man who had once been his brother-in-law.

But more than that, Wulfgar Zimmerman had once been his friend. At least as much as a troubled juvenile delinquent and a straight-laced boy genius could be friends.

"What are you doing here, Z?" he asked.

"Saving your ass, what else?" He tossed him a towel.

Vince grabbed the towel and rubbed it against his dripping black hair. "And how did you find my ass?"

Z smiled at that. "I have my ways."

Vince glanced around the limo and remembered the kids they had been. Back in the run-down Staten Island neighborhood where they'd grown up, they had only dreamed of ever being inside a car like this. Z had earned his limo through hard work and legal investments.

Vince had earned his in much less refined and legal ways.

But he had to admit, he was strangely proud of Z, who had been a scrawny kid. Vince had spent most of their childhood beating the shit out of the other kids who wanted to pick on Z.

There was no trace of that skinny kid now. Z was one of the richest men in the country. His black Armani power suit and black silk shirt were refined. With long, dark brown hair, a small goatee and a muscular build that would rival his own, Z looked like he could now beat the shit out of anyone dumb enough to cross him.

Z offered him a silver flask.

Draping the towel over his shoulder, Vince grabbed it without asking what it was and took a drink to find it contained brandy. The good stuff. He wiped his mouth with the back of his hand before he took another drink.

"I moved your mother into my house," Z said. "I've got security guards all over her."

Vince choked as his stomach sank. "She knows?"

"No. I told her that I was the one under threat and that since she's my mother-in-law someone might hurt her wanting to get to me. She didn't question it."

She wouldn't. His father had once been a bagman for the family, which meant she was used to obeying without asking questions.

Vince was relieved at the news. The last thing on earth he wanted was for his mother to learn the truth about him or, God forbid, be hurt because he was an idiot.

He narrowed his eyes on Z. "How did *you* know about me?"

His bland expression didn't change. "I know everything you've done since you left the Marines, Vince. *Everything.*"

He expected condemnation from Z, but he didn't get it.

Z merely sat there, quietly watching him as his driver moved them through the busy city streets.

"Did you ever tell Susan?" he asked Z.

"No. I loved my wife too much for that. It would have killed her to know what her big brother was doing with his life. I let her think you were a legitimate businessman."

He inclined his head in gratitude. Z had always been a good man. Since Vince's sister Susan had died, Z had spent his life honoring her memory and watching out for Vince's mother. "Thanks, Z. I owe you."

"No you don't. I owe you for all the years you kept watch over my sisters and Susan . . . not to mention all the ass-beatings you took on my behalf."

Vince snorted. "No one ever got the better of me, Wulf. You know that."

Z smiled in agreement.

Vince took another swig of brandy, then returned his .45 to his concealed holster. "Where are you taking me anyway?"

"I have a private plane waiting at the airport. No one but me knows the destination. The pilot has the coordinates in a sealed envelope and he won't open them until after takeoff. Then he'll be routed off for a two-month vacation on an island someplace where no one can find him. Believe me, I'm sending you somewhere safe."

Vince had a hard time believing that. He knew the people who wanted him dead, and his life didn't lend itself to optimism. "What about Gino?"

"I'll take care of it."

"How?"

"Don't worry. There are things in life a hell of a lot more frightening than cops and death to a man like him."

Yes, there were. But Vince wasn't stupid enough to believe for one minute that Gino would ever let him go no matter what Z threatened him with.

Vince knew too much.

He had done too much.

Still, this was his best bet for extending his life beyond tonight. So long as he was in New York, his life expectancy was about eight seconds. Here he was in the heart of Gino's territory.

Anywhere else, and Gino would be at a disadvantage.

It was a long shot Vince was willing to take.

CHAPTER ONE

*I*f there was a Richter scale for erotic experiences, this one would shatter the record.

Robin Daniels moaned deep in her throat as her lover's hand slid slowly up the inside of her thigh in an electrifying caress that culminated with his long, lean fingers stroking her between her thighs where she was wet and hot, waiting for him. She'd been craving him for weeks now. This man with the perfect male body, killer smile and eyes so green they didn't seem to be real.

Perfect lips that quirked up with a wicked charm. Lips that did naughty things to her body. She couldn't wait to feel his cock deep and hard inside her. To hold him close while he thrust himself into her over and over until they were both sweaty and spent.

His touch set her on fire.

But if either one of them were ever caught during one of their secret meetings, their lives would be over.

Their love would be over.

So he came to her at night like some incubus who needed to feed from her body.

She could deny him nothing. Whatever he asked, she would gladly cede.

Opening her legs, Robin gave him full access to the part of her that craved him most. The part of her that was aching and wet, desperate for his touch.

It was an invitation he took boldly as he slid his fingers even deeper inside her, seeking out her warmth and making her body burn with frenzied lust.

Robin hissed, arching her back. Her breasts tightened, straining against the cotton of her T-shirt.

"That's it," he said, his voice deep and husky. "Show me how much you want me."

"I want you, baby," she murmured, barely recognizing her own voice as she took his hard cock into her hand and toyed with the sensitive tip of it.

Oh yes, he felt good there. She let his wetness coat her fingers while she stroked him, exploring the hard, long length of him. She ran her hungry fingers over the thick, heavy vein, down lower until she could cup his sac in her palm.

He groaned at her gentle caress.

She captured his lips with hers, tugging his bottom lip between her teeth as she tasted him fully.

Before this night was over, she would make him hers for all eternity.

After tonight, Brendan would never want another woman.

She was going to ride him until he begged her for mercy. . . .

"Allison. Cleanup, aisle five."

Allison George jerked her head up from her book as she heard her name called over the intercom. It wasn't until the manager had repeated his command that she left her dream world completely.

Damn. She was just getting to the really good part.

It never failed.

Sighing, she flipped to the front of the book and looked wistfully at the advertisement.

What's your fantasy?

Do you ever dream of getting away from it all? Just for a week or two?

Have you ever read a romance novel and thought . . .

What if?

Have you ever, just once, wanted to be the heroine in a book and to have the man of your dreams come in and rock your world?

Your dreams could come true. Enter the Hideaway Heroine Sweepstakes and you too could be headed off to be the heroine in your favorite romance novel. Just send in your name, address and phone number, the title and author of your favorite book and the reason(s) why you need a break from your everyday life.

Two lucky winners will be selected every three months. No purchase necessary. Enter as many times as you like.

For more information, please visit HideawayHeroine.com.

Good luck!

Allison ran her hand over the words. Had she ever dreamed of getting away?

Was Brendan about to give Robin the best sex of her life?

Was he primo fabuloso?

Of course she dreamed of getting away. Every minute of every day. Unfortunately, that seemed about as likely as Brendan stepping out of his book and making her his fantasy lover.

Or of a house landing on top of her evil floor manager during a tornado and putting him out of her misery.

And speaking of the devil, he was headed straight for her. Allison hid her novel behind her back as her manager came down the book aisle with a stern grimace on his face. At fifty-two with salt and pepper hair, Dan might have been attractive at some point, but the constant disdainful sneer robbed him of any appeal.

"Allison, there's a toddler who threw up on aisle five. Move your butt. We can't leave it there for someone to step in." He barely looked her way as he went past her.

Oh yeah, her life was just one great big bowl full of cherries.

If she was really lucky, maybe on her way home some uninsured driver would plow into her beat-up Dodge Neon and total it while leaving her completely hale and whole enough to walk back to work tomorrow and mop up more vomit. She sighed in disgust.

Wondering if she had just in fact conjured up another visit from the Bad Luck Fairy, Allison tucked the romance novel into her smock pocket.

For weeks now she'd been carrying it around, rereading the entry form and debating on whether or not she should enter.

But why bother?

No one like her ever won anything anyway. It was always some rich doctor or lawyer. Someone other than her. Someone who didn't really need the money or the break.

Still that tiny voice in her head kept saying, "Yeah, but maybe this once . . ."

She hated that voice. It had gotten her into plenty of trouble in her life.

Grabbing a broom and the special dry solution she needed to clean up the mess, Allison went to the aisle and tried not to think about just how much she truly hated her job.

As she worked, a small smile hovered at her lips. *Hey look, I'm already Cinderella. All they need to do is send me over to housewares with the fireplaces and have me clean those out and I'm in business.*

"Ally?"

She looked up and it took a full second for the voice to register. It was one she hadn't heard in way too long.

Margaret Dale.

The two of them had been best friends in high school. And in the ten years since they had graduated, Margaret hadn't changed a bit.

"Maggie May!" she exclaimed, using her old nickname for her friend.

The broom forgotten, Allison hugged her tight, grateful to see a friendly face again. "Good Lord, how long has it been?"

"Six or seven years, at least."

Allison's eyes teared up as she stepped back. Maggie's elegant blond hair was pulled back in a sleek ponytail. She wore a black pair of slacks and a chic, short-sleeved black sweater. But then Maggie had always looked like some fashion model walking away from a shoot. "You look fantastic!"

Maggie beamed, until she looked Allison up and down

and then the smile faltered. Not in a condescending way, but in a way that said, "I'm sorry I got out and you got trapped in this godforsaken place."

Allison offered her a joking grin, even though a part of her was mortified at what she knew Maggie saw.

She stood in front of her elegant friend in her dark blue polyester smock, ill-fitting jeans and faded-out, oversized shirt. Worse, her own frizzy blond hair was in bad need of a trim and deep conditioning. Neither of which she could afford at the moment.

"I'm sorry about your mom," Margaret said quietly. "Had I known, I would have been here for the funeral."

Allison patted her arm as her throat tightened. She'd loved her mother more than anything. Ten years ago when she and Maggie had graduated high school, Maggie had gone to the University of Georgia, then moved off to New York after graduation to be an editor. Meanwhile, Allison had stayed home to help her mother, who was dying of cancer. For nine years her mother had fought hard and then last spring, she'd lost the war.

God, how she missed her. It was still a raw, aching pain inside her. Her mother had been everything to her.

"I know," she said, rubbing Maggie's arm. "I'm sorry. I didn't even think about sending word to you until after the funeral was over. I just wasn't in my right mind."

Maggie nodded in understanding. "You've been busy. My mom told me that you're engaged to Gary Mitchell. Congrats. I know how much you always loved him."

Allison drew a shaky breath as she thought about her rattlesnake ex. "Yeah," she said in an overly exaggerated tone. "Just l-o-v-e him to pieces."

"Uh-oh. That sounds ominous."

She sighed as she picked up the broom. "Well, I found the dog in bed a week ago with one of the strippers from the Night Owl."

Maggie's face showed the horror Allison had felt when she'd stumbled in late from work to find the two of them going at it in her bed. "No!"

"Oh yeah."

"What did you do?"

"I grabbed my broom, swept both pieces of trash out of my house, then I went through and decided it was time to do a little fall cleaning. I gathered up everything of his I could find, threw it into a pile on my front lawn and then proceeded to have a weenie roast. I'm told you could see the flames for up to a mile away."

Maggie laughed. "What did Gary do?"

"He called the cops and I spent the night in jail. But it was so worth it. I just wish I'd been able to get my shotgun loaded before the police got there and had had a chance to fill his backside with buckshot. . . ."

"Allison? Are you on break?"

Allison cringed at Dan's voice coming from behind her. She looked around to see his soured frown. "I'm just helping a customer, Dan. She wanted to know where the lightbulbs were."

He didn't buy it for a minute.

Allison led Maggie away from his hearing. "Sorry, Maggie, I can't really talk right now."

Nodding, Maggie let her gaze dip down to the pocket of Allison's smock where the top of her book was peeking out. She smiled. *"Sugar and Spice* by Rachel Fire. You like it?"

"I love it. It's a great book."

Maggie's smile widened. "I edited it."

"You did not!"

"Yes, I did. She's one of the authors I discovered last year." Maggie tilted her head and looked back down the aisle to where Dan was still watching them. "Look, I don't want to get you into trouble. What time do you get off work?"

"Midnight."

"Okay, I'll be waiting out in the front lot with a pizza, a pack of Ho Hos and beer. Sound good?"

Allison laughed. When Maggie had been a college student, they would always celebrate her homecomings with pizza, Ho Hos and beer. A disgusting and yet somehow quite tasty salute.

"Sounds great. I'll see you in three hours."

Maggie stepped away from Allison, and headed straight toward the middle-aged floor manager who had been eyeballing them with tangible rancor.

"That's a great employee you have there," Maggie said to him. "She really knows the store."

He gave her a semi-hostile glare and walked off, leaving her with the childish desire to stick her tongue out at the soured beast.

But that would wait.

Pulling her phone out of her pocket, Maggie turned to see Allison straightening shelves.

She checked her wristwatch.

It was right at nine o'clock, and she knew exactly where her boss would be. Where he always was . . . sitting at his desk, working late into the night.

Z answered his cell phone on the third ring.

"Hey, Mr. Z, shouldn't you be at home?" It was an old joke between them. In truth, she was just as bad to work late as he was. But then she loved her job as an editor and as the head contest coordinator, and as a result, she had a hard time leaving her work behind at the end of the day.

"And why are you calling me at nine o'clock when you're supposed to be on vacation?" he asked in that deep sexy/provocative voice that always made her shiver.

But not nearly as much as the breathtaking man who held it. At six foot four, with a lean, rippling body that had been built for sweaty, exhausting sex, Wulfgar Zimmerman was one of the sexiest men who had ever been born.

"Oh because I've found us a live one," Maggie said. "Allison George. I went to high school with her and if she isn't a prime candidate for Hideaway Heroine, then I'm not a workaholic and you're not rich."

Z was silent.

Maggie imagined him sitting at his large mahogany desk, staring out onto his breathtaking view of the New York skyline with the light of his desk lamp cutting across the chiseled planes of his face.

Wulfgar Zimmerman, Z to his friends and family, was one of the richest men in the world.

He was also the loneliest.

Though to be honest, Maggie couldn't figure out why. There were plenty of women, herself included, who would practically sell their souls to call him their own. But Z wasn't interested. Ever since his wife had died three years ago, he'd withdrawn from the world.

She wondered if anyone would ever be able to reach him again.

"Island B is open," he said at last. "You set things up on your end and let me know what you need to do to put this plan into motion."

"You got it, boss."

"And Maggie?"

"Yes?"

"Try not to work too much while you're at home. Enjoy your family. There's nothing else like them in the world."

She smiled. Z was also the kindest man she'd ever known. No wonder everyone in the company was so loyal to him. He didn't believe in treating them like employees. He treated them like family.

"I will. 'Night."

He answered in kind, then hung up.

Maggie turned her phone off as she glanced back to where Allison was helping a customer.

Little did her friend know, her life was about to take an unexpected turn.

Nothing would ever be the same for Allison again.

CHAPTER TWO

Three weeks later

"What exactly is Hideaway Heroine?" Allison asked Maggie while they sat inside the famed Elizabeth Arden Beauty Salon, where Allison was being pampered like a queen.

Allison had only dreamed of ever coming to New York, never mind having a makeover at one of the most prestigious beauty salons in the world.

She still couldn't believe she'd won the drawing. Any more than she could believe the size of the limo that had picked her up at the Newark airport and brought her to the Waldorf-Astoria where she would stay for the next two days while they bought her a wardrobe and made her into Robin Daniels from the book.

It was a dream come true.

"Hideaway Heroine is kind of like Fantasy Island," Maggie explained. "For one week, you get to live there as anyone you want to be. You can do anything you want to do,

eat anything that appeals to you and best of all, you're surrounded by nothing but gorgeous men who will wait on
you hand and foot."

Now that sounded like something far beyond wonderful.
Imagine an island of men at your beck and call . . . yum!

"Are you serious?"

"Oh yeah." Maggie smiled. "Just wait until you see these
guys. You are going to think you've died and gone to heaven."

She already had that feeling. "Is it safe?"

"Absolutely. There will be security guards hidden among
the men. Nothing happens on the island unless you want it
to. Everything there is geared for you and your tastes. Only
your favorite foods will be offered, all the places you stay will
be the colors you choose—that's why you filled out that
stack of forms when you won."

Allison leaned back in the chair as the pedicurist came
over and started to work on her feet.

Wow. This was the most unbelievable moment of her life.
The sweepstakes had really paid off for her. In addition to
the week of heaven, she'd also received ten thousand dollars
in cash and a brand-new car. It was more than she'd ever
dreamed of having.

"Thank you, Maggie."

"For what?"

"For letting me win this."

Maggie looked aghast at her. "I had nothing to do with
it."

Yeah, right. Allison waved her words away. "I'm not stupid, you know. I've never won anything in my life. Then

you show up, make me fill out the entry form and the next thing I know, I'm getting a phone call telling me I've won. I know you pulled a few strings and I really appreciate it."

"I promise you, it wasn't me. If you want to thank someone, thank Mr. Z when he picks you up at the hotel and takes you to the airport. He's the one who bought the islands and set this up for the winners."

Allison thought about the mysterious billionaire whose acts of charity were legendary. The tabloids and papers were full of how Wulfgar Zimmerman spent more money than he kept.

"How many islands are there?" she asked Maggie.

"There are three where you're going. All of them linked together by bridges. Z owns eight of them altogether in different parts of the world."

"And they're set up just to make someone's dreams come true?"

"Yes."

Allison had never believed in fairy tales before. But for the first time in her life, she was beginning to. "You must have a great boss."

"You have no idea."

"Ma'am?" the pedicurist asked.

Allison turned toward her. "Yes?"

"What color would you like your toenails?"

"Red," she said without hesitation. "Fire-engine red." Robin Daniels wouldn't be caught dead in anything less than that. And for the next week, she was going to toss off her old shell and bust loose.

Watch out world, Allison George was going to sow some wild oats.

Or at the very least scatter a few dandelions.

She looked back at Maggie while the lady began painting her toenails. "So what happens to me when I get to the island?"

"Your biker group will meet you at the airport and 'Harry,' Robin's supposed biker boyfriend, will put you on his motorcycle. You and the gang will ride out to Dino's Bar and Grill, where you'll have dinner and play some pool."

"Until Brendan shows up?"

"Just like in the book."

Allison liked the sound of that until she remembered what else was in the book. Robin and Brendan made out like bunnies whose only mission in life was to create their own population explosion.

She wasn't a virgin, but her sex life had never been much to talk about. She'd always been painfully shy and body-conscious—something her ex hadn't helped as he complained about her extra pounds. Unlike Robin, the real life Allison wasn't some svelte bombshell. She was a nice and even size fourteen, which at five foot five wasn't fat, but it was a far, far cry from the skinny ideal.

And if the guy pretending to be Brendan really looked like the "god" Brendan in the book, he was more likely to run in the other direction than he was to approach her.

This was not good.

"Will I be expected to . . ." She bit her lip as she looked uncomfortably at the woman at her feet. "You know," Allison tried again, "will he treat me like Brendan treated Robin . . . and as many times as Brendan treated Robin?"

Maggie laughed as she caught her meaning. "What happens between you and Brendan is up to you and you alone. What you do period on the island is up to you. Everyone there is a consenting adult and no one will ever be forced to do what they don't want to. But when it comes to *that,* we have a strict don't ask, don't tell policy. Everything is in your hands. You can take your fantasy just as far as you want to."

"What if he doesn't like me?"

"What's not to like? Besides, this is your fantasy, girl. You can rewrite the book any way you desire. Believe me, there will be plenty of other guys around so that if you and Brendan don't hit it off, I'm sure you can find someone appealing. I've seen some of these guys. They will all curl those red toenails until your feet look like corkscrews."

Allison liked the sound of that. In her small Georgia town, there were only a handful of truly spectacular men and all of them were taken.

She couldn't imagine being anywhere with an abundance of perfect male specimens.

She shivered in excitement.

The hairdresser returned. "I need to put her under the dryer for a few minutes."

Maggie nodded. "I'll go grab us some Cokes."

Allison got up and dutifully followed the beautician to her new seat. She leaned back as the beautician lowered the hood and turned the heat on.

Closing her eyes, she conjured up an image of Brendan from the book. Oh yeah. Tall, blond and gorgeous, he was the kind of guy that could make a woman melt.

What would it be like to actually touch that body? To kiss those lips and run her hands over his naked skin? To run her tongue over his stubbled cheek and glide his rigid shaft into her body?

She'd never had the kind of mind-blowing, stop-the-clock sex she read about in books. Gary had made her happy before she found out about his extracurricular activities, but he had never made her burn. Never made her scream out in a blinding orgasm.

She wasn't really sure if any man was able to do that to a woman.

Maybe it was all a myth.

But what if it's not?

Three weeks ago, she would never have believed that a minimum-wage worker from backwoods Georgia would be sitting in Elizabeth Arden in New York getting a pedicure either.

Imagine. Her on an island full of men whose only job was to make her happy.

Allison shook with nervous expectation and excitement. Forget her shy, awkward self. For the next week, she was going to be Robin Daniels. Femme fatale. Woman of the world who could get any man she wanted.

Watch out island. This little country girl was finally going to get her due!

★   ★   ★

Allison spent the next two days with Maggie, shopping and preparing herself mentally and physically for the coming week of fun.

When Wednesday morning arrived, she was as nervous as a three-tailed cat in a rocking chair factory. All of her new clothes had been taken first thing to the airport.

Now she was waiting for the mysterious Wulfgar Zimmerman to appear.

Maggie had warned her that Z never spoke much and that he always greeted the winners personally. She couldn't imagine what he must be like. Maggie hadn't really gone into it.

Someone knocked on the door.

Allison jumped up and rushed toward it, then reminded herself that she was Robin.

Robin never ran, she moved slowly, seductively.

Oh to hell with that, she ran to the door and opened it, then gaped like an idiot as she caught sight of the most incredibly handsome man she'd ever seen.

Z stood a good six foot four in a pair of faded jeans that hugged a body made for nibbling. He wore his dark brown hair just past his shoulders in a careless style that said he wasn't into his looks.

Still, it was devastating.

He was devastating.

A pair of black sunglasses covered his eyes and he had at least three days' worth of stubble on his face. He looked dark, mysterious.

Dangerous.

In no way did he resemble some billionaire tycoon who spent his life trying to make other people's dreams come true. He looked more like a movie star heartbreaker.

No wonder Maggie had told her most people in his office building thought he worked in the mail room. Rich men were not supposed to look like *this*.

"Hi," she said, her heart pounding.

He inclined his head. "You ready?"

All she could do was nod.

Z held the door open for her as she numbly walked through it. Then he pulled the door closed and led her toward the elevators. "Have you enjoyed your stay here?"

She nodded again while he pushed the button for the elevator.

Of its own accord, her gaze swept down the back of him . . . over his black motorcycle jacket that displayed his wide shoulders to perfection, to his lean hips and butt that were covered in denim.

Oh yeah, this man had one finely shaped rump.

Grrrrowl . . .

Suddenly, she realized Z was watching her from the mirror on the wall between the elevators. That he could see her blatant case of Ogle-the-Stud.

Covering her face, she felt her cheeks grow hot. Please, please let her die now before she embarrassed herself even worse!

Z didn't say a word as the elevator doors on the right opened.

Following him inside, she struggled hard to regain her

dignity. He removed his sunglasses and pressed the button for the lobby.

As the elevator doors closed behind them, she tried not to stare at how blue his eyes were. Were those real or contacts? Surely no one had eyes that color.

"Will you be coming to the island too?" she asked.

He certainly looked like what she thought a biker should look like. Especially with that deadly air of darkness that seemed ingrained in him.

"No. I'll be in touch though, just to make sure everything is going the way you want it to. If you have any problems, there will be a man there named Vince. Tell Vince and he'll get ahold of me ASAP."

Pity he wouldn't be there. Not that it mattered.

An average woman like her would never appeal to a man like this one. Just being near him made her sweat.

He led her out of the hotel and down to the street where she expected another limo. Instead, he took her toward a shiny black Harley.

"We're riding this?"

Again he inclined his head with a smile. "You wanted to be a biker's moll. No time like now to get into the spirit of it."

He handed her a helmet. Z straddled the bike, pulled his own helmet on, then kick-started the Harley.

Allison put her helmet on before climbing onto the bike behind him.

"Hold tight," he said over his shoulder.

Oh baby, she did. She held on to every inch of his lean,

muscular body and wondered if Brendan would feel this good between her legs.

Allison!

She grinned at herself and the lascivious thoughts in her mind. To the devil with her bashful past. She was Robin now and Robin grabbed life with both hands. She took what she wanted and enjoyed life to the fullest.

For the next seven days, Allison would too.

Determined to put the past behind her, she watched them speed past the New York traffic. At long last, she really was headed into her wildest fantasies.

Watch out Brendan Tucker. Allison George was about to let loose every inhibition she ever had. Before she was through, she fully intended to ride something other than his Harley.

CHAPTER THREE

*V*ince Cappelleti had never been anyone's fool, but as he stood out on the tarmac waiting for the private jet to land, he felt like the biggest jackass ever born.

What the hell was he doing here?

He rubbed his jaw as he surveyed the "men" around him. Jeremy Winslow—Vince didn't even want to contemplate the white-bread, prep-school cadence of that name—stood to his left, dressed in ragged jeans and a biker jacket. The blond man's hair was cut like a politician's and his smile gleamed so bright that Vince figured every tooth in the man's head had to be a cap.

Jeremy was to play Brendan Tucker, DEA agent, who was trying to infiltrate the biker gang he suspected of killing his brother.

The only thing Vince suspected Jeremy wanted to infiltrate was Bobby Sloan, the guy who was supposed to play Harry Braxton, biker leader.

It was enough to make him laugh.

The ten actors around him were too neat and clean to be the kind of men they portrayed. Men he'd known all his life. The kind of guys who lived hard and if they were lucky, died young.

"The plane's on its way in," Jeremy said, smiling that capped-tooth smile. "I'll head out and meet up with you guys later. Ta-ta."

Vince ground his teeth. *Ta-freakin'-ta?* What the hell was that? Man, in the Staten Island neighborhood where he'd grown up, they would have eaten this pack of guys for breakfast and used their bones to pick their teeth.

Suddenly the idea of handing himself over to Gino Martelli started to look appealing.

What were a few bullet holes and torture when compared to *this*?

"Okay," Bobby said, turning to face them. "Remember, we are Hell's Angels and we're supposed to be dark and deadly." Bobby nodded at Vince. "Follow Vince's lead. He has the look down to a fine art."

If the kid only knew.

Vince's menacing presence wasn't from practice. It was from growing up hard on the streets where any weakness was quickly found and either exploited or eliminated.

In Vince's case, he'd eliminated his before he'd started kindergarten.

He watched as the actors fell into their roles. Each man on the island had been handpicked to lead a double life. Every place and person here had but one function.

They were to make someone's dreams come true.

And as hokey and stupid as it sounded, a part of him admired Z for what he'd accomplished.

Even more so because Z had done it to honor Susan. Only she could have conceived of something this preposterous, and God love Z for having loved her enough to carry out her dreams of helping other women.

Susan had held a heart unlike any person Vince had ever known. His sister had been as good as he was bad.

All their lives, she'd tried to explain to him that it was wrong to use people. That other people's lives, no matter how insignificant they seemed, mattered.

He'd never understood that until one night eight months ago when he'd come face-to-face with himself in the back room of a Portuguese restaurant down in the Ironbound in Jersey.

In one instant, he had seen himself for what he really was: a cold-blooded killer who had sold himself to the devil.

Now he was trying to buy his soul back, only the devil didn't seem real keen on the thought of letting him go.

So here he was, hidden on an island paradise where he hoped no one would ever find him again. No one except a bunch of odd actors who were pretending to be characters out of a book.

Just what kind of crazy fantasy was this anyway?

"Go with it, Vince," Z had said. *"All you have to do is add flavor to the group. Ride around for a week on a Harley and just look like your normal, ruthless self."*

Vince still didn't know how Z had talked him into this. But then talking people into stuff was what Z did best.

The plane landed.

Vince wasn't sure what to expect from the woman who had won the sweepstakes. Even though he'd been on the island now for eight months, he had yet to meet one of the winners.

He imagined most women who read romances to be like his mother, who'd always been addicted to them. Older women who kept their books sandwiched between plastic covers so that no one would know what they read.

If he was right and some matronly woman stepped off that plane, then Bobby and Jeremy certainly had their jobs cut out for them. They were about to earn every cent of their exorbitant salaries.

And the more he thought about it, the more he hoped the woman on the plane was some matronly grandmother. That he could cope with.

God help him if she were attractive. It'd been almost a year since he'd last had a woman in his bed, and he was seriously getting tired of going without. Damn Z for not having women on the island. The only ones he'd seen to date had been Z's two sisters, and as hard up as he was, he wasn't about to trespass there. Shanna and Aislinn were definitely knockouts, but touching them would be like dating his own sister.

He shuddered at the thought.

The stairs came down and out of the plane emerged a woman.

Vince cursed as soon as he saw her. "Someone grab a gun and kill me," he muttered under his breath. This wasn't fair.

No doubt this was God's way of getting back at him for the life he'd been living.

The woman coming down those stairs was the very thing a *fannullone* like him didn't deserve to even look at.

She was blond and curvy like a wholesome dairy maid from some middle-American state like Wisconsin. Hell, he half expected her to have a quart of milk in one hand and a piece of cheese in the other.

Her long blond hair was braided down each side of her face and she had the biggest pair of blue eyes he'd ever seen.

Sweet. That was the only word to describe her. And he desperately wanted to take a bite out of that lush, luminescent skin to see if she tasted as good as she looked.

His cock hardened instantly, straining against his fly in a demanding need to sample some of that dairy maid's cream.

It was hard for him to breathe.

She came toward them hesitantly. He could tell by the uneasy way she moved that someone had dressed her in a pair of leather pants and jacket with a white T-shirt. She didn't wear those clothes comfortably. Rather, they were like an alien skin.

But he had to admit that she looked damn good in them. Especially the jacket. The rough leather edges of it rubbed up against her nipples, making them hard and obvious underneath the thin cotton tee.

He swallowed as he imagined taking one of those hard nipples into his mouth and sucking and teasing the taut edges of it with his tongue until she came for him.

Better yet, he would love to taste her orgasm. To watch

her head rolling back and forth on a pillow as he drove himself deep inside her sweet, round body.

His erection throbbed with a predator's need.

This wholesome piece of pie was nothing like the confident women he'd known in his life. Women who had been users like him. Women who were after a better life, or a quick lay.

The Dairy Maid just looked like . . .

Peaches and cream. Most of all, she was unattainable and that made some inner part of him shrivel.

She chewed her nail nervously. He shifted his feet, trying to alleviate some of the pain of his engorged cock. Did she have any idea how sexy she looked when she did that?

Her guileless blue eyes said that she was completely clueless.

"Harry?" she asked, her voice tinged with a southern lilt that shivered like electricity down his spine.

Bobby stepped forward. "Hi, Robin. You ready to ride?"

She might not be, but Vince most certainly was ready to ride.

Her anyway.

Her smile flashed a set of dimples. Oh man, now that was truly cruel. *Damn you, Z.*

Vince ground his teeth as she climbed up on the back of Bobby's bike. The leather cupped her ass in a way that should have been illegal.

Oh yeah. He stared at her with an aching hunger he hadn't felt in a long, long time.

All too easily, he could imagine walking up to her and

running his hands over her hips, sliding those leather pants off until he had her naked in his arms.

Better still, he imagined her spreading her legs and sliding up over his seat. . . .

Vince hissed in appreciation.

This woman stirred the predator inside him. The part of him that was willing to do *anything* to get what it wanted. It was a part of him that scared him because he knew exactly how far he would go when he saw something he lusted for. And the last thing a woman like her needed was to be sullied with something like him.

No. Dairy maids and farm girls with smooth Southern drawls belonged to clean-cut prep boys like Jeremy and Bobby. They didn't belong with an ex-Mafia hit man whose life would be forfeit as soon as Gino found the right person to bribe or torture.

Vince slung his long leg over his black Harley and kick-started it as he watched her wrap her arms around Bobby's waist.

Envy stabbed him.

At the end of the day, Vince was still nothing more than that half-starved kid standing out on the street corner, looking up at the rich brownstones owned by the private school kids.

The kids who got to go to the prom in limos and wearing tuxes that didn't come from Uncle Sal's mortuary.

He'd dreamed then of being rich enough to one day walk down those streets without decent women crossing the road to avoid him, or nervous housekeepers eyeballing him from the windows, afraid he was casing their places for a hit.

What he'd found was that all the money in the world had never erased the taint of what his father had been.

What Vince himself had become.

Z had been lucky. He had somehow managed to escape their blighted past. Vince never had.

And he never would.

Allison was simply giddy as they rode over the beautiful island. It was like something out of a dream.

Even though it was fall, everything was still lush and green. Not too hot. Not too cold.

Perfect!

Just like the biker she rode behind.

Don't anyone pinch me, because if I wake up from this, I'm going to punch someone's lights out.

She laughed as they rode into a parking lot that was filled with more motorcycles. The roadhouse club was a dive. Complete with run-down boards that had been spray-painted and a sign exalting its exotic dancers.

It was just like the book.

She had to remind herself to get off the bike slowly and to saunter after Harry.

He led her into the dark bar where there were more bikers dressed in leather and denim. Some sat at the bar drinking. Others sat at tables and booths where they were playing cards and eating while others were playing pool or just lounging. There were no women anywhere to be found, and every guy there was absolutely stunning.

Jackson, the bartender was at the bar, using a rag to mop out glasses. He snarled at Harry, who grimaced back.

Allison beamed. This was better than a movie. Oh how she loved it.

Harry led his men to the vacant tables in the back corner. Tables that were always left open in the event they showed up—that's because in the book everyone was afraid of Harry. It was rumored he had killed a dozen DEA agents who were trying to bust him for running drugs.

And two of them because they had looked at Robin with lust in their eyes.

Allison had to admit the man playing Harry didn't look like he could even step on a cockroach without having guilt, never mind kill a man, but he was cute. There was something about him that vaguely reminded her of her ex-boyfriend, Gary.

She sat down at their table and watched as the rest of their gang filed in. The guys inclined their heads to her respectfully. In a strange way, they reminded her of Boy Scouts.

Until she saw the one pulling up the rear.

Now he looked deadly.

Dark.

Dangerous.

And he made the blood pound through her veins. Standing just over six feet, he had long hair as black as jet. His tanned, masculine skin was stretched tight over one of the most beguiling bodies she'd ever seen in her life.

Black jeans hugged long legs and his black T-shirt only

emphasized the width of his shoulders, and the definition of his well-developed pecs and abs. A pair of dark glasses obscured his eyes, but they only accentuated the sharp, clean cut of his face.

This was the kind of guy you might find on a soap opera, except for the fact that he seemed more sinister than a cobra lying across your foot.

And the way he moved . . .

Sinful and decadent.

He moved like a man who was at home with himself. Like a man who knew his way around a woman's body and how to get what he wanted out of life.

She was completely captivated by his deadly predator's swagger. Allison swallowed.

Unlike the others, he didn't glance at her. He just slid with refined masculine grace into a chair and propped one booted foot up on the vacant seat across from him.

The other guys didn't seem friendly toward him and he didn't seem to care. He pulled his sunglasses off, displaying a face that would make an actor weep with envy. She'd never seen a man more attractive. His eyes were a beautiful hazel green that contrasted sharply with his olive skin.

But what riveted her was what she saw inside those eyes. They looked lethal and cold as they assessed everyone and everything in the bar as if it could be a possible threat.

Boy, this man certainly had his part down. He should be the one playing Harry. There was no doubt he could kill someone.

"Beer?"

She blinked as she realized Harry was speaking to her. "Excuse me?"

"Would you like a beer, Robin?" he asked again.

Allison smiled. In the book, Harry ruled Robin like a true alpha jerk and would never have asked her opinion about anything. She had to admit, she was grateful this Harry was kinder. "Sure, whatever you have that's light."

The hair on the back of Allison's neck stood up, letting her know someone was watching her intently.

She glanced over to find those deep hazel green eyes focused on her with interest.

He didn't look away.

Instead, he boldly swept her body with his gaze. One corner of his mouth lifted as if he enjoyed what he saw.

An unexpected rush of lust burned through Allison. It was potent and hot, and it made her want to have the guts to get up from her chair, walk over to him and kiss those finely shaped lips of his.

Better yet, she would love to give that man a naked lap dance.

Still he stared at her.

Allison shifted nervously as her body heated up even more. Her body clenched and throbbed, aching for him to do something other than look.

What would it be like to make love to a man like him? He was all sinuous power. All masculine beauty.

"Hey, Vince," Harry snapped angrily. "Get your eyes off my woman, or we're going to have a talk."

The man staring at her laughed at the threat. "Sure,

Harry. God knows, I wouldn't want to tangle with *you*."

Allison would have needed a Ginsu knife to cut through that sarcasm.

Vince paid the waiter as he brought him his beer.

"Who is he?" she asked Harry.

"He's just a straggler we picked up. Don't know much about him, really. No one even knows his last name."

Allison wondered how much of that was true. For some reason, she didn't doubt any of it. She thanked her waiter as the man handed her a beer and watched as Vince got up and left.

From behind, that man had the best butt she'd ever seen in her life. He cut a very intimidating and striking pose as he strode from the bar.

Before she even realized what she was doing, she followed after him.

He was heading back toward their motorcycles.

"Vince?"

He paused and turned to face her. "You need something?"

"Are you the man Mr. Zimmerman told me to contact if I had a problem?"

He took a swig of his beer before he answered. "Why? You got a problem already?"

"No, I was just wondering."

"Yeah. I'm the lucky bastard."

She forced herself to move closer to him. If Mr. Zimmerman had designated this man to oversee the others, then he couldn't be as fearsome as he seemed.

She held her hand out to him. "Allison George. Nice to meet you."

He looked at her hand, then swept his magnetic gaze back up to her face without taking her hand in his. "Nice meeting you too."

He turned away from her.

"Wait. You're not going to shake my hand?"

He faced her and the hot, lustful look in his eyes burned her all the way to her toes. "Look, lady, I've been stuck here on this island for far too long without seeing anything as scrumptious as you are. If I touch your hand I'm going to kiss your lips. If I kiss your lips, I'm going to run my hands all over your body. And after I get tired of running my hands over you, then I'm going to strip your clothes off and lick on you until you scream. So unless you want to have sex with me, I suggest you keep your hands to yourself and just let me go and find a cold shower."

Heat exploded across her face. "Are you always this outspoken and crude?"

"If you want a refined college boy"—he glanced at the bar—"those are inside. If you want a man . . ." He gave her a wicked grin that set fire to her blood. "Then baby, I've got what you need. You just give me a yell whenever you're ready for it."

Allison shivered at his words as he sauntered away from her.

Never in her life had she felt temptation like this. She didn't know Vince at all, but part of her craved him powerfully.

Robin would already be after him, her hands caressing those broad, muscled shoulders. She would be pulling his tight T-shirt off his body and licking his hard, defined abs.

Allison would run for cover and hide.

It was time for her to make a decision.

Was she going to be a lioness or a mouse? A frightened wimp who had never dared reach for what she wanted, or the wild woman who lived in her heart?

Allison took a step, then heard a motorcycle roaring down the road.

That would be Brendan approaching.

Brendan—the hero from the book.

She looked back at Vince and his deadly, dangerous walk.

Decisions, decisions, decisions.

What *should* she do?

CHAPTER FOUR

*A*llison went running after Vince. He turned as she drew near him and actually looked sick to his stomach. A part of her was highly offended by that, but it was mitigated by the fact that she knew he was attracted to her.

"Why aren't you the one playing Brendan?"

He let out a tired breath. "Look, baby, I'm just here as window dressing and the muscle in the event one of these *gavones* gets out of line with you. If I'm the one who gets out of line, there's no one to make me back off, *capisce?*"

A shiver went over her at the deep sound of his pronunciation of those foreign words. It was exotic and hot. "Are you Italian?"

He looked baffled by her question. "What?"

"Are you Italian?"

"Yeah. Extremely."

She smiled. "Wow! That's so neat. I've never met a real Italian before. There just aren't any in Georgia where I live. Can you do one of those really thick New York City accents like Danny Aiello? I love whenever I hear that on TV. I think it's so sexy."

He shook his head with a short laugh. "Lady, you seem really nice, but did you miss the part about how horny I am? That wasn't a joke."

"I'm sorry. I just . . . I don't know. I'm sorry."

Vince ground his teeth as he saw the hurt in her eyes an instant before she turned around to head back toward the bar. He was such an ass.

He wanted to apologize, but that would be even worse. He didn't want to encourage her. She really was a nice lady. Too nice for someone like him. The last thing she needed was to hook up with a gangster.

It wasn't like he had a future of any kind he could offer her. *Hey, baby, let's date until Gino finds me and kills me. Shall we? And if he happens to find me with a woman, he'll rape and kill her before he gets to me.*

No, there could be no women for him in the foreseeable future. It was one thing to risk his own life and quite another to endanger the Dairy Maid.

His heart heavy, he watched as she hooked up with the college boy and they returned inside. That was where she belonged . . . in her nice homogenized world.

Vince leaned his head back to guzzle his beer. Then as an image of her and the geek getting together went through his mind, he turned and tossed the bottle toward a tree where it shattered. Just once in his life, he wished he could taste something wholesome. Maybe if he'd had someone like her in his corner, his life would have been different.

Instead, he'd been surrounded by other pieces of cheap trash who had pushed him into an occupation he'd never wanted. But in the end, he couldn't blame them for it. He'd been the one who had finally succumbed to Gino's pressures. After he'd left the Marines behind, he'd spent a year looking for a job.

Nothing had been there for him. There wasn't a lot an infantryman could do in the civilian world. Especially not when he had a juvenile arrest record. Granted those files were sealed, but when he'd applied for the police academy and a job as a security guard, the background search had uncovered his past.

The only people who'd been willing to hire him had been "family." And after a year of living off his mother and burning through his savings, he'd had no choice except to take what they'd offered. At first it'd been harmless enough. Pick up this, drop this off, drive Gino around . . .

And then they'd dangled the one carrot before him he couldn't deny. The one carrot that had started him down the pathway to hell, and once he'd stepped onto it, his life had been over.

Disgusted with the choices he'd made, Vince raked his hands through his hair. He had to get out of here for a little while and clear his head.

Allison was listening to Harry and Brendan argue over some pretended slight as she watched Vince get on his motorcycle and roar off. She didn't know why the sight of his leaving hurt, but it did.

What is wrong with me?

You don't really want to sleep with a guy you don't know, do you?

Well, it would be a new experience. It was definitely not something she'd ever done before. But she wasn't really that kind of woman.

And so she stayed there while the guys acted out the book.

"Robin!"

She snapped her head up to see Harry glaring at her. "What?"

"I said it was time for us to go." And then as if he remembered that he wasn't really Harry, his gaze softened. "That is, if you're ready to go . . ."

"Sure." Trying not to laugh as he fell back into his tough-guy role, she got up and followed him out of the bar back to their motorcycles.

Neither of them spoke as the rest of the guys surrounded them, mounted their bikes and then roared down the road a few miles to a really nice hotel. As they pulled into the parking lot, she looked around wide-eyed. Modeled after the famed Hotel Del Coronado in San Diego, it had the same white building and sloping red roof. Only it was a lot smaller, but still every bit as impressive.

"Is this where we're staying?" she asked Harry.

He nodded as he got off the bike and waited on her to pull her helmet off.

Wow. This was much better than the sleazy hotels the characters in the book stayed in.

As the men headed inside, she saw Brendan giving her a hot once-over like he was supposed to do. But strangely enough, it left her cold. It was nothing like the hot flash she'd gotten from Vince.

Not willing to think about that, she followed the men. And as they approached the glass door, she realized that Vince was here too. His black motorcycle was parked off to the side.

Oddly enough, that gave her a tingle.

Yeah, there was something seriously wrong with her. Unlike the real Harry, who would have slammed the door in her face, the actor held the door open for her. A handsome desk clerk was already waiting for her and had the key to her room ready.

"You're right on the beach," he said kindly as he handed the key to her. "All of your belongings are unpacked and waiting in your room. The rest of the day and night is yours to do with as you please, and the fantasy will officially begin tomorrow. We have a card in your room that you can fill out and we'll start in the morning, whenever you're ready. Just let us know what you want for breakfast and remember that we're here to serve you. Anything you need. Anything at all, just let us know and we'll bring it right to you."

It was really weird to have someone say that to her. In all her life, Allison had never had anyone wait on her. Not even Gary had been willing to help her after her appendectomy. In fact, he'd had the nerve to ask her what she was going to make for dinner just an hour after she'd come home from the hospital. So it was nice to have someone who was willing to wait on her now.

She wondered how rich people dealt with this kind of attention. Something about it was just unsettling.

"Thank you," she said before she headed toward her room down the hallway.

After kindly saying goodbye to her, the biker gang dissipated. Come to think of it, she was glad to have some alone time to adjust to the new place. The plane ride had worn her out and she could use a shower and a nap.

Not to mention a walk on the beach. She'd always loved the beach, but she hadn't been to one since she was eight years old. Not since her father had run off and left them. Before that, they'd always made the yearly trek to Panama City. But afterward, her mother had been too heartbroken, too poor and then later too sick to make the trip.

Allison opened the door to her room, then froze. There were several dozen roses and bottles of champagne and wine on the entryway table. Along with a giant box of Godiva chocolate! She'd never had those before.

She felt like a kid on Christmas morning as she walked around the large room that had a king-size bed, a little living-room area, kitchen and study.

"Dang, this is nicer than my house." It was bigger too. But what really stunned her was the view out the window. She went to the sliding glass door to open it so that she could listen to the surf and watch the waves crash onto the perfectly beautiful beach.

This was so unreal. She felt like Alice after falling down the hole. It was like being in a movie, only it was real and it was definitely the best moment of her entire life. Closing her eyes, she let herself absorb the sound of the ocean and the scent of the roses and sea salt that hung in the air.

Oh, it was going to be hard to go home again after all this and return to her job.

Not wanting to think about that, she headed for the shower and tried not to wonder where Mr. Vince had gone off to and if he might be skinny-dipping on that beach.

Vince was sitting in the lounge chair on the small patio of his room as he watched the surf rolling in. He didn't know how many beers he'd downed at this point, but he was finally starting to get a little buzz going.

But not even that was enough to dull the fire in his groin that demanded he go find his Dairy Maid.

He tipped the beer back and tried to think disgusting thoughts.

At least until he saw something move out of the corner of his eye. Turning his head, he almost choked on the beer as he saw the source of his discomfort. There she stood, completely oblivious to him. But the worst part was that she was wearing the same thing he was . . .

Nothing but a damned bathrobe.

And he couldn't help but wonder if she were naked under that terry cloth.

"Nice view, huh?" he said, his voice down an octave from his beer and lust.

She jumped as if he'd startled her. A becoming blush spread over her face. "I'm sorry. I didn't know anyone was there."

"It's all right." But actually it wasn't, as the robe parted just enough to really piss him off by teasing him with the thought that he might glimpse a part of her.

Allison knew she should run back into her room, but she couldn't quite manage it. Vince was sitting on a white chair in a white monogrammed bathrobe that matched her own. Leaning back in his padded chair, he had his long legs spread open with a beer resting on one thigh. Like hers, his hair was wet, letting her know he'd had a shower himself.

But what burned her was the intense look on his face.

"You're not running away?"

"Should I?" she challenged him back.

His eyes twinkled at her. "If you were wise, Little Red Riding Hood, you'd know to avoid the wolf." That danger-ously hot gaze swept over her body, making her throb again. "So you must be feeling daring . . ."

Run!

But she refused. For once in her life, she wasn't going to be a coward. He wasn't some insane killer. He was the man Mr. Zimmerman had chosen to oversee her safety. Surely he wouldn't have picked Vince if Vince were really dangerous.

"Maybe."

A warm laugh rippled out of him. "Just how daring are you?"

She shrugged. "I don't know. What are you thinking?"

He took a drink of beer before he turned his head toward the beach. She could see him debating what he should say next. He had his tongue in his cheek as he ran it around, thinking.

Finally, he scratched his chin and flashed her a devilish grin that absolutely melted her. "I'm sitting here wondering if you're naked underneath your robe."

She bit her lip. *Don't say it. Don't you dare. . . .* But the words were out before she turned chicken. "I was wondering the same about you."

His look intensified, and she swore the air between them had solidified. She shivered with anticipation.

"Well, there's one way to find out."

She looked about nervously. "What do you mean?"

"I'll show you mine if you show me yours."

She let out a small squeak at the idea. "No! We're not the only people staying here, you know? What if one of the others comes out?"

"They won't."

"How do you know?"

"'Cause I sit out here every evening at this time and no one has come out yet except you."

Like she was going to take *his* word for that. "For all I know, you're lying."

He tsked at her, but still his eyes held that warm, playful air. Mercy, that man was more tempting than sin itself. "You know, I read that book of yours that you're reenacting. Robin would do it in a heartbeat."

"I'm not Robin."

"Aren't you?"

Allison toyed with her belt as she considered that. No, she really wasn't, but she'd promised herself that she wouldn't be so damned straight this week.

C'mon, Allison. You've never done anything wicked in your entire life. Just once, walk on the bad side. . . .

That was so much easier said than done. It took a lot to undo a lifetime of timidity. But there was no time like the present to work on it.

"Okay. You first." She didn't really expect him to agree, but before she could blink, he opened his robe.

Allison's jaw dropped. Yeah, he was naked all right. Totally. Completely. And she couldn't take her eyes off him. He had that kind of lean, hard body that they used in movies. The kind that said he was a man who liked to work out. She'd never seen a real eight-pack of abs in the flesh before, but he had one. And those golden muscles were dusted with enough black hair to be attractive and not gross.

But what kept her gaping was the size of his obvious erection. The man was huge, and like he'd said, he was definitely interested.

Holy. Cripes.

"Your turn, princess."

Allison bit her lip as fear consumed her. "No one better come out here."

He gave her a lopsided grin. "If they do, I'll kill them for you. Promise."

Yeah, right. Taking a deep breath, she glanced around the area nervously, before she reached for her belt.

Vince couldn't breathe as she hesitated. Oh man, this really was cruel. "Don't tease me, princess."

With a slowness that was sheer torture, she unfolded her

belt. He swore his heart stopped beating as he watched her open that belt, then slowly part her robe.

The sight of her hit him like a fist in the gut.

He expelled an appreciative breath at the sight of her naked body. She wasn't skinny, but rather she had lush curves. Her breasts were a bit small, but they were big enough to fill his hand and that was all that mattered.

Before he could stop himself, he set the bottle down and got up.

Allison knew she should run away as Vince approached her, but she couldn't.

He hesitated before her so close that she could feel the heat of his body. Smell the beer. It was all she could do not to step into the warmth of him. To press her body against his . . .

Frozen to the spot, she didn't move as he bent toward her and drew a deep breath against her neck. He pulled back ever so slightly. "You smell like roses and wine."

And he smelled like beer, sun and all masculine skin. Her breasts tightening at the thought, Allison turned her head and before she knew what he was doing, he lowered his lips to hers. She moaned at the decadent taste of him.

He cupped her face in his hands as his tongue hungrily explored every inch of her mouth. She shivered. This man certainly knew how to kiss. Her head swimming, she buried her hands in his damp hair.

Vince's heart pounded as he had his first taste of goodness. He drank it in from her lips and he knew he was lost. Between the beer and his lust, there was no way he could stop. He pulled back only a tiny bit to nibble the corner of that delectable mouth.

"Push me away, Allison," he whispered against her lips.

She didn't. Instead, she recaptured his lips with hers. Growling, he dipped himself down so that he could pick her up.

Allison felt a wave of giddy joy as Vince lifted her up without groaning because she was heavy and set her down on the concrete support for the patio. He pushed her robe open more while his hands caressed her breasts. Every part of her burned.

She'd never done anything like this before and honestly she didn't know why she was doing it now except that there was something so sad and yet safe about him.

And then he did what had to be the most tender thing a man had ever done to her. He wrapped his arms around her and just held her. Something inside her melted at the feeling of being held like this . . . as if she were precious.

Vince closed his eyes as he reveled in the sensation of her naked skin against his. Her breasts were flattened against his chest while her thighs pressed against his bare hips. God, it'd been so long since he'd just had a woman hold him and never had he held one so sweet.

Most of the women he'd dated would be clawing at him by now, wanting their satisfaction. But Allison merely held him as if they were something more than strangers.

He pulled back to return to her lips before he took her hand into his and led it to the part of him that was craving her the most.

Allison nibbled at Vince's lips as she gently explored the length of his cock. It was so strange to be this intimate with a man she didn't know and yet she felt some strange connection to him. It didn't make any sense. It was almost like love at first sight or at the very least lust at first sight.

Oh yeah, definitely lust.

"You are so beautiful," he whispered against her ear.

"It's the makeup."

He shook his head. "It's you." He picked her up then and carried her into her room where he laid her back on the bed. Her heart pounding, she watched as he shrugged off his bathrobe and dropped it to the floor.

He paused at her nightstand to open the drawer.

Allison frowned until she saw him grab a condom. Stunned, she rolled over to open the drawer wider where she saw a whole box of them.

Now she was offended. "Months, my heinie!"

Nonplussed, he frowned at her. "What?"

She narrowed her gaze on him as anger coiled through her. "If you haven't had a woman for months, then how did you know about—"

"They're in my room too."

"Sure they are."

"Allison," he said, his eyes deeply sincere, "they are. You can go see for yourself. And they've been killing me every night. I'm not a player anymore, okay?"

An image of her boyfriend in bed with his stripper tore through her. "Why don't I believe you?"

He cupped her cheek in his hand before he gave her a sizzling kiss. "I promise. I haven't been a player since I got out of the Marines four years ago. I haven't been celibate, but I haven't been a horn-dog either."

She was a bit surprised by his confession. "You were a Marine?"

"Yeah."

She started to ask him another question, but he chose that moment to dip his head down to her breast. Allison's thoughts scattered as he teased her.

Wanting more of him, she laid back, drawing him with her.

Vince was completely dazed by the taste of this woman and by the fact she wasn't shoving him away. In fact, she pushed him back and took the condom from his hand.

He sucked his breath in sharply as she took him in her hand. She placed a blistering kiss to his stomach before she opened the pouch and pulled the condom over him. He really shouldn't be doing this. She didn't strike him as the kind of woman to have sex and then walk away.

And that was what he liked most about her. His emotions didn't want her to walk away, but his common sense knew it was stupid to even think about dating a woman right now.

Why was he doing this?

Because she was the epitome of everything he'd ever craved. She was that sweet, wholesome, middle-American dream. She wasn't a city-born hustler. She was a doe-eyed innocent.

And God help him, he was helpless before her.

Allison moaned as Vince rolled onto his back and pulled

her against him. It felt so good to be with a man again. To be held, even if they were strangers. For some reason, he really made her feel beautiful. It didn't make sense, but she did.

Wanting to please him, she straddled his hips before she slowly slid her body onto his.

He hissed before he bit his lip and lifted his hips to drive himself even deeper into her. The look of pure pleasure on his face thrilled her. She couldn't remember the last time a man had been this happy to be with her.

She took his hand in hers and held it close. She understood that she meant nothing to him and that when this was over, he'd probably walk away. The thought hurt and yet she still couldn't bring herself to stop this.

She didn't know why, but she really wanted to be with him even if it was only temporary.

Vince sighed as he teased her lips while her damp hair fell around them. Oh yeah, this was what he'd needed in the worst sort of way. No woman had ever felt better than Allison did. She rode him slow and easy, at least in the beginning. But after a few minutes, she quickened her strokes.

Sensing what she needed, he rolled over with her until she was beneath him.

Allison arched her back as Vince leaned back and thrust himself deep inside her. He moved faster and faster, spurring her pleasure on until she couldn't take it anymore. When she came, her orgasm was so fierce that she screamed out from it.

She saw the fire in his eyes as he smiled down at her. He

moved even faster until he joined her in that perfect moment of bliss. She cradled him with her whole body as she drifted back from the rippling edge. He felt so wickedly good as she ran her hand over the muscles of his back.

She hadn't felt so at peace in a long time and for that she was truly grateful. Overwhelmed by the feeling she pressed her cheek to his so that she could feel his prickly whiskers. This really was a fantasy come true. . . .

Vince lay himself against her body while his heart raced. For the first time in years he felt a deep-seated peace and he didn't even know why. There was something magical about this moment. Something magical about her.

He lay on top of her, unwilling to move while she played with his hair and ran her other hand over his back. "I'm not too heavy, am I?"

"Definitely not," she said dreamily. "I like the way you feel."

Growling as another wave of desire hit him, he wiggled his hips against hers, driving himself in a bit more. "I like the way you feel too."

Allison smiled at him as he traced small circles around her breast. "I don't ever want to get up from here."

"Well," he said, drawing the word out, "they do have room service and there's a whole box of condoms in the drawer." He gave her a hopeful look.

She laughed at him. "You're so bad."

She had no idea.

Vince lifted himself up to kiss her, then paused as he heard something strange. . . .

It sounded like someone was in his room next door.

"Where is he?"

The voice was faint through the wall, but it was an unmistakable accent. He started to reach for his weapon only to realize that it was in his room . . . along with the men.

Damn.

He heard them kick open the bathroom door, looking for him. His anger mounting, he also realized he and Allison had left the sliding glass doors open.

It wouldn't take the men next door long to figure out where he was. . . .

Sliding off of Allison, he held his finger to his lips to warn her to silence.

"What's going on?" she mouthed.

He held his hand up to caution her again before he gathered her clothes and tossed them to her. And then he remembered that all of his clothes were in his room next door.

Double damn. He'd have to think of something quick or else the two of them were dead.

As soon as she was dressed, he put her in the far back of her closet. "Stay here," he whispered, his tone barely audible, "and whatever you do, don't move until I come back for you. Do you understand?"

Her blue eyes wide, she nodded.

Kissing her hand, Vince grabbed the bathrobe from the floor, then made his way into the hallway. He was slinking toward his room when all of sudden two doors opened at the same time.

His and Jeremy's.

And Gino's number one thug was heading out.

CHAPTER FIVE

Reacting on pure instinct, Vince grabbed Jeremy into a tight embrace and turned his back to Paulie. "Just play along," he whispered into Jeremy's ear.

Jeremy looked as if he'd just handed him the five-hundred-million-dollar winning lottery ticket. His face beaming, Jeremy wrapped his arms around him. "You got it."

Vince heard Paulie make a sound of disgust behind his back. "Yo, faggots, take it into the room."

That was his undoing. It let Vince know two important things. One, the bastard was distracted and two, exactly where Paulie was standing.

With reflexes honed from the military and the streets, Vince lifted his arm and elbowed Paulie in the face. Staggering back, Paulie cursed as he realized who it was and went for his weapon. Vince caught the hand Paulie had under his jacket and slammed his fist into Paulie's jaw.

The second thug, Gino's nephew Frankie, came out of the room behind them. Tall, thin and wiry, Frankie reached for his own gun. Before Vince could move, Jeremy karate-kicked him into the wall so hard, Frankie broke through the plaster.

Dazed, Frankie slid to the ground to land in a thud on his ass.

As Paulie started to get up, Jeremy kicked him in the head and knocked him unconscious. His eyes blazing, he met Vince's impressed stare.

"No one calls me a faggot unless they're my friend or my lover."

Vince could respect that. He held his hands up in surrender. "No worries here." He looked at the two men on the floor and laughed. There weren't many men who could have gotten the drop on Gino's goons. It said a lot that Jeremy had kicked their asses. "You handle yourself pretty damn well, kid."

"Thanks. You too. Now you want to tell me why they were coming out of your room?"

"Absolutely not," Vince said as he checked the clip in Paulie's gun. Luckily it was fully loaded. He slammed it back into place. "But I can tell you this. They're most likely not alone. These two are muscle and I'm sure somewhere else around here is the brain who orders them into action. So we need to find some way to secure them and get some help onto this island before one of you guys gets hurt in the crossfire."

"Hurt how?"

"Dead hurt."

Jeremy's face lost some of its color. "Okay. Give me two seconds."

Vince went to check Frankie for more guns—he found one in an ankle and the other in a shoulder holster. He'd no sooner unarmed him than Jeremy returned with two pairs of handcuffs. He handed them to Vince.

"I don't even want to know," Vince said as he used one pair to cuff Paulie while Jeremy cuffed the other man.

Jeremy frowned at him. "Where were you going in your bathrobe anyway?"

"Where were you going in yours?"

Jeremy smiled, letting Vince know he was probably about to rendezvous with one of the other actors. "Touché. I'll go get security. . . ."

Vince grabbed his arm to stop him. "You're going to need more than security. If I were you guys, I'd get the hell off this island before things get any worse."

Jeremy nodded as he considered that. "What about you?"

"Trust me, we'll all live a lot longer if you don't know that one."

Jeremy inclined his head to him before he headed for the lobby.

Vince took a minute to search the two thugs one last time to make absolutely sure they were clean before he headed to his door, only to realize that he was locked out.

Oh yeah. That was good.

His disgust ended as he realized something. They hadn't had a key card on them. . . .

How the hell had they gotten into his room?

This didn't bode well. There was definitely another party pulling their chains. Sighing in disgust, he dodged out the side door back to the patio so that he could return to his room and dress.

Vince let out a tired breath as he fastened his shoulder holster around him—something he'd stupidly thought he was through doing, then secured the other three guns. He had no way of knowing how many men Gino had sent after him, but hopefully it wasn't too many.

He considered calling Z to let him know what was going on. Honestly though, he didn't have time. He needed to take cover before the brain came looking for Paulie and Frankie.

His nerves steely cold, he returned to Allison's room and opened the closet where she was still sitting, right where he'd left her. Damn, she was beautiful and far more trusting than anyone had a right to be.

He would kill anyone who hurt her.

She looked up with her eyes round.

He held his hand out to her. "It's okay. C'mon, we need to get out of here."

She frowned. "But the fantasy—"

"This isn't a fantasy, Allison, and I'm not an actor. I've been hiding on this island from people who want me dead and if they find us, they'll torture and kill us. Now, we need to go."

"Us?"

He nodded. "I knew I shouldn't have come over here to your room. If they ever find out about you, they'll hurt you just because you were with me."

Allison swallowed. If not for the dark sincerity of his

eyes, she would think it was part of the story. But one look at him said it wasn't.

He was serious.

"Why do they want you?" she asked as she took his hand and he pulled her to her feet.

"Because I know too much about them. Who they are. What they've done. How they screwed me over. And they're afraid I'm going to the Feds—it's the only thing in life that scares them. I'm sure you've seen enough movies to know exactly the kind of men I'm talking about."

"What are they? Mafia?"

He gave her a droll stare. "Mafia is a word invented by Hollywood. It's not a term people in the family use." He paused and let out a deep breath. "But yeah, they're Mafia."

"And what did you do for them?"

She saw the pain and guilt in his eyes as he looked away from her. "Things I know I shouldn't have. Look, I'm not proud of who I am, okay? I let them lie to me and I lied to myself. Then one night, I came to my senses and I tried to leave. Unfortunately, they're not willing to let me go. At least not while I'm living."

Her heart sank at his words. "Did you kill anyone?"

He met her gaze unflinchingly. "Only those who tried to kill me first. I swear." He cupped her face in his hand as his gaze asked her to forgive him. "I really wish I wasn't what I am, baby. Believe me. But unless we hit the road, we're both history."

"Why me? Can't I just stay here?"

"I don't dare take that chance. These aren't the kind of

men who just ask politely if you've seen me. I'm not going to leave you behind for them to question and torture for fun."

Allison narrowed her eyes as anger welled up inside her. All her life, she'd been a good girl. She'd done what she was told. Had gone to church every Sunday. She'd worked a job she hated, had been loyal to a boyfriend who cheated on her and lied to her and in this moment, something inside her snapped.

She was through just taking crap. There was no way she was going to lie down and let these people kill her just because they could.

"Fine," she said, letting her anger swell even more. "You got a gun?"

"Yeah."

"Then give me one too. 'Cause if these assholes come after me, I intend to give them what for."

His expression turned even darker. Deadlier. "This isn't a game, Allison."

"Boy, don't I know it. But I'm a country girl, born and bred, who used to go hunting every weekend during the season with my grandfather. One thing he taught me early on is how to shoot straight and stand up for myself. Now give me a gun and put me on equal footing with these pricks."

Vince wasn't sure if he should be impressed or scared. Deciding on the former, he handed her the .22.

She wrinkled her nose at it. "What is this? A .22? You only shoot this if you're after a rodent or you just want to piss someone off. Don't you have a real weapon?"

"Where did you get that language?"

"The same place you got this crappy little gun. I don't normally talk like this, but when someone's out to kill me, I think it calls for a modicum of profanity. Now give me something good."

Vince was amazed by his little Dairy Maid. Smiling at her, he pulled out Frankie's .38 snub nose. She opened the barrel like a pro and pulled out one of the bullets. She nodded as she looked at it before she returned it to the chamber. "Hollow points, not bad." She slammed the barrel shut and tucked the gun into her jeans. "Okay. Where we going?"

She was taking this so much better than he'd ever hoped for. "Aren't you scared?"

"Shitless, pardon my French. But you don't know anything about me if you think I'm just going to lie down and take this. Nobody comes after me and threatens me and just walks off. I'm not a doormat. I might be female, but where I come from that doesn't make me the weaker sex. It just makes me the more vengeful sex."

He had to admire that about her. She was so much more than he'd even dared to hope. "All right, here's the plan. . . ." He hesitated as he thought over their options. Come to think of it, they didn't have many, or any. "Okay. There's not one. Basically the plan is we don't want to get killed and we find some way to get off this island before they find us."

"Gotcha. I definitely vote for the not-dying."

Shaking his head, Vince edged his way back toward the door to the patio so that he could check their perimeter. The surf was still peacefully crashing ashore while the seagulls called out to each other as if everything were normal. Only he knew the truth. This day was far from peaceful or serene.

But at least he didn't see anyone.

Then again, that didn't mean much. He knew from experience just how well someone like, oh say, *him* could blend into the background until he struck. Whoever was working with Paulie could be lurking around any corner, watching them. So they would have to move slowly to get out of here.

He turned back to find Allison staring at him. He offered her a smile. "We're going to work our way around to the front of the hotel and get on my motorcycle."

"Okay."

As they eased their way around to the side of the building, she proved herself. She must have been one hell of a hunter as a kid. The woman could move every bit as silently as he did. There were no missteps or mistakes. Allison handled herself like a pro.

Vince kept his eyes peeled as they stayed close to the wall, behind the shrubs. Luckily, he saw nothing. Everything was quiet and normal.

At least until they came around the last hedge. He froze instantly with Allison following suit. She ducked down, out of sight, while he continued to glare.

There was a man in front of the door, talking to "Harry." And as Vince watched them, his gaze turned red. It was Tony, Gino's son and right hand. If Gino couldn't come himself, he'd sent old Tone out to get him.

It figured.

And Tony knew the little prick who was playing Harry. Well, by the looks of things. They were too friendly, and he knew enough about Tony to know he was never friendly with strangers. Harry had to have been the one to let Gino know where he was. Most likely it was just a freak case of happenstance. . . . Or was it? If Z's people were hiring actors, they were probably hiring them out of New York where they were based. Yeah, it was a big city, but in some ways, it wasn't big enough.

It would actually be frighteningly easy, given the size of their families, to hire someone who knew someone.

Damn it. How could he be so stupid? He should have thought about this before now. Harry had only been on the island for the last four days, getting ready for Allison's arrival.

Now that he thought about it, he remembered little telltale clues that should have warned him Harry knew about him. The little bastard had even made a comment about Mafia families.

"I can't believe I didn't catch it," he muttered under his breath. But then it'd been easy. He'd wanted to be safe here and had convinced himself that no one would find him.

He was a first-rank ass.

Allison put her hand on his arm in a soothing gesture. Vince covered her hand with his and gave a light squeeze to reassure her. He kissed her lightly, before he looked back at Tony.

It wouldn't take him long to figure out what had happened. Any time now he'd check that watch and go after Paulie and Frankie.

Allison started to rise.

Vince grabbed her and shook his head no. She held her hand up in a placating gesture.

"Trust me," she whispered.

Trusting people wasn't something that came naturally to Vince. But at this point, he didn't have much choice. He pulled his gun out, preparing himself to fight his way out of this if he had to, and watched from the shadows as Allison walked over to the men.

"Hi, Harry," she said cheerfully, acting as if nothing were out of the normal. He had to give her credit, she was better than most of the actors here. "I'm really sorry to disturb the two of you, but I was wondering if I could take a ride on your bike? I'd really like to sight-see a bit before we get started tomorrow."

Harry looked around suspiciously. "You didn't hear anything a little while ago, did you?"

She shook her head innocently. "Just my radio. You ever listen to heavy metal? It's the best music in the world, but it's only good when it's really loud."

His face softened as he reached into his jean's pocket for his key and handed it over.

Without betraying a bit of nervousness, she thanked him, took the key and headed for his bike. Vince frowned as he watched her looking at the other bikes that were parked around it. She ran a loving hand over them as if she were admiring them.

Why on earth wasn't she hurrying a little bit more? It wasn't like someone was trying to kill them or anything. . . .

He glanced back at Harry and Tony who were again talking and not paying attention to Allison.

Suddenly, Jeremy came through the doors to grab Harry's arm. Jeremy wasn't quite as swift as Allison. Without hesitating, Jeremy asked the question that made Vince inwardly cringe. "Do either of you have the number for Mr. Zimmerman?"

Harry immediately clued in. "Is there a problem?"

"I would say so. Two guys just tried to kill Vince. He's got them hand—"

Before he could say anything more, Tony ran into the hotel. Harry, on the other hand, started looking around the parking lot. His attention went straight to Allison, who was starting up his motorcycle.

His eyes narrowed on her with deadly intent before he headed toward her with long, malicious strides.

"Hey?" Jeremy called after him. "Do you have the number?"

When Harry didn't respond, Jeremy started after him. Harry continued to head for Allison and as he did so, he reached beneath his lightweight jacket.

His only thought to protect her, Vince shot out from behind the shrubs to tackle him.

Jeremy jumped back and gaped as Vince quickly subdued Harry on the ground and knocked him unconscious. "He's one of them?"

"Apparently," Vince said, his tone full of sarcasm as he pulled Harry's gun out of its holster.

Jeremy cursed. "Fine, each man to himself. I'm out of here."

"In your bathrobe?"

Jeremy hesitated. "Okay, after I dress." He dodged back toward the hotel.

Allison rode the motorcycle over to Vince at about the same time he saw Frankie, Tony and Paulie returning. Damn it!

They started running toward him as Jeremy ran into the hotel.

Vince quickly jumped onto the bike while Allison slid back to make room for him. He took a heartbeat to savor the feeling of her arms around him, but a heartbeat was all they had.

Suddenly, bullets shattered around them. He could feel Allison cringing as he gunned the engine and took off out of the parking lot with squealing tires. He glanced over his shoulder to see the others head for more bikes.

Vince cursed.

"Don't worry," Allison shouted in his ear, over the sound of the engine.

"Don't worry?"

"When I was looking at the other bikes, I pulled the spark plug wires off. It should take them a few minutes to figure out what I did and why the bikes won't start."

Amazed by her, he laughed. "How did you know how to do that?"

"I'm a Southern girl, Vince. Every male in my family used to love his cars and bikes. They'd work on them in my mom's backyard and I paid attention over the years. Not to mention, pulling the spark plugs out was a good way to make sure my ex didn't go anywhere when I was mad at him."

He laughed again at that image. "You've got some spunk there, Allison."

"Piss and vinegar all the way, just like my mama."

Oddly enough, he liked that about her and right now he was truly grateful for it. Vince accelerated as they flew down the vacant road.

It wouldn't take the others long to figure out what'd happened and be after them again. They couldn't head for the small airstrip since Tony no doubt had a pilot there who was in the family. If he and Allison showed up, Vince was sure they'd kill them. Not to mention the small fact that he didn't know how to fly a plane and Z's pilot wouldn't be back until the end of the week.

Like it or not, they were stuck here. And right now, they needed to find some high ground so that they could face Tony and his thugs on equal footing. But where? There wasn't exactly an abundance of places to hide on this tiny island.

Except . . .

Vince paused as a thought occurred to him. He glanced over his shoulder to make sure the others weren't gaining on them before he headed toward the restricted area. It was a part of the island that Z rented out to some government group for training. Z had warned him that if they ever learned who and what he was, they'd be honor-bound to turn him over to the authorities. But being the adventurous sort, Vince had gone over there a few times just to check them out. Not to mention, he wanted to know their layout in the event they did come after him.

He'd even befriended one of the agency members, the

surly hotel manager who was usually alone with no one for company but his dog, Roscoe. To date, Vince had never seen any of the government people over there for training. But if it was a training ground, they were bound to have some supplies he could make use of.

Yeah, that would be their best bet. . . .

It only took a few minutes to make their way over to the other side of the island. Vince kept checking behind them, but so far, there had been no sign of Tony or the others.

He breathed in relief as they neared the parking lot. On the outside, the white stucco was reminiscent of a typical small hotel that had minimal landscaping. But inside it was really nice, if not overly spectacular.

Still it would give them some cover, especially since Roscoe was bound to start barking if anyone unusual approached.

Vince drove around back and pulled to a stop. After Allison got off, he hid the bike in some shrubs.

"What you doing, Vince?"

He jumped at the sound of Sam's gruff voice. He turned to see Sam standing off to the side, hidden mostly by the shrubs, while Roscoe was relieving himself a few feet away. Sam was the epitome of what a burly Scotsman should look like right down to the ruddy complexion and heavy jowls. He was also stout and powerful with bushy white eyebrows and white hair. As always, he wore a pair of black-rimmed glasses.

"I'm hiding my motorcycle."

Sam scratched his whiskered cheek that looked as if he hadn't shaved in a couple of days. "Why?"

"I have some people after me."

Sam seemed to take that in stride as he turned toward Allison. "She one of them sex maniacs from the contest?"

"Excuse me?" Allison said, her tone broken by disbelieving laughter.

Sam offered her a kind smile. "I didn't mean no offense to you. It's just you women come here and go wild on us poor men. Well, not me personally, but all the young bucks. It's scary what they do."

Allison gave another nervous laugh. She looked at Vince. "I think I'm offended."

"Ah now," Sam said good-naturedly, "don't be. I don't mean any harm. I usually dream of meeting a sex fiend on this island . . . but that's probably more than either of you wanted to know about me too."

Allison's dimples were shining brightly as she smiled at him. "Just a little."

Sam nodded before he turned his attention back to Vince. "So who you running from?"

"Hired killers. You got any guns?"

Sam scratched his chin as he thought about that. "What are we talking about? Handgun? Automatic? Semi-auto? Single action, double action? Water-cooled? Bolt action?"

"I'm not picky."

Sam gave him a patronizing look. "Well, you need to be 'cause we got all that and more. We even have claymores, rocket launchers, flamethrowers and high-tech explosives. You've got to tell me where to start."

Vince felt his jaw go slack. "Are you serious?"

Sam didn't flinch. "I never joke with or about artillery. That's how folks get hurt."

Yeah . . . this was better than anything Vince could have hoped for. "What exactly do you guys do over here?"

Sam was completely stone-faced. "Obviously, blow shit up. You need some plastique? We got that too."

Vince shook his head. "I'll stick to the guns. It's what I'm best at. And I could use a phone. I need to call Z and let him know he should evacuate Allison before she gets hurt."

Sam looked back at her. "There's not much Mr. Z can do from New York. But I'm thinking you don't need him anyway."

"Yeah, but Alli—"

"I heard you, boy. But we got agents here training today. Let me get to the radio inside to call them and I can assure you, not even a cockroach will be able to get to your little miss."

Vince wasn't so sure about that. Tony could be pretty persistent. "You're sure about that?"

"Oh believe me, these guys know what they're doing. I pity anyone dumb enough to cross them."

Sam whistled for Roscoe, who loped his way over to him. He patted the dog on the head, then led them in through the side door to the counter where he had several phones and walkie-talkies.

He picked up a yellow Motorola. "Yo, bossman, remember the guy I was telling you about last night? He's here and he's being tailed by some of those good-fers. He's got a woman with him who he doesn't want to get hurt. Can you guys lay aside training and lend a hand?"

Vince frowned at his words. "What's a good-fer?"

Allison offered him a wide smile. "Good-fer-nothings. You know, good-fers."

Vince laughed at that bit of Southern slang he'd never heard before.

Static sounded over the walkie-talkie before a deep masculine voice broke through. "We'll be there. ETA about three minutes, Sam."

Vince cocked his head at the sound of that voice. There was something vaguely familiar about it, but before Vince could ask, he heard the sound of motorcycles pulling up outside.

He glanced to Sam. "Is that your people?"

"I doubt it," he said as Roscoe started snarling and barking. Sam reached down to calm his dog.

Vince cringed at that implication. "Where can I stash Allison?"

Sam took her gently by the arm and pulled her around to his side of the counter, but it was too late. The others were already heading in.

Allison held her breath as Vince took aim, but before he could pull the trigger, the tallest man coming through the door opened fire on them. Gunfire rang in her ears as wood and glass exploded around them. Sam pulled her down behind the counter and she lost sight of Vince while Sam tied his dog to a hook so that Roscoe wouldn't get in the way or hurt.

Sam grabbed a gun that was hidden at the small of his back and stood up. He fired two rounds.

Her heart hammering as more shots rang out, Allison realized that there was a shotgun dead even with her behind the counter. Roscoe increased his howling as shot after shot was fired.

Sam ducked down to reload.

"Get 'em."

Reacting on pure instinct, she grabbed the shotgun while Sam reloaded and stood up.

There was one man headed straight for Vince while another was headed for her. She took aim at the one gunning for Vince and pulled the trigger.

The man flew back. She cocked the shotgun and turned it to the one nearing her.

"Drop it," she growled at him.

He didn't. Instead, he glared at her. "This ain't no game, sweetheart, and your boyfriend is out of ammo."

She glanced to see that Vince was on the floor wounded in his shoulder. He held his gun up and nodded to confirm that he was indeed out of ammunition. She tightened her grip on the trigger as she returned her attention to the other guy. "No, it isn't a game. Now drop it or I drop you."

Vince came to his feet. "You better do it, Paulie. She doesn't play."

Suddenly, applause broke out.

Behind her.

Still, Allison didn't look. She didn't dare.

"Tell your woman to drop the gun, Vince. No need in spraying her pretty little brains all over the old man and his dog."

Sam put his hand on her leg. "Put it down, Allison."

She saw the confirmation in Vince's eyes as he tossed his own gun to the floor. It was followed by Sam doing the same.

Her heart sinking, she reluctantly complied and turned to see another man behind her who was holding a gun straight at her head. Her heart literally stopped beating in terror.

It was the man who'd been talking to Harry outside the hotel. Which made her wonder what had happened to Harry, since there was no sign of him now.

The man holding the gun at her head tsked at them. He cast a condescending look toward Vince. "Vinnie . . . Vinnie, Vinnie, Vinnie. What am I going to do with you? You leave town. You don't say goodbye. You don't write. You don't call. Your poor mama is worried sick about you."

Vince's body went rigid as his face turned to steel. "You better leave my mother out of this, Tony. You touch her and so help me, I will kill you."

The man Vince had called Paulie walked closer so that he could take the guns that she and Sam had laid aside.

Tony ignored Vince's threat. "You know, I've got to give you credit, sending your mama off with that rich prick friend of yours was a good move. But sooner or later, she's going to want to go home. What's going to happen to her then?" He paused dramatically. "I guess you can die knowing that I plan to take real good care of your mother after you're gone. I'll also make sure she knows all about her son and how he's responsible for what happens to her."

"You bastard!" Vince took a step forward.

Tony cocked the gun he held to Allison's head. She squeaked as her eyes filled with tears, but she didn't move or make any real sound. She was terrified of making Tony nervous. The last thing she wanted was for that gun to go off.

Oh, God, please help me! In that moment, she wished she'd never won this trip. She wished she were still in Madison, Georgia, in her tiny, two-bedroom house where her biggest fear was the summer mosquitos.

But she wasn't . . .

Vince cast her an apologetic look.

"Now, now, Vinnie," Tony said in a mock parental tone. "You need to mind that temper of yours."

Vince froze, but if looks could kill Tony would be dead.

"Get on your knees, Vinnie."

He shook his head no. "If you're going to kill me, then you're going to shoot me standing."

Tony pressed the gun against her head. "On. Your. Knees. Asshole."

Allison held her breath as she expected Tony to kill her any second.

She could see the anger and pain in Vince's eyes. But for her, he knelt on the floor. She trembled as fear and gratitude mixed inside her.

Tony laughed. "You always were an arrogant bastard. All right, Paulie. Put him—"

The door to the lobby opened.

Allison swallowed as she watched an extremely attractive man in his early thirties walk nonchalantly into the lobby. He had long, dark hair that was pulled back into a ponytail and the palest blue eyes she'd ever seen. He was wearing a black pair of slacks and a black T-shirt that showed his ripped body off to perfection. Tattoos marked both of the arms he had crossed over his muscled chest.

He appeared to be unarmed and yet he walked into the firefight with an unfounded confidence.

He paused near Vince. "Little Vinnie. Long time no see. How's your mama doing? She still making that gravy that used to be so good that even the angels in heaven wept in envy?"

Vince gaped and stared in complete disbelief. Allison held her breath, waiting to see if the newcomer was a friend or a foe.

He turned toward her and looked at the man holding the gun as if there was nothing strange about it. "Cousin Tony?" he asked. "Is that you?"

Tony tightened the hand he had in her hair. "Who the hell are you?"

The man looked offended by that question. When he spoke it was in a thick New York accent. "Tone . . . tell me it ain't so. I know it's been awhile—fifteen, sixteen years or so—but damn. Surely you haven't forgotten me? *Me?*" He gestured at himself with both hands, and shook his head in disbelief. "I even took your little sister, Maria, to her first prom 'cause your father was afraid to let anyone else near her."

"Joe?"

"Yeah. Little Joseph. You oughta remember me. My grandfather, Big Joe, is the man your father replaced in the family."

Vince's jaw dropped as he stared up at the man. Allison didn't know what to think. She still didn't know whose side Joe was on.

"I heard you was dead," Tony said in an angry tone.

Joe shrugged. "Not yet. But if you don't drop that gun, *you* will be."

Tony laughed as he surveyed Joe's tough, unarmed stance. "Yeah, right. Whatcha gonna do, Joe? Talk me to death?"

Joe duplicated his laughter. "Nah. You know me, Tone. I'm Big Joe's grandson. We don't talk, we act." His face sobered as he glared dead at Tony. "And you, if you have any brains, should be afraid. Remember, I took a bullet for you and you threw me to the dogs, you bastard. I owe you one. Now drop the freakin' gun and I might let you live."

"Fuck you, Joey." Tony moved the gun away from her head to shoot at Joe.

Allison acted without thinking it through. She elbowed Tony hard in the ribs and shoved his arm away. A shot fired into the wall. Tony hit her hard with one hand before he started to bring the gun back toward her.

Vince launched himself over the counter, knocking Tony to the ground where they wrestled. Joe was only two steps behind as Allison scrambled to get clear of the chaos.

Sam grabbed the shotgun and angled it toward Paulie who froze instantly. Two seconds later, a gunshot sounded.

Allison held her breath as terror sliced through her. Who was hit? She stared at the three men on the floor in horror, waiting to see who it was.

Joe got up first with the gun in his hand. "Vinnie?"

"It wasn't me," Vince said as he pushed himself up.

Tony lay on the floor, groaning as he held his hand to his bleeding stomach.

Joe looked at him with no sympathy whatsoever. "Hurts like a mother, don't it? Now you know how I felt when you walked off and left me to die. But you're lucky, you bastard. I'm at least going to call you an ambulance."

Vince didn't respond as he grabbed Allison to him and held her in a crushing embrace. "Are you okay?"

Before she could answer, a dozen people, male and female, came running in with guns in their hands. They were dressed like a SWAT team, in black clothes with flak jackets. They quickly surveyed what was going on as they swarmed into the lobby. Two of them checked on the man Allison had shot while two covered Paulie and two more went to stand over Tony.

A small Vietnamese-American woman glanced at Sam. "You okay, buddy?"

"Like a peach, Tee."

She smiled, then looked at Joe. "What about you? Did you get shot again, Joseph?"

"No," he said drily. "The only person who's ever shot me on the job, Tee, is you."

Tee arched a brow at him. "What about Moscow?"

"That was luck."

"Egypt?"

Joe made a noise of annoyance. "Just secure them and call to the other side for a medic."

She nodded before she complied and called for help.

Allison stepped back to look at Vince's shoulder. "How bad does it hurt?"

"You ever slammed your hand in a door?"

"Yes."

"That doesn't even come close. But I'm alive, so I'm not complaining." He kissed her lightly on the lips. "Thanks."

Joe came over to them. "I ditto that. Good reflexes for a civilian."

She gave a nervous laugh. "I don't know. I think it was pretty stupid myself. I could have gotten us all killed."

"But you didn't," Joe said. "I appreciate that."

"Well," Allison said with a lightness she didn't really feel. "I appreciate the fact I didn't get us all killed too."

Vince smiled, until he looked back at Joe, then his face sobered.

"Same Vincenzo," Joe said with a sigh and a heavy accent. "You never could keep your nose clean."

Vince narrowed his eyes on Joe. "I'm not the one who went to jail."

Something passed between them. Something that was laced with pain and sadness.

Joe cocked his head slightly and narrowed his eyes on Vince. "I thought you knew better than to let Gino get his hooks into you."

Vince gave Allison a sheepish look before he answered. "He dangled a carrot I couldn't refuse."

"And that was?"

"He said he knew who killed my father."

Joe scowled at him. "Gino's the one who killed your father, Vin, and most likely, mine too. Didn't you know that?"

"Yeah, I learned it a few months back when I went to kill Jimmy Tatalia. Lucky for him, he came clean and I let him live."

"Jimmy is a lying sack of shit," Tony snarled from the floor.

"Yeah, right," Vince yelled back. "He had proof that you and your father took out mine. It was a fucking initiation for you." Vince started for Tony, but before he could reach him, Joe pulled him back.

Vince glared at Joe. "Give me a gun, Joe, and let me blow his ass away."

"I can't do that, Vin."

An angry tic worked in Vince's jaw.

Allison saw the pain in Vince's eyes and it made her ache for him.

"I just wanted out and away from you people," Vince snarled at Tony.

"Yeah, sure. You were going to the Feds to rat us out. Little Sal heard the whole thing."

Vince looked ill at that as he scowled at Tony. "I don't know why Sal lied, but he did. I had no intention of going to them. Ever. But I will now."

"And we'll kill you," Tony snarled.

"Hey, hey," Joe snapped, holding up his hand. "If anyone here is going to make a threat against someone's life, it's going to be me. Besides that, both of you are talking to the

Feds right now and that'd be me too." He curled his lip at Tony. "Now why don't you be a good boy and just lie there quietly and bleed." He glanced over to Tee. "He opens his mouth again, shoot him."

Tee's dark eyes twinkled as she moved to stand over Tony. She pulled out her gun and checked the clip. "With pleasure."

The door opened to admit a small group of paramedics who quickly went to Frankie, Tony and Vince.

Allison stepped back as they had Vince lie down on a gurney so that they could cut his shirt off and apply a pressure bandage to his wound.

She didn't say anything while they worked on Vince, but she hoped he'd be okay. Given how well he was dealing with the wound, she took it as a good sign.

Joe came over to stand beside her. "How are you holding up?"

"I'm okay, I think."

"Good."

She glanced over to Tee and the other agents. "Just who are you people anyway?"

Joe laughed, but didn't answer. "You want to ride to the hospital with Vince? I'm sure they'll have to air-lift them out of here to the mainland for a hospital."

She glanced nervously at Vince, not sure what he'd want. "I would like to."

"Yo, Vin," Joe said as they lifted the gurney up. "You want some company for the ride to the hospital?"

"Not if it's your ugly ass. I'd rather be alone. But I'll take Allison in a heartbeat."

Joe made a noise of disagreement. "My ass may be ugly but at least it ain't hairy like somebody else's I know. . . ."

It was Allison's turn to duplicate Joe's snort. "Trust me, his butt's not hairy. I know that for a fact."

Joe gaped while Vince gave him a shit-eating grin. Smiling, Allison followed the medics out to the helicopter that was just coming in for a landing.

While they waited, she moved to Vince's side. He took her hand in his and offered her a tender smile. "I'm glad you didn't get hurt."

"I'm sorry you did."

"Ah, it's okay. Better since you're still speaking to me."

"Why wouldn't I speak to you?"

His eyes darkened with shame. "I've had a bad past, Allison."

"You ever beat small children?"

He frowned at her. "No."

"You ever knock around a girlfriend?"

"Hell no!"

"You ever shoot someone who was defenseless?"

"No. Never."

She reached out and took his hand into hers. "We all make mistakes, Vince. *All* of us. The past shapes us, but it's what we do with our future that defines us."

He gaped as he looked at her. "You're an amazing woman, Allison."

"I have my moments," she said with a smile and a wink.

The medics returned to lift him into the helicopter. Allison didn't get a chance to say much more to Vince as they flew to the hospital and as soon as they landed, he was whisked away for surgery to remove the bullet in his shoulder.

She paced the waiting room and was on the verge of complete boredom when the doors opened to admit Joe, Mr. Zimmerman and Tee.

Mr. Zimmerman headed straight for her. "Are you all right?"

"I'm fine."

"I told you," Joe said.

Mr. Zimmerman glared at him. "Yeah, but you lie."

"Only to Tee."

Tee snorted. "No you don't. You know I'll shoot you if you do."

"Well, there is that."

Mr. Zimmerman ignored them. "I want you to know that the actor playing Harry has been fired and if you'd like to go on with your fantasy—"

"That's okay," she said, feeling a strange sense of peace. "I think I'd rather stay here with Vince, just in case he needs something."

Mr. Zimmerman looked pleased by that.

Joe and Tee handed her a picnic basket that had a sweater and food inside. But more than that, it had a portable DVD player and a case full of movies.

"I've spent way too much time in one of these things," Tee said. "I know how tedious the wait is and there's never anything good to eat or watch."

"Thank you." Allison set it aside and as time passed while they waited for word, she found out that Mr. Zimmerman—

Z—was Vince's brother-in-law and Joe was his cousin.

It wasn't until the next morning that they were able to see Vince again.

Allison paused in the doorway of his room. He looked groggy and tired, but at least his color was good and the doctor had told them that he would be back to normal in no time.

Vince froze as he saw Allison hesitating. Her clothes were wrinkled and her face flushed. It was obvious she'd spent the night here. He didn't know why, but that thought made something warm run through his veins.

"Hi, angel," he said softly.

Her smile made him forget about the pain of his wound. But it started a whole other pain that wanted a taste of her.

"Hi." She came into the room, followed by Joe and Z.

The men moved to the foot of his bed while Allison came to stand beside him. "You need anything?"

He took her hand into his and kissed her knuckles before he rubbed it against his cheek. "Nope, what I need just came in."

Her blush deepened.

"You know," Joe said, exchanging a look with Z, "there are some of us in here who don't want to go blind from the PDA. So could you two be a little less sweet before my teeth rot out?"

Vince shook his head at him. "By the way, where the hell have you been all these years, Joey?"

Joe shrugged. "I got out and I got legit."

"And you just forgot about all the rest of us?"

"No," Joe said, his eyes dark in sincerity. "I didn't. I've

kept in touch with Z, which is why I'm here now. He's the one who got my head on straight back when I was working for Gino. He tossed me a lifeline and I took it."

Vince looked at Z as his gratitude swelled. "Then we have a lot in common."

"Yeah, we do."

Vince took a deep breath. "So you're one of the federal agents who rents the island from Z?"

Joe gave a solemn nod.

And Vince could see where this was headed. His stomach knotted as he stroked Allison's palm with his thumb. "So what are you going to do with Tony and the rest?"

"Don't worry. They won't be coming after you again. Ever. They're going to have much bigger problems to worry about. I called my friends in the FBI and Treasury Department. They're already here and watching them." Joe shifted uncomfortably. "It's why I made myself scarce and cut all ties to the family. Had I stayed in New York, I would have done my job and brought down all of you."

The knot tightened even more. "So you're sending me to jail too, I take it."

"No." The word stunned Vince. "Z handed me his file on you last night. He told me the two men you took out were under indictment for various illicit crimes and that they tried to kill you first. That makes it self-defense in my book."

Vince couldn't believe it. "You're just going to let me go?"

"Not exactly."

Vince narrowed his gaze. "What?"

"I could use you in my division. I run an interesting government task force. When you're feeling better, we'll talk more about it."

Vince looked up at Allison. "What about Allison?"

"I'll be talking to her too."

"But I don't have any education," she said, hanging her head. "All I did was graduate high school."

"Hey," Vince said, shaking her hand until she looked at him. "You're the smartest woman I know. Don't you ever be ashamed that you didn't go to college."

Joe agreed. "We can educate you on the job. But for a woman with no academy training, you handled yourself incredibly well under pressure. You have a natural ability to cope and that makes you desirable for what we do."

Z stepped forward. "Well, now that we know you're going to live, we'll leave you two alone."

Joe nodded. "We'll be back to harass you later."

"I'm sure you will."

Vince watched as the two men left, then he turned his full attention back to Allison, who absolutely took his breath away. "I can't believe you haven't gone back to your fantasy."

"Why would I want to do that?"

Before he could respond, she leaned over and whispered softly in his ear. "Baby, you are my fantasy and there's no place else I'd rather be than right here with you."

EPILOGUE

*A*llison had a strange sense of déjà vu as she entered the Wal-Mart where she used to work. She hadn't been home in almost five months . . . not since she and Vince had rented an apartment in Nashville so that they could begin training to be agents for the Bureau of American Defense.

The last few months had all been a whirl in her mind. Between training during the day and spending her nights with Vince, she hadn't had any time to spare.

But now it was time to put her past to rest. She'd come back home to sign the papers to sell her house and she'd wanted to say goodbye to a couple of friends who'd worked here with her.

As she neared the book aisle, she paused. There was a new employee who was holding a Rachel Fire romance novel open and reading a passage out of it. The woman was probably a couple of years younger than her with long dark hair. Allison knew the wistful look in her eyes.

Before she could stop herself, she walked over to her. "It's a great book, isn't it?"

"Yeah," the woman said, smiling.

Allison flipped to the last page where the entry form for the contest was. "You should definitely enter."

"Nobody ever wins those things except women who don't need them."

She smiled knowingly. "Oh hon, trust me, they do. . . . I did."

The woman gaped at her. "Did you really?"

"Oh yeah, and it was the best time I've ever had."

She saw the woman's gaze go past her, toward someone else. Allison turned her head to find Vince drawing near. He didn't pause until he pulled her back in his arms and kissed the back of her head. "Are you ready?"

"I am."

The woman's gaze dropped down to Allison's hand, where her engagement ring rested. "You're a lucky woman."

"Believe me, I know, but never, ever stop thinking for one minute that you can't be too. Dreams really do come true. You just have to have the courage to see them through."

The woman scoffed. "That's easy for you to say."

"Maybe, but you know, my whole life was changed because of one postage stamp." Allison reached into her purse and pulled out a stamp book. "I hope it brings you the same luck it brought me."

"Carla, cleanup on aisle eight."

She saw the woman cringe as Dan's voice sounded over

the PA system. She tucked her book into the pocket of her apron. "I better go."

Allison stopped her. "Oh no, honey, let me handle this."

Vince frowned as she pulled away from him. With determined strides, Allison went to the cleaning station and pulled down the broom and dry solution. Then she made her way over to where Dan was at the front of the store.

His eyes widened as he saw her. Before he could say anything, Allison handed it to him. "You know, Dan, for once in your life try and be a decent human being to someone. People work a lot better and harder when you treat them with dignity."

And with that said, she headed for the doors.

Vince took her hand as they entered the parking lot. "Are you all right?"

Allison nodded as she took her last look around. "Yeah, I am." She pulled him to a stop and faced him. "You do know how much I love you, right?"

"I hope as much as I love you." Then, he pulled her into his arms for a quick kiss and as their lips met, Allison realized that what she'd said to Vince really was the truth. The past had definitely left its mark on her, but the future was entirely up to her and she planned on making it a great one.

And it was one that would definitely include him.

Hunter's Oath

JAID BLACK

To Patty Marks,
a graceful fighter in every sense of the word.
Thanks for everything, Mom.

Prepare thyselves for the inevitable demise of the wicked. Hunt down and steal as many wenches from the Outsiders as needed for the continuity of our line. To prevail, we must breed women and bear much fruit.

'Tis not I, a humble servant of the gods, who decree this, but the gods themselves:

Go forth and hunt, men.

—Viking Legend

CHAPTER ONE

Alaska

*T*hirty-two-year-old Sofia Rowley sat in the back of the taxi, gazing out the window but seeing nothing. Leaving Alaska today wasn't possible, since Fairbanks was at least two hours from the army base. She'd have to stay in a motel near the airport and catch the first flight back home tomorrow.

She welcomed the thought of the sun beating down on her face when the plane landed in Tampa. Alaska in February was bone-chillingly frigid.

This is where Sam died, she thought, gazing at the treacherous, icy terrain all around her. Snowcapped mountains thrust up everywhere, creating a picturesque but deadly panorama. She didn't know how the cabbie was plowing through this stuff. Experience, she supposed—and strong chains on his tires.

Exhausted from jet lag, grief and lack of sleep, Sofia raked her crimson fingernails through her long blond hair and sighed. She itched to tie the wild mane of curls back into a ponytail, but she hadn't remembered scrunchies when she'd hastily packed. Word of her brother's death had driven everything else from her mind.

I don't know what to do, Sam. I don't know how to go on without you.

Her life, so driven and purposeful, suddenly felt unfocused. Rowley Travel no longer held any allure. Her twenty-two-year-old brother's death had forced her to recognize that work and Sam had been her sole sustenance.

It was time to start anew, to *live* instead of merely existing. Sam would have demanded no less. Indeed, her brother had been harping on her for years to go out and enjoy herself more often. She recalled a conversation they'd had just a few months ago, while he was here on a classified assignment.

"*You should get out and date more, Sis,*" Sam told her. "*I've always seen the way guys look at you. And while it kinda grosses me out—I mean, you are my sister, after all—I know why they do. You're the type of woman every man wants for his own: smart, kind, hardworking, gorgeous, and as much as I hate to say this out loud, you've got a killer body.*"

Sofia chuckled into the phone. "I think you're being generous. The looks in the family all landed on you, kiddo."

"*That's a bunch of bullshit and we both know it.*"

"*Oh? Then how come men rarely ask me out?*"

"*Because you always put out you-don't-stand-a-chance-with-me vibes. Men are basically pathetic and insecure. Trust me on that one, Sof.*"

She shook her head and grinned. "Am I really that bad? I don't mean to be."

Sam's voice grew serious. "You raised me after Mom and Dad died, and I can never thank you enough for it—"

"Sam, you don't need to—"

"—But I'm grown up now and you deserve to find your happy ending. Don't waste your life behind a desk, Sis."

Sofia smiled sadly. Her brother had been her best friend, her only real friend. His death had left a gaping hole in her heart and her life that might never be mended.

Fatigue overwhelming her, Sofia's eyelids slowly closed, thick dark lashes fanning down. The pain inside was raw and powerful; she welcomed the respite a short nap would bring.

No matter how old I live to be, Sam, I will carry you in my heart and memories forever.

Sofia's eyelids slowly batted open. She stretched and yawned, feeling a bit more refreshed. Wondering how long she'd been asleep, she glanced at her wristwatch. She stilled.

Four hours?

They should have reached Fairbanks by now.

Her gaze darted outside the taxi. Sofia's pulse soared when she realized that nothing looked familiar. It was dark outside, but she could see that the terrain had become impossibly harsher and more mountainous. The road—were they even on a road? Sofia's eyes widened. She didn't think they were.

"Sir," she called out to the back of the taxi driver's bald

head. "I don't think you're going the right way. I wanted to go to Fairbanks."

He said nothing. Her heartbeat picked up as an ominous feeling stole over her.

"Sir!" Sofia yelled, her voice sounding hysterical even to her own ears. "Where are you going?"

Their gazes locked through the rearview mirror. Again, the cabbie said nothing. His driving increased in speed, and true panic set in.

He was kidnapping her! The thought was stunning, numbing. A sense of surreality set in. This just couldn't be happening. She had to be dreaming!

A thick, opaque barrier of glass kept Sofia from lunging at him. Thinking quickly, she fumbled for the door handles, preparing to jump out of the taxi. If the fall killed her, it didn't matter. She'd rather jump to her own death than be raped and murdered by this evil, grotesque little bastard.

But the door handles wouldn't budge. Making small, terrified sounds, Sofia rattled the handles harder to no avail. The driver must possess a mechanism that kept backseat passengers from opening the doors until they paid their fares.

Oh no.

God, help me!

Sofia kicked against the door with all her might. "Let me out!" she screamed, her heart hammering loudly in her ears. Her fists pounded against the glass divide that separated them. *"Open the fucking door!"*

The cabbie didn't even acknowledge that she'd spoken. His silence was more frightening than any words he could have spat back at her.

She was going to die. Perhaps slow and torturously.

Her heart slamming against her breasts, Sofia slumped helplessly back against the seat.

CHAPTER TWO

Hannu, New Sweden
Present Day

*T*he bride-hunter lied to me!" a disgruntled Viking
spat.

"They always lie!" another angry male voice boomed in.
"'Tis treachery that they are permitted to deceive us,
milord!"

"It costs us nigh unto our last coins to purchase a bride.
The bride-hunters should make certain that the wenches are
prime candidates to bear Viking fruit. Not just physically,
but emotionally as well!"

Enraged demands that the bride-hunters be whipped and
imprisoned erupted in the hall. Lord Johen Stefsson sat in
his chair at the apex of it, soldiers surrounding him on all
sides of the raised platform.

Not that Johen required their protection; a more skilled
warlord did not exist.

Johen stood seven feet tall, his battle-scarred body honed

of three-hundred-twenty pounds of solid muscle. He wore black leather boots and braes, and a sleeveless green silk tunic that stood in stark contrast against his naturally bronze skin. The emblem of a dragon was emblazed on the gold bangles clasped around his powerful biceps, signifying his authority.

Lord Stefsson could defend himself with deadly skill did the situation require it. In this instance crowd control would not be a problem, as Johen was firmly on the side of the people who looked to him for leadership and guidance.

"Enough!" Johen bellowed, his eyes narrowed into gray slits. Two braids plaited back against his temples served to keep his dark brown hair out of his eyes; the shiny mane fell to mid-back. "I hear your cries, men, and I do not take them lightly. I will speak to our king about this issue on the morrow."

The crowd of fifty quieted, appeased mumbles rippling through the gathering like a wave. Nods of approval and respect told him they would give him time to find a solution before taking matters into their own hands.

Not that talking to the jarl would do them any good, Johen thought, disgruntled. Toki was of a mind to make coins, not friends.

One day his corrupt rule would come to an end. Until that time arrived, all Johen could do was act as an intermediary between Toki and the people of his sector. Failing that, there would be no choice but to revolt again.

The Revolution had been won less than two fortnights ago, the old, corrupt jarl dead and deposed. Under the former king's rule, bride-hunters had gotten away with far too much, sharing the profits of very little work with the crooked jarl.

But now a new government was in power and lots of changes were to be made. It would take time, though. Years and years of neglect and abuse couldn't be turned around in less than one month.

Lord Stefsson assessed the crowd, his battle-trained mind accustomed to sizing up war opponents rather than men he was meant to rule. 'Twas a vastly different role, one that would take some time to grow accustomed to, yet he was eager for the challenge. His people had been neglected for far too long and deserved to be governed by a noble who had their best interests at heart.

The Revolution had been both necessity and inevitability. In the Viking world that existed below the earth's dirt and leaves, where none from the Outside knew of its existence, war was not taken lightly. 'Twas resorted to only when obligation dictated.

For mayhap two thousand years, the Viking clans of New Sweden, New Norway and New Daneland had thrived below the ground deep in the earth's belly. 'Twas the decree of the gods that they go there and dwell, the ancient prophets predicting that one day soon, mayhap in Johen's lifetime, the number of wenches who lived above the ground would dwindle to near extinction.

The Vikings would live on, the Terrible Northmen destined to rule the world once again. Their people had been forewarned by the gods of the events to come. 'Twas their duty to preserve their way of life, which could only be done if those who dwelled above the ground knew naught of their existence.

The king of New Sweden, Toki, had flirted with being discovered by Outsiders one too many times. For that, and for his brutal tyranny, Lord Stefsson, commander of the independent sector of Hannu, had thus far refused to let his people be swallowed into the belly of New Sweden. Toki hadn't dared gainsay him for fear that Johen would throw his weight toward the jarl's enemy—the king of New Daneland.

The warriors of Hannu had revolted after Toki claimed the throne, declaring Johen their leader instead. Situated between mainland New Sweden and the barbaric kingdom of New Daneland, their small but well fortified zone thrived.

His people were dependent on New Sweden for nothing—except for brides. Until a new jarl overthrew the corrupt one, 'twas unlikely any significant changes would be demanded of the bride-hunters.

"'Tis a bride-hunter's job to ensure that the wenches they steal from above the ground are not wed to Outsider men." Johen frowned, his face grim. "If they are not doing what they earn their high wages to do, there will be hellfire to pay for it."

Cheers ensued.

Johen inclined his head. He meant every word of it.

He grew as tired as his sector's people were of waiting for New Sweden's Revolution to erupt. Did the rebels not overthrow Toki soon, Johen would swear his allegiance to the New Danish jarl.

"I would not trade in my Jennifer even if I could," one man grumbled. "Yet her heart is with another. 'Tis difficult to warm her up to her new life with me."

The laws of the Underground did not recognize Outsider matrimony as binding, yet Johen understood the anger these Viking men felt upon learning that their wives were already married. It made wooing them into Viking culture and ensuring their eventual marital happiness a difficult task.

Once a wench was captured, she could never return to the Outside; 'twould be foolhardy and mayhap cause the collapse of their civilization. 'Twas why bride-hunters were to go to such great lengths to do all they could reasonably do to guarantee a lack of marriage.

None from the Outside could know of their existence— a point that couldn't be stressed enough. On the few occasions when the colonies had been stumbled upon by accident, the people in question were either killed or incorporated into their culture by matrimony.

Johen was the product of one such marriage. His sire, Eemil Stefsson, was a Viking from Hannu. His mother, Amani, was an Outsider who originally heralded from the country of Saudi Arabia.

His mother had been on vacation with her only living relative, a sister, in what the Outsiders called Alaska, when she and Aunt Affra had accidentally stumbled upon a door that led to the Underground. They had been caught and sold on the marriage auction block.

Eventually, after much perseverance by their husbands, both women had happily settled into Viking life. It made the transition easier that neither wench had given her heart to another man prior to being captured.

The bride-hunters had done grievous injustice to the men standing before Johen today. 'Twas not, however, Lord Stefsson's place to judge the fates of the bride-hunters; that would be the jarl's decision. If he refused to listen, Lord Stefsson would have no recourse but to rebel.

"I will speak with the king on the morrow," Johen said, standing up to take his leave. His silver gaze swept the audience a final time. "You have my vow."

CHAPTER THREE

*T*error having deserted her long ago in favor of numbness, Sofia wasn't certain how much time had ticked by before the taxi pulled up in front of a remote log cabin.

Icy mountains thrust up all around her. She was in the middle of nowhere, deep in the heart of rural Alaska. She hadn't seen another cabin since she'd awakened.

Snow began to fall, soft tranquil puffs looking at odds with their deadly ability to freeze people. What she wouldn't give to be back home in Florida, the sun beating down on her face.

As if in a dream, Sofia watched her hijacker alight from the taxi and close the door behind him. The thudding sound caused her to blink; the blink forced reality to come crashing back down on her.

He was going to murder her, probably rape her first. There was no other explanation for this.

Sofia's teeth began to chatter. Watching the taxi driver walk into the log cabin and shut the door behind him, she forced herself to concentrate on how she might overpower him.

He was short, fat and aging. She stood five-feet-eight-inches tall and had a more athletic physique. She had always been on the voluptuous side, but she was in excellent shape.

But what could she use as a weapon . . . Of course—her keys! She fumbled through her faux leather purse, relieved when she found the keys to her car. They didn't make much of a weapon, but they were better than nothing.

When he opened the backseat door, she would attack him. She took one of the keys off the ring, palmed it, and prepared to strike.

Driving a taxi didn't earn Willy the money he needed to support his cocaine and booze habit. Fuck, it barely covered the bills. Luckily, he knew what he had to do and who he had to go to in order to get paid nicely.

The pair of tall, weird mountain men who lived out here in the middle of no-fucking-where regularly paid him a lot of cash for young, pretty, fuckable bitches. Black, white, Asian, Spanish . . . they liked it all. But over the years he'd learned what they paid the most for, and the lady in the back of his cab was it.

The mountain men with the weirdo foreign accents didn't pay much for the skinny ones. They preferred rounded asses and hips, and big ole titties. An exceptionally beautiful face was always a requirement. Color didn't matter.

Willy didn't know what the mysterious men did with the women after they bought them, nor did he care. It was obvious the ladies were killed after they were fucked good and decent for a few days because the cabin was always devoid of females when he showed up . . . and he couldn't kidnap the bitches fast enough to suit the foreigners.

Willy waited with more patience than he felt as the foreigners stalked outside and inspected the new chattel.

Sofia clutched the key so tightly her knuckles turned white. Expecting to do battle with the short, out-of-shape taxi driver, she gasped when two huge men draped in polar bear furs emerged from the log cabin instead. They looked straight at her and her heart leapt into her chest.

They wore their hair in an odd fashion—a braid plaited on either side of their temples to keep their hair out of their line of vision. Obviously, they'd watched Mel Gibson in *Braveheart* one too many times. The polar bear furs obscured what they wore beneath them and whether or not they were carrying weapons.

The closer the giants got to the car, the sweatier Sofia's palms became. They had to be six-and-a-half-feet tall! She willed her heart to stop thumping so madly, but couldn't control it. The excess adrenaline was making her hands so clammy she could scarcely keep the key palmed.

One of the men threw open the front door of the taxicab. He pressed a button and Sofia heard the locks click open. Her teeth sank down into her lower lip, drawing blood. Her heart was beating so fast, she felt close to passing out. She didn't know what to do.

"Leave me alone!" she demanded, her voice guttural with desperation. "Go away!"

The front door slammed shut. The two brutes began to converse in a foreign tongue she couldn't place. One of them inclined his head to the other, then threw open the backseat door.

Sofia's breasts heaved up and down with her labored breathing. Did she strike now, or after he pulled her from the cab?

A second later, a big, meaty hand grabbed her by the arm and roughly pulled her from the backseat and onto her feet. Two seconds later, she was stabbing his hand with the key, breaking free of his hold while he bellowed.

"*Fan, hon skar mig!*"

"*Var inte så mesig!*"

Sofia took off running, blindly fleeing into the night, as far away from her new captors as her four-inch black high heels would carry her.

"*Jag kommer att fixa henne!*"

"*Det är ingen större problem!*"

She could hear their raised voices shouting at each other. Her arms pumped madly as she ran, breasts jiggling, her feet already close to frostbite. Her black pantyhose and high heels offered no protection against the subzero conditions. She was dressed for a funeral—not for highspeed running.

Where do I go? Sofia hysterically wondered.

There was nowhere to run to. The log cabin was in such a remote area, it was impossible for most people to find.

Her eyes widened in terror when she heard the telltale crunch of boots on snow gaining on her. Oh God, this wasn't happening. It couldn't be!

She ran with everything she had in her, heart drumming like mad, breath coming out in pants. Sofia screamed when two strong hands seized her from behind, effectively bringing a halt to her escape.

She struck out at him blindly with the key, but this time the giant merely snatched it out of her grasp and pocketed it with his free hand.

"Enough," he said gruffly, frowning. His accent was thick, its origin indiscernible. "Calm yourself, wench."

Wench? Oh God, he really *had* watched *Braveheart* too many times. The psycho believed he was living in medieval times!

Sofia kicked and flailed when he lifted her from the ground and threw her over his shoulder. It was like a mouse hammering against an unyielding brick wall.

"Help me!" she wailed, hysterical. "Somebody please help me!"

The big man was unperturbed by her cries as he carried her back toward the cabin. It forced her to wonder how often he did this to women, for it seemed like all in a day's work to him.

The giant she'd injured was waiting at the threshold. The colossal man carrying her said something to his comrade in their odd language, then followed him into an adjoining room.

The door shut firmly, terrifyingly, behind the three of them. A light flicked on. Sofia was hoisted off her captor's shoulder and made to stand before them. Her teeth started chattering again.

Her heart pounded like mad in her chest as the duo took their time studying her. They walked around her in circles as if inspecting a new horse they were considering purchasing. They forced open her mouth and eyed her teeth, then palmed her breasts and squeezed them a little. A hand on her butt, another one feeling up and down her legs . . .

"Please," she gasped, her voice catching in the back of her throat. "Don't hurt me."

One of the men blinked, then had the nerve to look affronted. "No harm shall come to you, wench." He frowned. "'Twould lower the price you can fetch us below the ground."

Lower the price they could sell her for? Like some modern day sex slave? But . . . but why would they take her below the ground? Would they talk so freely if they weren't absolutely certain she'd never escape them alive?

Oh God. Oh God. Oh God.

Perspiration drenched her forehead and cleavage. Unable to endure another moment, Sofia kneed one of the kidnappers in the groin and ran for the door as he bellowed in pain.

A pair of hands confidently seized her from behind. One moment she was kicking, screaming and punching anything within striking distance, and the next she had a handkerchief over her nose, breathing in what could only be chloroform.

Sofia could feel blackness stealing over her. As her legs and hands slowly went limp, her last conscious thought was that she hoped she never woke up again.

★   ★   ★

Willy's beady little eyes lit up as the two foreigners handed him a wad of hundreds. He whistled as he counted the cash. Yep, he'd known that girl would fetch him a pretty penny the moment she plopped down in the back of his cab.

What Willy didn't yet know was that this time, he wouldn't get a chance to snort that money away. The tall, mysterious men had decided that the cabbie knew too much, had seen too much.

And that was something they wouldn't tolerate.

CHAPTER FOUR

*L*ord Stefsson emerged from the jarl's dwelling place, furious he and the king were not of the same mind where the bride-hunters were concerned. The penalty for perjury under Hunter's Oath should result in whipping, imprisonment and confiscation of property for the guilty—not a slap on the wrist.

Bride-hunters who went out of their way to excel at their craft should earn higher wages. 'Twould offset the cost of the time-consuming work they must do and should have been doing all the while.

Unfortunately, a bride auction was slated for this eve. As always, the bride-hunters could legally sell off wenches to the auctioneer tonight, regardless of how little research they'd done before stealing the females. Johen would be there with his soldiers to ensure crowd control. 'Twas the best he could offer the men from his sector who were of a mind to bid on an Outsider bride this eve.

Right now he had another duty to attend to, of the familial sort.

Johen had promised his parents that he would arrive at their dwelling in time for the noon repast; they hadn't been able to see their son but twice in two fortnights. The price of power, he supposed.

He loved his sire and mama fiercely, but truth be told, Johen was not looking forward to this meal. Both of his parents had been pressing him to marry for ages. He had insisted on not buying a bride until after the rebels' Revolution had been won. That hadn't come to pass, but his parents expected him to continue their lineage regardless.

And, indeed, when he left Lokitown and arrived in the colony of Hannu forty-five minutes later, the marriage conversation began. Johen stifled a sigh as his sire droned on about the importance of settling down. Johen understood his duty and had given more thought to marriage as of late, but he preferred to give the rebels another couple of years. 'Twas much to be done in New Sweden and he would be responsible for much of it did they win.

Johen respectfully listened as he wolfed down his mother's impeccable cooking.

"You are a noble, son. The status of our entire line depends upon a marriage that bears fruit." Eemil Stefsson looked at his son pointedly. "'Twould be a shame for the glory of the Stefsson name to die out with you."

"Really, Eemil," his mother, Amani, said with exasperation. "Can we not discuss this after Johen finishes eating?"

His sire frowned, but grumbled agreement. Johen winked at his mother.

Gods, but he'd missed his mother's cooking. Leastways,

'twas decent fare to be had all over Lokitown, but none of it measured up to his mother's Viking-Arabian style of cuisine.

His sire resumed needling him about marriage the very moment Johen's platter was empty. His mother smiled, knowing her husband very well. There would be no help forthcoming from her camp, he mused.

"'Tis a matter of honor," his sire barked. "Not to mention pride. The Stefsson name cannot carry on without a bride to give you heirs. And furthermore . . ."

Johen listened with a patience he did not feel as his sire droned on. He sat back in his chair, resigned to the tongue thrashing no man save Eemil Stefsson would dare give him.

Leastways, his mother's cooking had been worth it.

Johen gathered up his warriors and soldiers, motioning for them to follow him toward the bride auction. If the gossip his men had overhead was to be believed, crowd control might very well be an issue this eve.

'Twas apparent that the men of Hannu were not the only ones upset about the bride-hunters' inept work as of late; the Vikings from mainland New Sweden were growing increasingly furious as well. The bride auction could very well turn ugly.

He didn't like traveling to Lokitown. He had come here once today already to speak to the wretched king. Twice was taxing to the nerves. Johen didn't think Toki would be so daft as to attempt his assassination, but 'twas best to always proceed with caution. Killing Johen would result in Hannu throwing its allegiance toward New Daneland, but the jarl of New Sweden was known for his idiocy.

Johen's gray eyes narrowed as he walked. "Do not wield blunt force unless absolutely necessary," he instructed his men.

Making their way to the coliseum, Johen reflected on the nooning meal he'd shared a few hours ago with his parents. As much as he hated admitting it, his sire did have a valid point.

Johen was possessed of three married sisters. Unless he took a bride, their line would die out—a fate worse than death to proud Vikings.

He supposed it wouldn't kill him to assess the wenches up for bid this eve as potential brides for himself. Ten of the fifteen to be auctioned off were natives of New Sweden, accustomed to the ways of the Underground Viking world. They wouldn't spend days, months or mayhap even years, grieving for life above the ground.

Unfortunately, Outsider wenches had always held an allure to Johen. Even as a boy barely in the throes of puberty, he'd sneak into bride auctions, hide in the shadows and lust after them. Their exotic beauty and unfamiliar backgrounds were too much an enticement to pass up.

Johen's tastes hadn't changed over the years. Outsider wenches continued to fascinate him. Mayhap he could at least consider the possibility of . . .

He frowned. Nay, 'twas impractical. At least in this phase of his life.

Helping Niko depose of Toki was not only his mission,

but his duty. He needed to be at the ready when the rebels were ready to strike. A troublesome wife at such a crucial juncture was a recipe for disaster.

And *all* Outsider brides were difficult until they settled into the Viking way of things. No matter how intriguing any of the Outsider brides up for auction might be, he would only consider native wenches as potential wives. 'Twould appease his parents while permitting him to concentrate on his duties to Hannu.

"We are here," Johen told his men. "Keep your swords at the ready."

His course firmly decided, Johen entered the arena, his fighters close on his heels. Should he purchase a bride this eve, 'twould be a native wench and no other.

CHAPTER FIVE

*A*re you sure?" she gasped. "M-maybe it's a mistake? Maybe Sam wasn't on that chopper?"

"Ma'am, I'm sorry. I can't tell you how sorry I am. But there is no way your brother survived that helicopter crash. None of the four victims could have."

She closed her eyes, indescribable grief ripping through her gut. Sofia had tried so hard to talk Sam out of joining the army, but he couldn't be swayed. Naïve and patriotic, her brother had wanted to make a difference for his country. He hadn't gotten that chance.

And wasn't the military supposed to deliver news like this in person? *Sofia thought, angry at everyone and everything. That's the way it always happened in the movies.*

"Ma'am?" Jacobs's voice gentled. "I know this is difficult for you, but as Specialist Rowley's only living family member, we really need you to come to Alaska and attempt to identify your brother's remains."

"Attempt?" she breathed out. An ice-cold chill worked up and down her spine. "Can't you tell from his dog tags?"

Every person in the military wore those small pieces of metal dangling from their necks. They were used for identification purposes, namely for awful situations like this.

Jacobs stilled on the other end of the telephone connection. "We didn't find his head," he said softly, "so there wasn't a dog tag to retrieve."

Sofia's eyes widened. She slapped a palm over her mouth, and screamed behind it.

Her eyes flew open. Breathing heavily, Sofia jolted upright on the bed. *Sam . . .*

Her heart sank as she realized anew that her brother was dead. It had been this way every night since she'd received that horrible telephone call. Despite her current predicament, the nightmares still came.

She took a deep breath and slowly exhaled as her gaze darted around and another reality slowly took hold—she was still being held captive.

Sofia had been a prisoner in the bizarre Underground world for five very long days and nights. She hadn't seen much of the civilization, but the trip from the log cabin to this undiscovered enclave in the earth's belly was enough to send icy fear lancing through her.

Each day in captivity felt as long as a year. The first day was still a numb blur, as she'd been too shell-shocked to comprehend what was going on.

The numbness waned on the second day and was replaced with a mixture of anger and terror. She physically and verbally attacked anyone who dared to enter the tiny room she'd been sequestered in, not caring whether they were male or female, young or old.

They claimed to be Vikings. These people were insane, and she wanted no part of their lunacy.

An old healer named Myria had mixed a brew to calm Sofia's raging nerves, and explained where she was and why she was here as Sofia sipped from it. The woman had told her that the people of the Underground had dwelled below the earth's surface for centuries as a result of ancient prophecies. They believed that one day the women who lived above the ground would become all but extinct.

Sofia could have cared less about how their people chose to exist. She cared mightily, however, that they meant to envelop her into their peculiar world.

"You are to become the bride of whatever Viking bids the most coins on you," Myria told her.

"You can't be serious," Sofia retorted. She managed to keep her voice from shaking, but it took a lot of effort. "I'm going to be sold off . . . like a slave?"

"Nay, like a wife." The old healer frowned, her wrinkles all but enveloping her lips. "'Tis an honor."

Sofia didn't think it was an honor. She had spent days three and four plotting methods of escape. Determined to be back in sunny Florida before she was auctioned off to some throwback barbarian on night five, she had attempted to break out and run away at least a dozen times.

She had failed every time. Deep down inside, she had known she would. After all, these people continued to exist and thrive because nobody knew about them—it was as simple and ugly as that. Sofia wasn't naïve enough to believe that these Underground dwellers hadn't thought and rethought out every possible escape . . . and made them foolproof.

Still, she owed it to herself to try, so try she did. She didn't give up the ship until this morning, when a group of female groomers entered the room she was confined in and made her strip off her clothes. Then they bathed her, shaved her mons of all hair and worked rich oils into her skin that smelled of vanilla and honey.

They were preparing her for the marriage auction block. That knowledge was as sobering as it was frightening.

Later, toward evening, the group of females returned for a final inspection of Sophia. She asked them for clothes; they told her all brides went to the block naked. Sophia paled, praying for death.

Physically exhausted and mentally resigned, Sofia didn't know what to do as she examined her reflection in the jagged, cracked mirror on the wall.

She closed her eyes and sighed. She wished her prayer for death had been answered. Even going back to the surreal, numb phase would have been welcomed. It would be easier to get through this auction if she wasn't so painfully aware of everything transpiring around her.

" 'Twill be all right," an old voice crooned.

Sofia's eyes flew open. She hadn't heard Myria come in. "I doubt that, but thanks for trying to make me feel better." Her turquoise gaze rounded. "I've never been this scared."

She wasn't the type to admit to fear, but confiding in the

old woman was easy. She had been with Sofia so much over the past five days that her presence almost felt normal.

"I vow that no harm will come to you." The healer shut the door behind her and waddled into the room. She was the only female Sofia'd seen around here that wasn't dressed in skimpy attire. She always wore a black-hooded cowl that covered everything, its solemn color a stark contrast against the white crinkles of her skin. "Viking husbands are patient and kind. Leastways, they try to be."

Sofia snorted at that. "How encouraging," she muttered, running both hands through her unruly mane of blond curls.

"Drink this," Myria instructed, handing her a mug of something she could tell was alcoholic. Apparently Sofia wasn't good at hiding her emotions under moments of extreme distress. "Drink," Myria again prodded. "'Twill calm your nerves considerably."

Sofia had no problem following that dictate. She was grateful that the old woman had intervened with her impending fate in whatever small way she could. And, she thought as she swallowed down the contents of the tankard, the healer was right. It *was* calming her nerves. A few minutes later Sofia realized it was doing something else too, though. She frowned quizzically.

"What's in this?" Sofia asked before downing the remainder of the sweet, potent liquid.

"Mead laced with honey," Myria informed her. "And a few herbs from my private garden. I must take my leave. Good luck, girl. May the gods smile upon you and deliver you unto a fair, kind master."

Master—an interchangeable word for husband in this queer world. Sofia didn't know what to say beyond "Thank you."

A weird sensation hit her belly, and she squeezed her thighs together. "Uh, Myria . . . what kind of herbs from your garden are in this?"

The old healer cackled as she opened the door, then winked. "I like you and I want you to thrive in Lokitown. I gave you a little aid to see you through the wedding night. Your future husband will expect to bed you this eve."

Sofia stilled. Her eyes narrowed. "What. Kind. Of. Aid?"

Myria shrugged as she prepared to exit the room. "'Tis known to Vikings as *erotisk.*" Her shaggy gray eyebrows shot up. "Our ancestors said 'twas like something called Spanish Fly—"

Sofia gasped. And stifled a moan.

"—yet far more powerful a sexual aphrodisiac."

Sophia believed her. Her hands balled at her sides, jaw clenching, as she determinedly attempted to thwart the increasing arousal.

All ten of the natives had been auctioned off and Lord Stefsson found himself intrigued by a grand total of zero. They were all quite striking in their beauty, but they lacked a certain feistiness that he found attractive in wenches.

Johen stilled as the Outsiders were led up onto the stage. All five were exotically striking. All five were feisty. But only one of them snagged his attention from the moment he saw her.

He frowned grimly. He would not bid on her. No matter how bedeviling her beauty and proud her stance, no matter how defiantly stiff his cock became in his braes from just looking at her . . .

"Cease this," he muttered to himself. He had made a vow and he meant to keep it. Johen's jaw tightened as he willed himself to look away, but 'twas useless.

She wasn't a classic beauty, but that didn't make her allure any less potent. Possessed of bewitching blue-green eyes the color of which he'd never before seen, her gaze was heavy-lidded like a sexual wanton's. 'Twas an irresistible combination.

Her hair was long and blond with springy, wild curls—further bringing to mind an untamable, exotic beauty made for his hard, lusty lovemaking. Her skin was a gorgeous honey-gold that glistened of the rich oils the groomers had no doubt slicked her down with. Her lips were full and naturally red. Johen blew out a breath as he glanced down and took in the rest of her.

Her breasts were firm for their large size, two luscious globes that he wanted to spend hours kneading, kissing and sucking. Her nipples were pink and very stiff, so swollen that just looking at them made his cock throb.

The naked, blond captive was voluptuously built, her body like that of a fabled beauty from Viking folklore. Big breasts, flat belly, curvy hips . . .

And a gorgeous, bald pussy.

He unapologetically stared at her glistening, oiled-down cunt. He needed to fuck her so badly he ached with it.

The auctioneer instructed the wenches to turn around, and Johen got a painfully arousing view of her plump, perfectly rounded arse. Once they were bade to face front again, the bride auction for the captives began.

She was the first Outsider to go up for bid. The wench stood there proud, her back straight and chin held high, despite the frenzied shouts, cheers and whistles erupting from within the arena.

His narrowed, silver gaze clashed with the captive's. Her eyes widened and she quickly looked away.

"This gorgeous wench is named Sofia!" the auctioneer cried out in their people's tongue. "With big tits and a plump arse, she's worth your last coins, men!"

Laughter echoed throughout the arena. The auctioneer winked. "Milords, as always, you have first inspection and bidding rights. You may now approach the marriage chattel!"

Lord Stefsson's nostrils flared when he saw every bedamned noble in the coliseum approach Sofia. This captive wench would not be bid on by those of the lower classes—the auction would never make it that far. The rouge-lipped blonde with the rounded turquoise eyes would become the wife of a noble this very eve.

You are a noble. You can bid on her, too. . . .

Johen's muscles tensed, fighting the way his cock throbbed from just gazing at her.

CHAPTER SIX

S ofia didn't know whether to scream or masturbate. She wanted to wring Myria's neck for putting that damn *erotisk* in her drink.

Every moment worked her higher into frenzied sexual arousal. Surely the herb would wear off soon—it just had to! Even the bald, obese men in the crowd gawking up at her were starting to look like acceptable lovers.

Oh, God, this was just awful! Anger fought arousal inside Sofia, but it looked to be losing.

There was one man in particular that Sofia found her gaze inadvertently straying to. If she had thought the men that stole her were giants, well, that was before she saw *him*.

Dressed in a sleeveless, silver, chain-mail tunic with two dragon-crested bangles clasped unforgivingly around his bulging biceps, he had to stand seven feet tall. His black leather pants and boots covered the lower portion of his body, but didn't hide the honed, powerful musculature beneath them.

His hair was a sleek dark brown and fell to mid-back, with a braid at either temple. And those eyes . . .

Merciless gray slits devoid of all emotion.

Their gazes clashed and Sofia felt decidedly nervous. He was assessing her and she didn't like it. Her sex-hungry libido recognized that he was undeniably handsome, but the part of her brain not glutted with the herb realized how powerfully built he was.

If one of the fat, bald men bid on her, at least she could still carry the hope of escaping this madhouse one day. If that giant bid on her, she'd never see Florida again. He didn't look like the type that gave up easily, if at all.

She quickly glanced away and blew out an edgy breath. Arousal knotted fiercely in her belly, forcing her to squeeze her thighs together again.

The auctioneer called out something in their Viking tongue, and the spectators cheered and whistled. Sofia swallowed roughly as men began to ascend the stage, their attentions trained directly on her. Clearly, she was the first of the unwilling brides to go up for bid.

I can't believe this is happening. I lost my brother and my freedom in two day's time. . . .

And now, five days later, she was being sold at an auction like a common animal.

So much grieving and soul-searching had occurred after Sam's death. So many "what ifs" and "if onlys." She'd realized that she needed to get a new life—but if *this* was her new life, she'd take the old one back in a heartbeat.

* * *

The proud, beautiful Outsider wench was starting to get frightened. Her eyes were round, her breasts heaving up and down in time with her labored breathing. Johen had seen that look of apprehension on the faces of countless other females before they were sold to their masters, so he couldn't say why this woman in particular struck a chord of sympathy with him. And yet she did.

Johen sighed. He would *not* bid on her.

Lord Mikael Aleksson approached the platform. A longtime friend, he would take excellent care of any bride he purchased. But why was he here? Mikael had always been too much of a ladies' man to settle down with one female.

But Sofia was . . . intoxicating. There was no other word to describe her, and even that was sadly lacking.

As Mikael approached the Outsider wench, she warily eyed him up and down. It took her a suspended moment, but she eventually granted his friend a small, if nervous, smile.

Wenches loved Mikael—it was ever the way of it. Young maidens swooned at his feet, all of them praying she would be the one he bid on when at last 'twas her turn to stand on the marriage auction block.

The native girls would be heartbroken. Mikael had his sights fixed on Sofia.

Johen's nostrils flared. He didn't even know the Outsider wench, yet he found himself detesting the thought of another Viking touching her. 'Twould have been bad enough watching her sold off to a man he scarcely knew, but to a noble he counted among his closest friends?

Johen envisioned being greeted at Mikael's dwelling by Sofia, all soft curves and swelled breasts. He would be forced to watch as his comrade made lusty eyes at her over the evening repast. Mikael would be thinking ahead, to the time after Johen departed, anticipating thrusting into the body he now owned by the law. . . .

His stomach muscles clenched. Johen couldn't explain his powerful reaction to Sofia, but it was all-consuming. No man should touch her. No man but him.

Despite his vow, Johen's feet carried him to the raised platform where she stood.

The potency of the *erotisk* all but made Sofia moan. She felt like a trapped animal in heat. There was but one cure to the desperation gnawing in her belly and battling that need only served to work her up that much more intensely.

A man approached her. A big man, and quite handsome, though not so formidable as the unsmiling one possessed of gray eyes and an emotionless face. She knew this man wouldn't do. Like the Viking her damned libido kept forcing her gaze to stray back to, the new male threat was too powerful a foe to ever escape from.

Sofia swallowed as he eyed her up and down. He looked his fill at her naked body and face, and she couldn't help but notice his erection through the leather pants he wore. Tall, raven-haired, and forbiddingly muscular, he was as frightening-looking as he was handsome.

The last thing on earth she wanted was for this man to bid on her. Nevertheless, she granted him a small, barely there smile as a safeguard.

If he married her, she didn't want him on his guard any more than he would already be.

She would pretend compliance. Or at least attempt to.

He winked down at her, and she swallowed again.

Just when she thought the situation couldn't possibly get grimmer, *he* ascended the stage—the man with the silver eyes and stoic face.

Tall and broad, his lethal musculature was a heady sight. Their gazes clashed and she felt close to hyperventilating. An aura of power surrounded him. She'd never met a harder, more determined and dangerous male in all of her life.

His gaze raked over her, his eyelids heavy with desire. It was the only emotion Sofia'd seen him betray thus far, and the very last one she wanted.

Her body reacted to his stare against her volition, her nipples stabbing out farther until they were swollen and aching. Her hands balled into fists at her sides, fingernails digging into her palms.

There was no denying his impressive good looks, but she didn't want a husband like him! Short, overweight and out-of-shape was the ideal ticket—getting through the wedding night with such a man wouldn't even be necessary because she could knock him out and run. She hoped.

But this man?

Her worried gaze flicked between the two potential buyers. They would both bid on her. Without a doubt these Viking men wanted her.

The *erotisk* continued to work its dark magic and she closed her eyes briefly, praying the worst of the herb would wear off soon.

She needed her wits about her. The hours to come would be crucial ones.

CHAPTER SEVEN

*S*ofia . . .

Her name was as exotic and beautiful as she was. Johen imagined himself calling it out as he slammed in and out of her, his cock jerking and throbbing as he came into her body.

"Milords," the auctioneer said with a respectful bow, "we've a lot of brides up for sale this eve and so the auction must proceed anon. Do I hear a first bid?"

"Ten thousand," Mikael announced without a pause.

"Fifteen," another said.

Every muscle in Johen's body tensed. The vow he'd made to himself was forgotten. "Twenty."

Mikael's surprised gaze darted over to Johen; his attention had been trained on Sofia.

Mikael's eyebrows slowly rose. His half-smile was amused, and bedamn it, quite smug. Mikael wasn't the only warlord in New Sweden with a rogue's reputation. Leastways, the other noble was as astonished to espy Johen bidding on a bride as Johen had been to see him doing so.

"Twenty-five," Mikael said, his eyes dancing.

Johen grunted. "Thirty."

He could hear the murmurings of the crowd. 'Twas a heady sum to pay for a bride, and every man present knew it.

Johen's gaze strayed to Sofia. She looked scared, and he couldn't fault her for it. All conversation was transpiring in a language she knew naught of. In time she would come to know the Viking tongue; for now, all that mattered was ensuring he would be the one teaching it to her.

"Does any noble amongst you bid thirty-five?"

Johen's gaze swept over the other men, his possessive expression speaking volumes. Wisely, no man thought to gainsay him.

Not even Mikael. Surprising, considering how much they enjoyed baiting each other.

"Going once. Going twice . . ."

Gods, she is beautiful. His cock was so hard it ached.

"The bride Sofia Rowley is sold to Lord Stefsson for thirty thousand coins!"

And now she was his! All his.

Johen barely noticed when Mikael affectionately thumped him on the back; he was too occupied with staring at the wench standing before him. His wife.

She was scared. Sofia mayhap spoke nary a word of their tongue, yet her expression told him that she understood her fate.

Sofia didn't need to speak their language to know what was happening. If the congratulatory pats on the back given to

Silver Eyes weren't obvious enough, the auctioneer placing her hand in his spoke volumes.

She was married to him. By the laws of this bizarre world, the barbarian with the unsmiling face was now her husband.

She shivered, though she didn't know if it was from fear engulfing her brain, the *erotisk* smothering every nerve in her body or both. Her turquoise eyes widened as he gently tugged on her hands.

"I am Johen," the giant said softly, his gaze finding hers. "Your master."

He spoke English. She didn't know if that was a good thing or not. She also didn't know what to say in reply. Her master? Good lord.

Sofia swallowed heavily, her breasts heaving up and down with her heavy breathing. Perspiration broke out on her forehead as her pulse picked up in tempo. Again, she didn't know if the changes were a result of terror or arousal.

Her heart told her this couldn't be happening, but her mind knew that it was. This was no dream. Her brother was dead, and she had been kidnapped mere minutes after his funeral. Stripped of clothes and her dignity, she now stood before a man telling her that she was his possession.

The herb hit her in the belly hard, forcing her to stifle a gasp. "My name is Sofia Rowley," she said quickly, trying to cover up her intense arousal. She squeezed her thighs together as if trying to juice a lemon. If she ever got her hands on Myria . . .

"Stefsson," the man countered, snagging her attention. "Lady Sofia Stefsson is your name."

She would deal with the implications of his declaration later. For now, she was too busy trying to thwart the *erotisk*.

"I'm not feeling well," she gasped, stifling a moan. God, how she needed to come! "Please . . . I need to lie down."

Preferably someplace private, where she could masturbate like there was no tomorrow. Once replete, she could concentrate on what her intuition screamed was impossible: escaping the man who called himself her husband.

Johen's cock had never been so hard.

Though he had purchased an Outsider bride who would try to escape from him if he ever lowered his guard, he didn't care. She was his fantasy, with lush, full hips, a rounded arse, plump tits, and a face he would never tire of drinking in.

At this moment, she feared and mayhap loathed him. Given time and patience, she would grow to love him just as his mother had come to love his sire.

"I'm not feeling well," she said, her voice sounding choked. "Please . . . I need to lie down."

Her fear was to be expected. 'Twould nearly kill him to delay the consummation of their marriage, but it was the honorable thing to do. If he wanted her to grow to love and trust him, he had to earn it.

"Come," he said quietly, trying not to scare her with his usual gruff tone of voice. His passion-drunk gaze swept over her face, her body, unable to resist staring at those ripe, stiff nipples. "I will take you to our dwelling."

CHAPTER EIGHT

*T*he trip to Johen's sector was quite lengthy, surprising her as to the vastness of this unknown world. Methods of Underground travel were proving to be efficient and complex.

Johen had explained to a distracted Sofia that when trekking from one village to another within New Sweden, a mine car could take you wherever it was you needed to go. The Viking version of a subway, she supposed. But when traveling outside the colony, as they were now to Hannu, a boat that braved the icy Viking rivers belowground was necessary.

The air was frigid, mercilessly lashing against her face. Thankfully, Johen had removed his chain-mail tunic and covered her with it before leaving the bride auction. It was heavy, bulky and scratchy, but it was keeping her pretty warm. The *erotisk* was doing a good job of that too.

Sofia closed her eyes and held onto the boat rail, telling herself she wasn't aroused. The icy air beating her face should have acted as a deterrent, but it didn't. Every second of every minute passed like a year. She repeatedly squeezed her thighs together, praying the boat would soon dock and Johen would leave her alone in a bedroom where she could take matters into her own hands—literally.

"We've five minutes more and we'll be home," Johen announced, threading her fingers through his. "Our dwelling lies close to the docks."

Good. If she didn't get to a private room soon, she was liable to start masturbating like a lunatic right here and now.

"Okay," Sofia breathed out.

Her clit was pulsing, throbbing. She needed to touch herself so badly. Just when she thought she couldn't take it anymore, the boat docked.

Sofia expected Johen's home to be as simple and rustic as the room she'd been locked in for five days and nights. It was surprising to be led into a lavish Underground house bursting at the seams with luxury.

Silk pillows and draperies of every color imaginable filled each room, bringing to mind the extravagant home of an Arabian sultan. Servants lingered everywhere, seeing to various chores, humming tunes to themselves as if pleased in their work.

Sofia blew out a none-too-subtle breath as Johen steered her into his bedroom. The bed was huge—at least double the size of her king bed back in Florida—and ornately carved from a black material she couldn't name. Proud dragon heads had been sculpted into the foot of it. Sheer blue and green silks draped down from the eight posters that thrust up from the gargantuan-size bed.

"I do not expect that we will consummate our union this eve," Johen said softly as he turned her around to stand before him. "Yet we will always sleep under the same bed furs, never to be separated."

Those silver eyes betrayed his desire. He was controlled enough to keep his hands off of her, but Sofia realized it was the last thing he wanted to do.

The self-preserving part of her brain was thankful that he didn't want to have sex tonight, since she planned to run. She knew that being intimate with him might make him all the more territorial where she was concerned.

Two strong hands landed on her shoulders and her gaze flew up to meet his. Johen tugged at the chain mail she wore, his eyes filled with unapologetic lust as he removed it.

"What are you doing?" Sofia breathed out. Her pulse soared, heart thumping in her chest. "I-I thought . . ."

"I will not breach you," he said, his voice hoarse. His gaze drank her in as she stood before him naked. "I just want to touch you."

His callused palms rested at the juncture of her neck. Slowly his hands trailed down, feeling every curve of her breasts. His palms scraped her sensitive nipples and Sofia couldn't suppress the small moan that escaped.

"So beautiful," Johen murmured, gently massaging her stiff nipples. "And so mine."

He played with her breasts and nipples for torturously long minutes. Every second felt like an hour, destroying Sofia's concentration. She was this close to coming and knew it wasn't wise. She had to fight the arousal—refuse to give into it.

His fingers found her vaginal lips. He played slowly with them while she sucked in a deep tug of air.

"Please," Sofia begged, her voice shaky. His forefinger found her clit and began rubbing her tantalizingly. "Please stop."

Her plea didn't sound credible even to her own ears. She could see his large erection swollen against his leather pants and wondered if he'd be able to pull himself back.

"You are wet with need," Johen said hoarsely, "yet I will respect your wishes."

He rubbed her clit a few more times, then withdrew. Sofia whimpered—in relief or misery?

Lord help her, a saint couldn't withstand torture like this! Desire clawed at her belly; she would never survive this night with her sanity intact!

Her eyes frenzied, her entire body on fire, she ached so badly that she was in actual pain.

Unable to endure it another moment, her brain too frazzled to consider the consequences, Sofia scrambled up onto the bed, spread her thighs wide, and began vigorously masturbating.

Beads of sweat broke out on Johen's forehead at the carnal sight. How could she expect him not to consummate with her this eve when she was stroking her pussy right there in front of him? His jaw steeled.

Sweet Odin.

"Oh, God," Sofia moaned, rubbing her clit in urgent circles. *"Oh, yes."*

She was lying on her back, golden ringlets of hair fanned

out around her head. Her legs were wide open, showing him the tight flesh he wanted to impale more than he wanted to breathe. Her nipples stabbed straight up, beckoning to his mouth.

Johen's teeth gritted. Why was she doing this to him?

Sofia came on a loud groan, her nipples growing impossibly harder. Her neck arched and her eyes closed, yet she still wanted more.

"It's not enough," she gasped, her voice sounding almost terrified. "When will it wear off?"

She continued her relentless quest for satiation, nearly killing him. What man could resist this?

Then Johen stilled as her words sank in. When will it wear off? When will *what* wear off?

The answer slowly dawned on him. Old Myria was chiefly responsible for the captive brides' well-being until they were put up for auction. Old Myria . . . the herbalist.

Sofia had been pumped full of *erotisk.*

Sweet, sweet Odin.

Johen peeled off his clothes until he wore nothing but his gold, jewel-encrusted bicep bands. His cock was stone-hard, and more than eager to help his wife out of her carnal predicament.

He got onto the bed beside her, resting his weight on an elbow. "'Twill be all right," he said reassuringly, his free hand massaging her nipples. He couldn't help but lower his mouth to one. He closed his eyes briefly as he suckled it, firmly drawing on the swollen nub.

She moaned, coming loudly. He nigh unto spilled himself

at the sound, at her scent. Suppressing a moan of his own, he released her nipple with a popping sound and laved attention on the neglected one.

"Ohgggggooooooood!"

She came. And came and came and came.

Gods, but he'd never seen a sexier wench.

"I had thought to give you time to adjust to the thought of consummating our marriage," Johen rasped, "yet your need will not pass for a few days."

She whimpered. His cock throbbed, knowing he was up for the challenge. Pre-cum dripped from the tiny hole, desperation to be inside of her scraping at his gut.

"Come, little one," Johen said thickly as she resumed playing with herself. His hand recommenced playing with her breasts, massaging her stiff nipples.

Sofia burst on yet another loud groan, her head falling back and mouth ajar. Her breathing was heavy, her need still great.

"Please," she said in a little voice that got to him in a way no wench before her ever had. "Help me."

She looked so scared, so defenseless. It moved him in a way he couldn't name. Wide, innocent eyes and a wanton's body—'twas a heady combination.

Johen blew out a breath. He didn't want to take her like this, but he didn't want her in unnecessary pain, either.

Hard and ready, he moved between his wife's thighs. Preparing to enter her, he threaded his rough fingers through the soft silk of her golden hair, his eyes finding her amazing green-blue gaze.

"Do you want me to help?" He positioned the tip of his cock at the opening of her pussy. If she said nay, he might not be able to stop. "Do you desire this consummation?"

"Yes!" she wailed. Her hands grabbed his buttocks, pulling him closer. Her eyes were wide, desperate. *"Please get inside of me!"*

Teeth gritting, muscles tensing, Johen slowly pushed his long, thick cock into her pussy. He groaned as he impaled her, seating himself to the hilt in hot, wet paradise.

Sofia came immediately. Violently. She screamed, fingernails digging into the rigid flesh of his arse.

Already close to coming, Johen utilized every drop of self-will to hold back his orgasm. He began to move slowly within her tight flesh, his entire body clenched in a pleasure that was almost an agony. He had to concentrate on his wife's needs rather than his own.

"Faster," Sofia panted. She threw her hips up at him, pounding against him. *"Faster, harder,"* she ground out.

Johen growled, giving her what she needed. He drove deep, impaling her in long, fast strokes. She keened in response, coming more times than he could count.

"You belong to me," Johen said possessively, riding her hard. "Your pussy, your everything—never forget that you are mine."

Later he would work on claiming her heart, her soul. For now all he could do was bask in her tight depths, gluttonously devouring every inch of her.

Sofia's hips rose to his, meeting him thrust for thrust. "I won't forget—*just don't stop!"*

Johen took her impossibly harder. He moaned as he rode her, the sound of flesh slapping against flesh as arousing as the scent of her orgasms. Over and over, deeper and faster, possessively branding her as his.

He could no longer hold himself back. The orgasm was ripping through him and he couldn't stop it. *"I'm coming, here I come, little one."*

He came on a loud roar as she milked every last drop of him. His entire body convulsed atop hers, tense muscles loosening in the all-consuming explosion.

Johen held her closely, his breathing heavy, his body slick with sweat. He murmured to her of her sexiness, of her beauty . . . and of his promise that one day soon she would love him.

He could only hope his words proved true.

They were husband and wife. Master and cherished one. He would have it no other way.

CHAPTER NINE

Three days later

I vow to you that they will not bite," Johen said with a wink as, hand-in-hand, he steered Sofia toward his parents' house. " 'Twill be all right."

Sofia doubted it. For one, the *erotisk* still hadn't totally worn off. Her urges weren't as all-consuming as they'd been over the past three days, but they still simmered. Her cheeks suffused with heat, thinking about the possible embarassments.

Second, she was still feeling shell-shocked. In a little over a week Sofia had borne the death of her only relative, survived a kidnapping, been stripped of her clothing and possessions, then sold to the highest bidder on an auction block.

The clothes Johen had given her in replacement were shockingly indecent. The gold tunic was undeniably beautiful, but much too sheer for Sofia's peace of mind. The barely–there dress was supported at the top by an elastic band that began just above her cleavage line and draped down to her ankles. Red rope crisscrossed at her hips and kept the hemline from falling all the way to her toes. Her nipples pressed against the sheer top, stiff and aroused. To say she was mortified by her attire was the millenium's greatest understatement.

All in all, there were plenty of times when she felt like she was in the midst of a long, weird dream.

And Sofia felt uncomfortable pretending to be compliant while plotting her escape all the while. It would have been so much easier if she could hate Lord Johen Stefsson.

If he'd mistreated or abused her. If he'd forced her into having sex. Or withheld it, knowing the potent herb was driving her crazy. Hell, even being ugly would have helped!

You're simply going through Stockholm syndrome. You aren't the first woman alive to start identifying with her captor, and you won't be the last. Fight against it. . . .

She had nothing to feel guilty about. She had been kidnapped, and it was normal to want her freedom.

And yet the guilt was there whenever the giant gazed down at her with stars in his eyes and she smiled back at him.

Why did he do that? *Why?* He'd known her all of three days. He couldn't possibly be in love with her!

Johen was a battle-honed soldier, a wise and respected leader of his people. He was not a young boy who couldn't separate lust from love. At thirty-six, Johen was not only four years her senior, but judging by his skill in bed, he'd been around the block more times than the ice-cream man.

And yet . . .

Despite his brains, regardless of his brawn, there was something inexplicably naïve about him. Johen looked at her with such hope, such longing—as if she wielded the power to make him or break him. Sofia couldn't understand why, but it was getting to her.

She didn't want to hurt him. Despite everything, she truly didn't. Call it Stockholm syndrome, call it something else altogether, but she had no desire at all to wound this man who called himself her husband.

"I'll survive this meal somehow," Sofia said quietly. A pang of arousal lanced through her, forcing her to clench her vaginal muscles. "Preferably without making a fool of myself."

Johen chuckled. It was the first time she'd ever heard him do that, and she found herself giving him a genuine smile.

Stop it! Don't you understand that I need to hate you?

"The only fool here is I," Johen replied, coming to a stop before the door to his parents' house. He drew her hand up to his lips and softly kissed it. "I'm fool-crazy over you."

Sofia mentally sighed. Apparently he *didn't* understand.

The door abruptly opened. Startled, Sofia's gaze landed on the handsome couple standing there—his parents.

They eyed her up and down, as if assessing her worthiness for their son. Stupid as it was, she found their scrutiny even more nerve-racking than the bride auction three days past. Sofia had no reason to be bothered by what these people thought of her, and part of her wished they disliked what they saw, so she'd feel better when she ran from Johen.

It didn't look like that would be happening.

The father's smile was wide, the mother's all but beaming. "Greetings, daughter," the older man said, his eyes dancing. "I am Eemil and this is my wife, Amani." He respectfully inclined his head. "Welcome to our dwelling."

Sofia forced a smile to her lips, every nerve in her body frayed. "Thank you."

As Johen's parents led her into their home, Sofia decided this had the makings of a long night. An aura of exuberance haloed the gathering, while she felt as though she'd ridden a twister into the land of Oz.

Dinner was unlike anything Sofia had ever tasted. As she listened to the conversation taking place, namely, the story of Amani's capture and marriage to the big Viking beside her, she understood why the flavor of the meal was so unique.

A mix of two cultures, the food was just like the house's decor—Conan the Barbarian meets Princess Jasmine of Arabia.

"My sister and I thought we might faint," Amani mused in a lyrical Arabic accent. "Arranged marriages were nothing new to us, but the Viking culture was much to take in, for two women who'd lived such sheltered lives."

Eemil chuckled at the memory. "I believe you did faint, my love. Leastways, I seem to remember reviving you, only to have you see me and faint dead away yet again."

The family shared a laugh and Sofia found her lips twitching, too, despite herself. She could empathize with Amani's plight only too well.

"I do not recall fainting," Johen's mother teasingly sniffed.

"Aye, you did," Eemil quickly countered. "Right at my bedamned feet."

"Oh shush!"

Sofia's gaze strayed to Johen's grinning face. It was obvious he and his parents were very close. The love and bond they shared was a tangible thing.

Johen looked like a younger, but strikingly similar version of his father. Same height and musculature, same teasing eyes and smile. From Amani he had inherited his dark hair and olive complexion.

Yet as much as Sofia found the conversation amusing and intriguing, it was also horribly alarming. In the first year of her marriage, Amani had run from Eemil several times, only to be recaptured by him in mere hours. She had raged against him, declaring her hatred toward him, his people and all that they stood for.

All to no avail.

Amani had possessed the advantage of hatred and fury, not to mention an ally in her sister, and yet still she had not escaped. Sofia briefly closed her eyes. She had no ally in this world, or any hatred toward Johen to conjure up and call upon. Even her fury seemed to come and go.

Don't let them break you, Sofia. Remember what it was to be free.

The more she watched them interact, the more she saw her own childhood family reflected in their smiles. She had forgotten what it felt like for mother and father, daughter and son, to gather around a dinner table and just enjoy being alive and together. It was appealing to her, and she didn't like it.

Oh, Sam, do you remember how good things were before Mom and Dad died? It's been so many years since I've allowed myself to remember.

Pancake breakfasts on Saturdays. Washing the family car on Sundays. Love, affection and a sense of belonging every day of the week.

All of that had been taken by a cruel twist of fate. For years she'd had no one but her brother. Now she didn't even have him. Above the ground, she was utterly and completely alone.

Johen's gaze strayed toward Sofia's. He looked at her questioningly, but thankfully didn't call attention to her. He could see the distress on her face, the unshed tears, and doubtless knew something was wrong—he just didn't know what it was.

Unable to endure his stare, Sofia blinked several times in rapid succession while she regained her composure. Looking away, she trained her eyes on her meal, feigning interest in the chunks of spicy meat, vegetables and bread set before her.

As Johen and Eemil engaged in a political conversation, Amani said, "I know it's overwhelming to you."

Sofia's gaze darted over to meet Johen's mother. A second ago she had been seated halfway across the table. A blink later and she was right beside her. "Yes, it is." She sighed. "Very overwhelming."

Amani nodded. Her hand found Sofia's atop the table and rested there. "You think to flee from my son."

She thought about denying it, but there was no point to that. "Yes, I do," Sofia admitted, pulling her hand back. "Surely you can understand."

"Oh yes," Amani agreed, her brown eyes gentle. The kindness she exuded made Sofia feel guilty. "I was you once, after all. I feel your every emotion and sympathize with it."

"I sense a 'but' coming on."

Amani's tone was tender, but firm. "But you cannot escape." When Sofia opened her mouth to rebut, Johen's mother placed a solitary finger to her lips. "You believe you can run successfully, and will believe so for some time to come. It's normal—we've all felt that way."

"I'm different," Sofia quietly insisted. A part of her wondered how many Outsider brides had all said the same thing to no avail, and she ruthlessly squelched the thought. "I can't just accept this without a fight!"

"Nor could I." Amani sighed. "I had thought to try and save you from all the marriage pains I endured when first wed, but I see now that it is not possible. You must learn these things for yourself."

Oh, God, don't say that I'm just like you! Please stop!

"Just know that I'm here if you need to talk. I've been in your shoes and I understand what it feels like to wear them."

Deep inside, Sofia knew Amani was being genuine with her, not trying to deceive her into believing that escape wasn't possible when it was. The truth was even more defeating than lies.

"Why?" Sofia asked, her voice shaking just a little. "Make me understand *why.*" She kept her voice low so as not to be overheard by the men. Johen and Eemil were too embroiled in conversation to notice her rising anger, though. "Do they have a shortage of women down here or something?"

"At times. Nothing noteworthy these days, though."

Her nostrils flared. "Then *why?*"

Sofia was nine-tenths rational logic and one tenth emotion. She loved and hated as strongly as the next person, but her brain wasn't wired in a stereotypical female fashion. She needed to understand, even in a world where reason might not exist.

"Why do the men of my home country marry several wives?" Amani softly asked. "Why do your Christian countrymen take but one wife?" She waved a hand. "Why do the Jews fight the Muslims for the rights to the Holy Land, and Muslims fight them back just as fiercely for those same rights?"

Sofia stilled. *Because of their deeply held belief that it's the will of their particular God.*

Her shoulders slumped, the fight going out of her. She was tired, mentally and emotionally.

"The Vikings believe in the will of the gods of Valhalla." Amani found Sofia's hand once again. "This culture is an ancient one, a civilization steeped in its own rules and doctrines. It is foreign to you, as it once was to me, but you will eventually see the Vikings for what they are—a good, family-oriented people."

"But the world above the ground . . ." Sofia shook her head, not comprehending. "How can you just give up all hope of ever seeing it again?"

Amani's smile was nostalgic. "Love can do many things to a woman."

Sofia mentally rolled her eyes. She didn't mean any disrespect to Johen's mother, but she wasn't the type of person to be ruled by sentiment.

"I'm happy for you that you fell in love with your husband," Sofia whispered, "but—"

"Yes, I did," Amani interrupted. "But it was not my love for Eemil that I spoke of."

Sofia raised a golden eyebrow.

"It was Eemil's love for *me* that I found impossible to keep waging war against." Amani's gaze seemed to gentle each time she spoke of her husband. "Vikings, as you have witnessed, are raised differently from any culture above the ground."

"That's an understatement," Sofia muttered.

Amani grinned. "Yes, it is." Her expression grew serious. "But that difference is also shown in the love they harbor for their wives."

"What do you mean?"

"I'm not certain I can explain it," Amani said thoughtfully. "It's the way men raise their sons, I suppose."

Sofia listened intently, a rapt audience.

"They are taught that their bride is the center of all life and meaning. Down here, a man isn't complete without one. Through the woman, their house is blessed and the continuity of their line promised.

"Emotionally," Amani continued, "a little boy is raised to dream of his future bride, romanticizing her perhaps a bit too much." She quietly chuckled. "Such tender emotions being taught to such a roughened group of males seems odd to us, but this is the way of it down here."

That certainly explained a lot, namely how Johen could look at her with such naïve love in his eyes. "Do they care if their love isn't returned?"

"I've yet to see that happen. They expect it will take time to earn their bride's love, but they know that if they are good and patient and thoughtful husbands, eventually they will be rewarded and have her love in return."

So they never gave up? Good grief.

Sofia's emotions were in chaos. How could Johen possibly love someone he didn't know outside of the biblical sense? It made no sense.

Then again, Sofia sighed, how could Johen—or any other Viking—marry and love a woman they'd never met before, based on a few moments at an auction? It was bizarre. This entire world was bizarre.

She needed to find an exit before she lost her mind altogether. Or, worse yet, before everything started to make sense.

What do I do? I feel so lost. . . .

Sofia ran her fingers through her hair, her mind racing. She needed to escape before Johen's feelings deepened. After listening to Amani's speech, she understood that he truly did care about her. Hurting him wasn't what she wanted to do.

Her gaze strayed to where her husband sat. He was laughing and happy, his former stoic impassiveness gone.

Because of me?

Johen had married Sofia against her will, perhaps, but if he hadn't bought her, another man would have. He had shown her nothing but kindness and understanding. For that reason alone, she owed him respect and consideration.

She would leave Johen's life with as few memories as possible. The quicker she clicked her ruby slippers and got back to Kansas, the less pain she would cause him.

"One day, you will love my son," Amani promised, affectionately patting her hand a final time before standing. "I promise you that he will make you happy beyond your wildest dreams."

CHAPTER TEN

S ofia couldn't get away from Johen's parents' house fast enough. Not only did she need to escape from Amani's words, but the *erotisk* was hitting her hard. Her pulse had picked up and perspiration beaded on her forehead and between her breasts.

"'Twill be all right," Johen murmured, leading her back toward his home. "We are almost there."

"I don't think I can wait," Sofia shakily admitted. She looked up at his profile. "It hit me so hard that my belly hurts."

His eyes seemed to gentle, though he didn't look down at her. He just kept walking, steering them away from the twenty-passenger mine car as quickly as possible.

"It really aches," she gasped.

They came to a halt before the metal elevator cages that would take them to the sector Johen called home. Sofia's teeth sank into her bottom lip, drawing blood as she watched two passengers disembark. Johen steered her into the metal contraption and closed the doors.

"It hurts so *bad*," Sofia wailed. The journey felt like it would last forever.

His jaw steeled as he guided the mechanism up half a floor, then brought it to a jarring stop. Johen made quick work of her dress, hoisting it over her head and trapping it just behind her neck.

Her body, now naked, was bared to him. He palmed her breasts with a low growl, popping one stiff nipple into his mouth and sucking it hard. Just like he knew she liked it.

It was a little alarming that he already knew her body so well, and was a master at manipulating it.

Sofia's hands found his pants and pulled them down, just below his hard buttocks. His long, thick erection sprang free, growing impossibly more rigid between her palms.

"You're so beautiful, Sofia," Johen said thickly, kissing her eyes, her nose, then her lips. "I'm so happy you belong to me."

He lifted her up and she wrapped her legs around his waist. Holding her buttocks, Johen pulled her down onto him, his huge penis quickly filling her aroused flesh.

"Oh, God," Sofia moaned, her head falling back as he drove himself up into her. "Oh, yes—Johen—*oh, God.*"

"You feel so good," he said hoarsely, his eyes coming to life again while inside her. There was a darkness in him, a pain that only seemed to recede when he was near her. "I need you, Sofia."

Her heart clenched. "Johen . . ."

As if sensing and understanding the emotional upheaval his words caused, Johen picked up the pace of his thrusting, concentrating on making her come. He succeeded admirably, just like always. Sofia cried out his name as she came, pushing herself down on his cock as fast and furiously as she could.

"I will always need you," Johen murmured as she rode out wave after wave of ecstasy. "Always."

He spoke to her of her beauty, of her eyes and smile. He thrust into her depths as if trying to reach her soul.

It was getting to her. *He* was getting to her.

Johen came in a roar, his cock jerking inside her. Sofia watched his eyes all the while, witnessing as life deserted them once again.

It was as if he understood that she would go back to plotting against him once the passion faded . . . and needed to fortify himself against any injury that knowledge might cause.

CHAPTER ELEVEN

*B*y the early hours of the sixth day of her marriage, the *erotisk* had completely run its course. Gone was the gnawing pain, the ache, the unquenchable lust. In its place was a soreness that made her feel like a young virgin again instead of like the mature woman that she was.

Sofia had never had so much sex in her life. Johen had made love to her nearly nonstop this past week, pausing only long enough to sleep and eat. He looked as exhausted as she felt, yet he still managed to rise to the occasion every time she moaned and called out for him.

He had taken her more times than she'd thought possible, in more places than she'd ever dreamt of letting a man invade her.

And she had begged for it. Like an animal in heat, she had needed Johen's hard cock as though her life itself depended on it.

The weirdest thing of all, though, was the trust she had begun feeling for her husband. He was big and powerful, deadly and gruff, yet tender and gentle at the same time. At least with her. If she was to never learn another new fact about him, she fully comprehended one thing:

He would never hurt her.

Too bad she couldn't say the same about herself, where he was concerned.

Sofia sighed softly as she gazed at Johen's sleeping face. She disliked the thought of causing this man any pain, but she owed it to herself to try and escape. Six days of great sex hardly made up for a lifetime in captivity.

Down here, she would never have choices. Johen would decide her every move. Any woman in her right mind would try to flee.

It's not like he can't replace you. Today he calls you his wife, but he'll forget you the moment you leave. . . .

If only she truly believed that.

For five days and nights, Lord Stefsson neglected his duties to New Sweden that he might remain by his wife's side. When he awakened on day six and found Sofia sleeping soundly beside him, Johen realized that the effects of the *erotisk* had passed.

The selfish part of him wished it otherwise, for he knew that so long as lust consumed her she would lie with him willingly, even initiate their lovemaking. Now that Sofia could shake the carnal cobwebs from her mind, the uphill battle would begin.

He had heard enough stories over the years about captive brides to know what a difficult time 'twould be in their dwelling until Sofia accepted New Sweden as her home and him as her husband. That was why he'd vowed to himself not to purchase an Outsider bride.

But as Johen watched Sofia sleep, golden ringlets framing her beautiful face, he knew it didn't matter. However long it took, whatever manner of willfulness she displayed, 'twould be worth it.

Something about Sofia had called to him from the moment he saw her. There was a look in her eyes he understood only too well: a void, an ache that resulted from feeling lifeless inside.

It took the dead to recognize the dead.

Johen had no knowledge of what Sofia had gone through prior to her capture by the bride-hunters, but whatever 'twas, it had caused a great sorrow within her. He faced eyes like those every time he glanced in a looking glass.

He had seen so much during his rise to power, mercilessly fighting Toki for Hannu's autonomy. Dead bodies strewn like fallen paper along the icy rivers. Children blown apart—innocent little victims who had done naught wrong to anyone. Mothers weeping. Mangled corpses everywhere so far as the eye could see . . .

Witnessing these sights in theory was altogether different than seeing them in reality. A part of Johen had died in the uprising, a piece of his soul he'd thought never to recover. Being with Sofia made him feel hopeful again, as though it hadn't been in vain after all.

"Let us take away each other's pain," he murmured, one hand gently sifting through her hair. As Johen watched his wife sleep, he knew he had made the right decision in choosing her for his bride. They bore more in common than either of them knew. "I cherish you more with each passing moment."

'Twas true. The way she smiled despite herself whenever she found him to be good company, every time he slid his cock inside of her and those blank, sad eyes sparkled their brilliant blue-green for those stolen minutes . . .

He loved her. With his whole heart he already loved her, though he couldn't tell her until she was ready to hear it.

Sofia had not been raised in his culture and therefore didn't understand his people's ways. His mother had told him about the conversation she'd engaged in with his wife three eves hence, and of Sofia's bewilderment that a man could love so fiercely, devoutly and quickly.

His mother had not lied to her. He cherished Sofia as though he'd known her all his life.

Johen blinked, recalling that he had duties he could no longer neglect. There were disputes to be settled, grievances to be heard and a sector to rule. With a sigh, he stood up and headed to his chest to fetch clean clothing.

'Twould be a long road with Lady Stefsson, but one his lordship felt certain was worth it.

As the doors to the vast bedroom quietly closed, Sofia's eyes slowly opened.

Long before Johen had touched her hair or uttered a word, she had known that his attention was fixed on her. Not sure of what to do or say, she had feigned sleep. His softly spoken words echoed in her heart:

Let us take away each other's pain . . . I cherish you more with each passing moment.

Did he know about her brother's death? About losing her parents so many years ago? Had she said something to him she couldn't recall? What pain was *he* carrying? Should she even care?

They hadn't engaged in much conversation, for most of their waking hours had been spent in bed. Yet somehow there didn't need to be any words between them. Somehow, some way, what they had together was, in its place and time, *right*.

Sofia sighed. She *had* to leave. Johen was affecting not only her mind, but her heart as well.

CHAPTER TWELVE

*S*ofia ran as fast as she could, running blindly into the unknown Viking world outside Johen's home. She didn't know where she was going. She didn't even know if she was trying to escape or if she was merely blowing off built-up steam. Tears welled in her eyes from the confusion she felt.

Staying below the ground with Johen was so alien as to be frightening. Returning to the icy world above was equally distressing. She was alone up there.

Down here she had Johen, Eemil and Amani—three people who very much wanted her in their family. Even knowing her anger and frustration, they had enveloped her into their fold, treating her as one of their own.

To them, she belonged.

She came to a sudden stop, panting for air. It was all she'd ever wanted—a real family. But at what price?

Grief overwhelmed her until she just had to cry. She hadn't lost control of her emotions since her parents had died, but now she couldn't seem to stop herself.

"Sofia."

The voice, so gentle, so concerned and familiar, soothed in a way that frightened her. Succumbing without a fight wasn't in her vocabulary, but she was so tempted. . . .

"Sofia," Johen murmured, coming to stand beside her. Thankfully he didn't touch her; she was overwrought enough as it was. "Are you all right?"

"No," she sobbed, trying to stop crying. She swiped at her tears, but they continued to fall. "I don't know what to do. I don't know what to think. I don't even know who I am anymore—and that is the scariest thing of all.

Johen didn't interrupt her, which she was oddly grateful for.

"Up there in my world, I had nothing. I lost everyone that ever mattered to me. My parents, my brother—all of them are dead."

"I am sorry," he said quietly. "Were they alive, I would go steal them for you."

Sofia stilled. She smiled through teary eyes. "Would you really?"

"Of course," Johen said as though he couldn't understand why she thought otherwise. "I want to make you happy, Sofia—the happiest you've ever been."

She looked away. "That wouldn't take much," she whispered.

Johen led her a few paces to a bench, and he gently pulled Sofia down beside him.

"I will not pretend to understand what you must be feeling. I have seen it on the faces of countless captive brides, but have never lived it for myself."

He sighed. "What you must understand is that my people will never let you go. They couldn't even if they wanted to. Once the bride-hunters captured you, your fate was sealed. I know you are angry at me—"

"No," Sofia said honestly, "I'm not. I realize that if you hadn't bought me, someone else would have. Still, I can't seem to get beyond the fact that it happened."

He nodded his head. "You are angry with me."

"Not at you specifically—I'm mad at this entire civilization." She splayed her hands. "Your ways are not normal to me, Johen. If you stole a woman above the ground, you'd go to prison."

He whistled through his teeth. "Prison? A cell of incarceration? For doing what the gods decreed?"

"No one believes in your gods up there," she said gently. "They haven't for thousands of years."

"More's the pity."

Johen threaded his fingers through Sofia's. "I know this is difficult for you," he murmured. "I vow to give you as much space and time as you need in order to find your happiness."

"What if I never find it?" she asked sadly.

He squeezed her hand. "You will. I would allow it to be no other way."

Sofia couldn't help but grin at his arrogance, and he winked down at her.

They sat in silence for a long time, neither of them saying a word. They held each other's hand, their souls finding a peace neither of them had experienced in years. After what felt like a lifetime to Johen, Sofia at last rested her head on his shoulder, allowing him to embrace her.

Old Myria, the herbalist, watched in the shadows, a smile parting the wrinkly folds of her face. She had known these two were right for each other the moment she met Sofia. Some called her gift a blessing, others a curse. Whatever it was, she had known.

Fate was ironic with its twists and turns, but in the end it always worked out right. That was difficult for the newly wedded couple to fathom now, but in another month, Sofia would love Johen with as much passion as he loved her. Another month later and she would be pregnant with his child.

Fate was indeed ironic, yet equally wise. There was no other person alive who could have recognized and understood the shadows that the other carried.

Clutching her hooded cowl tightly about her, old Myria crept away. Something portentous was about to grip New Sweden in the form of a wench. She could only pray to the gods in Valhalla that her people were ready for it.

EPILOGUE

Three months later

*Y*ou are definitely with child," Johen proclaimed.

He shouldn't feel so pleased with his fertile self whilst watching his poor wee wife try to ward off the morning sickness that had consumed her over the past couple of weeks, but he couldn't seem to help it. She was pregnant. No wench could ever hope to be sexier.

"Either that," he teased, "or you've succumbed to a new illness no Viking has ever heard tell of."

Sofia moaned as she clutched her rebellious stomach. "What kind of illness would that be?"

"Mayhap we would name it *wife-of-the-green-face.*"

"You are *not* funny."

"And here I thought myself a court jester in the making."

"You could use a few more lessons."

Johen rubbed Sofia's back, doing his best to comfort her. It was long moments before she felt relieved enough to sit up, and then took a seat in her favored place—his lap.

Smiling softly, she wrapped her arms around his neck. "I am very happy, you know."

He kissed her forehead. "Aye, I know," Johen murmured. "I can see it in your eyes." He gave his wife a gentle squeeze, not wishing to tempt nature and make her sick. Especially not whilst she was sitting upon his lap. "I have never felt more blessed, Sofia. Thank you for all the goodness you have brought to my life."

"That's so sweet—you're going to make me cry."

"You do that often, too, these days. Mayhap we should change the name of the ague to *wife-of-the-green-face-and-red-eyes.*"

Sofia gave him a good-natured thump on the chest. "You really do need more lessons."

A court jester he was not, but fool-crazy in love, he was. The past three months had been the most wondrous of his life. He and Sofia had become so close that Johen was hard-pressed to recall a life before her. 'Twas almost as though he hadn't lived before that fateful eve at the bride auction.

Truth be told, he hadn't. He had existed, but he had not truly lived.

"Thank you for having my child," Johen murmured, his gaze memorizing her face. "I love you, Sofia."

"You're welcome," she whispered back. She reached up and ran a hand over the contour of his jaw. "I love you, too." Her smile held the promise of a long, happy life together. "More than you'll ever know."

★　　★　　★

Later that afternoon, once the morning sickness had securely passed, Sofia and Johen took a mine car to a docking station on the far side of Hannu, where Johen's parents lived. Her in-laws took the news of Sofia's pregnancy just as she'd known they would: with hugs, kisses and tears of joy.

"I cannot begin to tell you how happy we are!" Amani laughed. "Eemil and I are to be grandparents!"

Eemil was equally thrilled, running a few homes down to pound on his brother's door and share the news of her pregnancy. Pretty soon Johen's entire extended family was there, with food and drinks brought in for an impromptu celebration.

Sofia grinned up at her husband as his father and uncle began singing and dancing, a bawdy Viking performance reserved for only the most special occasions. Johen threw his head back and laughed, then gave Sofia a contented squeeze.

She was happy. God help her, but she'd never been happier.

Life in the Underground had turned out to be more wonderful than Sofia had thought possible. It didn't hurt that she was married to the world's greatest man, but Johen aside, the kingdom still had a lot to recommend it.

Johen had given Sofia the most amazing present—the gift of being loved no matter what. They had only been married for three months, yet her heart felt as though they'd been together for three lifetimes. Everything between them had clicked that fast and that well.

She still thought about the world above the ground from time to time, and now was one of those times. Her mom and dad would have been as overjoyed as Johen's parents at the news of her pregnancy. And Sam would have been the world's greatest uncle.

Sofia smiled. She hoped that her family was looking down from the heavens and seeing this moment through their angels' eyes.

She blinked, then turned her attention back to the Viking performance. Laughing with her husband, she laid her head on Johen's shoulder, grateful to be a part of this wonderful family.

The Warlord
Wants
Forever

KRESLEY COLE

THE ORIGIN
OF THE VALKYRIE

*J*nto the blood-splattered snow, the lone warrior fell to one knee and shuddered with weakness. Still, an arm shot out to raise a sword against the oncoming legion.

Her dented breastplate swallowed her small form.

The winds howled, whipping her hair, but she heard the twang of the bowstring unleashed. She screamed in fury; the arrow punctured the center of her armor, the blow sending her flying back.

The arrow had pierced through metal, then barely through her breastbone, just enough that her heart met the point with each beat. The beating of her own brave heart was killing her.

But her scream had woken two nearby gods sleeping together through a brutal, wintry decade. They stirred and looked down upon the maiden, seeing in her eyes courage burning bright. Bravery and will had marked her entire life, but the light ebbed with death and they mourned it.

Freya, the female god, whispered that they should take her courage and preserve it for eternity because it was so precious.

Wóden agreed, and together they gave up lightning to cleave through the ether and strike the dying maiden.

The light was violent and slow to fade and made the army tremble.

When blackness cloyed once more, the healed maiden woke in a strange place. She was untouched, her human mortality unchanged. But soon an immortal daughter would be born from her—a daughter who possessed her courage, Wóden's wily brilliance, and Freya's mirth and fey beauty. Though this daughter enjoyed the power of lightning for sustenance, she also inherited Wóden's arrogance and Freya's acquisitiveness, which merely endeared her to them more.

The gods were content and the maiden adoring of her new baby. Yet after an age had flickered past, the gods heard another female call out for courage as she died from a battle against a dark enemy. She wasn't a human, but a Furie, one among the Lore—that strata of clever beings who have convinced humans that they exist only in imagination. Scarce moments had the creature—in the freezing night her breaths were no longer visible.

"Our halls are great, yet our family is small," Freya said, her eyes sparkling so brightly a mariner in the north was briefly blinded by the stars and almost lost his way.

Grim Wóden took her hand, unable to deny her. Those surrounding the dying Furie saw lightning rent the sky once more.

And it would strike again and again in the coming years, continuing on well after female warriors—be they human, demoness, siren, changeling or any brave creature from the Lore—knew to pray for it as they died.

Thus the Valkyrie were born.

CHAPTER ONE

*I*f the overgrown vampire didn't stop staring at her face, even his wicked talent with his sword wouldn't keep his head upon his shoulders.

The thought made Myst, an immortal known as the Coveted One, grin as she curled up in the windowsill of her cell. Leaning against the reinforced bars, she watched the two vampire armies battle below as she might a rumble from the back of bleachers.

The poor warlord with his broad shoulders and jet-black hair was about to join a legion of other males whose last sight on earth was her smiling face—

She frowned when he ducked and ran through his enemy. He was a big male, at least six and a half feet tall, but he was surprisingly fast. Tilting her head, she studied him. He was good. She knew fighting and liked his style. *Dirty.* He'd cut with his sword then strike out with his fist, or duck a parry then throw an elbow. It amused her to watch, but what she wouldn't give to be down there fighting. In the middle. Against both sides. Against *him*.

She fought dirtier.

His gaze continued to stray to her, and once he'd even killed while his eyes were *still on her*. She'd blown him a kiss, sincerely, choosing to see it as a tribute.

He found time to glance back even as he thundered orders and gave commands to the army of vampires around him, showing brilliance in strategy. She examined it all as though watching *Decisive Battles* on A&E and grudgingly noted the effectiveness of his army's acid grenades and guns.

The creatures of the Lore scorned human weapons like these. The only ones such weapons could kill were humans, which was beyond nonsporting. Yet that was the thing about bullets—aside from ruining perfectly good couture, they *hurt* and could immobilize an immortal for precious seconds. Long enough for a dirty fighter to take your head. Done enough times, they could help take an "untakable" castle like Ivo the Cruel's.

Myst hardly cared that Ivo, her jailer and tormentor, was about to have his ass handed to him by this warlord with his forbidden modern weapons. Her situation would not change, for these rebels, turned humans known as the Forbearers, were still vampires. *A blood foe is a blood foe is a blood foe. . . .*

An explosion rocked the castle, and sparks and bits of debris wafted down from the roof of Myst's cell. The low creatures in the dank holds down the corridor howled with impotent fury, increasing in urgency with each successive blast, until it was . . . over. Silence. An aftershock here and there, a muted whimper . . .

The defense of this castle was no more, its inhabitants having disappeared—by *tracing,* as the Lore called teleporting—leaving no more than an airy draft and the burned records of their Horde.

She could hear the rebels searching the bowels of this place but could've told them they wouldn't find any of their enemies. The denizens here had not been a fight-to-the-death sort, more of a *he who fights and runs away, lives to run away another day* type.

Shortly after, she heard heavy boots clicking on the stone floor of the dungeon and knew it was the warlord. He crossed directly to her cell and stood before it.

From her perch, curled in the window, she examined the vampire up close. He had thick, straight black hair that hung over his face in uneven sections, no doubt from where he'd sheared it off with his blade months ago, and never thought to cut it since. Some hanks were kept from his field of vision with those small ravel plaits like the berserkers used to wear. He had scars on his hands, and his big body was powerful and cut with muscle. She wanted to purr—because apparently central casting had just sent down the consummate virile warlord.

"Come down from there and show yourself." Deep voice. Russian accent, moneyed, aristocratic.

"Or what? You'll lock me away in a dungeon?"

"I might free you."

She was at the bars before he'd had time to lower his gaze

from the window. Had his squared jaw slackened just the smallest bit? She listened for a quickening of his heart, but found none because there was no heartbeat whatsoever. So the vampire was single? His eyes were clear of the red haze that marked bloodlust, which meant he had never drunk a being to death. But then a Forbearer eschewed taking living blood through the flesh altogether.

When he saw her face up close, the key wasn't immediately in the lock as it usually would have been, but his lips parted, exposing his fangs for her to see. Of course his would be sexy—not too prominent or even much longer than a human's canines.

When she saw the short splendid scar that passed down *both* of his lips, lightning struck just outside, but he didn't flinch at the bolt or even glance up—he was too busy staring back at her.

Scars, any external evidence of pain, attracted Myst. Pain forged strength. Strength begat electricity. This one could give it to her.

It was possible he was even missing an eye under a thick hank of hair.

She stifled a throaty growl as her hand shot out to brush his hair back. But he was quick, catching her wrist. She curled one finger in a beckoning gesture, and after a moment he released her, allowing her to reach forward. She brushed his hair back, revealing a hard-planed, masculine face covered with grit and ash from the battle.

He was still in possession of both of his eyes and they were *intense*. Gun-metal gray.

When her hand dropped, his brows drew together, per-haps at her blatant interest, or perhaps at her fingers already stroking the bars in invitation as she stared at his mouth. She was surprised by how carnal she found it, especially since the vampire could use it to hurt her.

The smooth gold chain that she'd worn at her waist for millennia now felt heavy on her.

"What are you?" he asked in his pleasingly low voice. She realized then that his accent wasn't Russian, but from that of neighboring Eesti. The general was Estonian, which made him a kind of Nordic Russian, though she was sure he wouldn't appreciate that description.

She frowned at his question and pulled back her hair to show him her pointed ear. "Nothing?" She parted her lips and tapped her tongue against her smaller dormant fangs. No recognition.

Apparently, the rumors were true. Here was a leader in this army, a general most likely, and he hadn't a clue that she was his mortal enemy. He would think she was fey or a nymph. She'd prefer fey because she'd cringe to be confused with one of those little hookers—

She shook her head. As long as he didn't know she was Valkyrie it worked for her.

Killing the unwitting Forbearers would be easy for her and her sisters. *Too* easy. Almost like being your own secret Santa.

Myst had just confirmed rumors in the Lore that whis-pered of asses and elbows and this Horde's inability to differ-entiate between the two.

*   *   *

"What are you?" Nikolai Wroth demanded again, surprised his voice was steady.

When he'd seen her in the light, he'd felt like exhaling a stunned breath—if his kind respired—for she was strikingly lovely, with a beauty only hinted at from the distance of the battlefield. He'd been attracted to that face to his reckless peril.

Though she had expected him to recognize her kind, all he could determine was that she wasn't human and that he hadn't a clue what she might be. Her ears said fey, but she also had the smallest *fangs*.

"Free me," the creature said. Flawless skin, coral pink lips, flame red hair. The eyes that flickered over him appraisingly were an impossible green.

The way she held the bars was suggestive—everything about her was . . . suggestive.

"Swear fealty to my king, and I will free you."

"I can't do that, but you've no right to keep me here."

His brother Murdoch passed by then, raised his eyebrows at Wroth's discovery, and muttered in Estonian, "Sweet Christ." Then he walked on. Why was Wroth unable to do the same?

"What's your name?" He wasn't used to his questions going unanswered.

Another stroke of the bars. "What do you want it to be?"

He scowled. "Are you a vampire?"

"Not the last time I checked." Her voice was sensual. He couldn't place her accent, but it was drawling, honeyed.

"Are you innocent of malice against us?"

She waved a dismissing hand. "Oh, good God, no! I love, love, *love* to kill leeches."

"Then rot in here." As if she could kill a vampire. She was scarcely over five feet tall and delicately built—aside from her generous breasts showcased in her tight shirt.

Just before he turned, he saw her eyes narrow. "I smell smoke," she called after him. "Ivo the Cruel burned his records before he fled, didn't he?"

Wroth stilled, clenching his fists because he'd have to return.

"He did," he grated at the cell once more.

"And this new king's army is full of Forbearers—turned humans? It matters little. I'm sure the king is very knowledgeable about the vampire Horde's *extensive* list of enemies within the Lore. He wouldn't need this castle's millennia's worth of records. In fact, I'm *positive* that that is *not* the reason you chose this stronghold over the four others, including the royal seat."

How did she know their agenda so well?

Wroth could plan battles and sieges—he'd earned his rank by this victory alone—but he knew nothing of this new world to advance the army. Unfortunately, he wasn't the only one.

The blind leading the blind. When they'd found the records reduced to a smoldering heap of ash, that's what Kristoff had muttered.

"You think to bargain for your freedom? If you do happen to have information, I can get it from you."

"Torture?" she asked with a laugh. "My first piece of information I'll divulge to you? I wouldn't recommend trying to torture me. I dislike it and grow sulky under pincers. It's a *fault.*"

The *things* in the cells, many of which he'd never even heard of, never could have envisioned, howled and grunted at that.

"Now let's not quarrel, vampire. Free me, and we'll go to your room and talk." She offered her fragile-looking hand out to him. A smudge of ash was stark against her alabaster skin.

"I don't think so."

"You'll call for me. You'll be lonely in your new quarters and will feel out of sorts. I could let you pet my hair until you fell asleep."

He drew in closer and lowered his voice to ask in all seriousness, "You're mad, aren't you?"

"As—a—hatter," she whispered back conspiratorially.

He felt a hint of sympathy for the creature. "How long have you been in here?"

"For four long . . . interminable . . . days."

He glowered at her.

"Which is why I want you to take me with you. I don't eat much."

The dungeon erupted with laughter again.

"Don't hold your breath."

"Certainly not like you, Forbearer."

"How do you know what I am?"

"I know *everything.*"

Then, if true, she had a wealth they didn't.

"Leave her," Murdoch called at the gateway of the dungeon. His brows were drawn, no doubt puzzled by his brother's interest. Wroth had never pursued women. As a human, they'd either come to him or he'd gone without. He'd had no time in wartime. As a vampire he had no such need. Not until he could find his Bride.

He shook his head at the insane, fey *creature,* then forced himself to walk on, though he thought he heard her whisper, *"Call for me, General,"* making the hair on the back of his neck stand up.

He followed his brother to Kristoff's new antechamber and found their king gazing out into the clear night from a generous window—that would be shuttered in the few hours till dawn. When he turned to them, his gaunt face looked weary.

Wroth suspected it had been difficult killing other natural born vampires, his own kindred, no matter how crazed they'd become, and no matter that they followed his uncle Demestriu, who'd stolen his crown centuries ago. Wroth had no such compunctions. He was weary but only from injury and his sword arm being overworked as he hacked through them.

"Were any of the records salvageable?" Wroth asked with little hope. If the vampires of this castle had spent as much energy fighting as burning, they might have kept Oblak. To his disgust, they'd fled. He didn't understand it. When defending your home, you defend to the death.

He had.

Kristoff answered, "None."

Without the records, their own ignorance would kill them. Kristoff, the rightful king, had been raised by humans far from Demestriu's reach. For centuries, he had lived among them, hiding his true nature yet learning little of the Lore. His army consisted of human warriors he'd turned as they died on the battlefield, so they knew nothing. Before Wroth had seen Kristoff standing over him like an angel of death, offering eternal life for eternal fealty, Wroth had thought vampires were mere myths.

The rules of this new world were complex and often counterintuitive, and their order knew little more than conjecture and what had been learned by painful trial over centuries. They were trapped in a kind of twilight—not human and yet universally shunned by all the factions of the Lore. Those beings hid in the shadows, fleeing from whatever land Kristoff's army occupied, working together to always be one step ahead. Wroth's human experience said they should have been able to get information by now, but the reality was that this was a different plane altogether. The same effort that went into hiding the Lore from humans for ages went into keeping Kristoff's soldiers in the dark as well.

"Any sign of Conrad or Sebastian?" Kristoff asked.

Wroth shook his head. He hadn't seen his brothers since shortly after they'd been turned, but he'd heard they'd been in a skirmish with natural born vampires. Though he and Murdoch hadn't expected to find their brothers here, they had hoped the two might be in the dungeons of the castle they'd strategically needed to take.

"Perhaps the next Horde stronghold."

Wroth nodded, though he doubted it. He sensed his youngest brother Bastian was dead and suspected the mind of the next oldest, Conrad, was unreachable even if he could be found. The two had not appreciated the eternal life their older brothers had forced on them.

Murdoch examined a gouge in his arm, seeming unconcerned with this blow, but then he generally seemed unconcerned about everything. Though they shared similar looks, he and Wroth couldn't be more different in personality. Wroth believed in Kristoff's cause, seeing many parallels to his own past, and wanted to continue to fight. Murdoch didn't particularly care. Wroth suspected his brother fought only as a favor to him—or because they had nothing else now.

"Wroth found a being in the dungeon," Murdoch said. "She seems to have extensive knowledge of the Lore."

"What kind of being?"

Wroth answered, "I have no idea. She appears fey, delicate, with sharply pointed ears. But she has these small *fangs* and her fingernails were more like . . . claws. She's not vampire."

Kristoff frowned at that. "Perhaps she's born of more than one species?"

"Perhaps." *More speculation.* Wroth was sick of it. He wanted to know the rules of the game so he could dominate it.

"Find out everything you can from her."

"She won't talk. I've interrogated enough to know she'll hint but never truly divulge. And she hates vampires."

Kristoff pinched his forehead. "Then tomorrow night if

we haven't gotten information from the rest of the prisoners, we treat her as the Horde she hates would. Torture her for the information if you can't get it any other way."

Wroth nodded, but the idea sat ill with him. As a human he'd been merciless to his enemies, but he'd never tortured a woman. She wasn't truly a woman, he reminded himself. She was a female among the Lore, and their army's survival could depend on the knowledge she held.

Perhaps he'd never tortured a woman because he'd never needed to.

The creature had been right, Wroth thought as a guard showed him to his new chambers. He *was* going to call her up to him.

To do what with her, he didn't know.

CHAPTER TWO

*D*id you miss me? Because *I* missed *you*," she said when the guard escorted her inside his bedroom. Out of habit, he stood when a lady entered, and she flashed him a brilliant smile. "A gentleman warrior. Who cleans up *very* well." She fanned herself with her hand. "I think I'm in love."

He didn't answer, and she didn't seem to mind as she casually scanned the room. "Retro Dracula. Not necessarily what I would have done, but then I'm not married to sunproof shutters like you might be. . . ." She shrugged, then headed for the bathroom. "Taking a shower if you don't mind," she said airily over her shoulder, making him raise his brows.

At the doorway, she unbuttoned her tight blouse and shrugged from it, leaving only a transparent black bra. She turned to him, revealing her scarcely covered breasts, he knew, just so he could see the creamy flesh spilling from the lace when she bent over to remove her boots. What he didn't know was why.

Was she truly mad? Most people who were mad didn't think they were, but she seemed to be proud of it. He was usually quick to determine people's motives. Yes, she wanted her freedom, but for some reason he knew she wouldn't sleep with him to receive it.

If he had to guess, he would say that she simply didn't see stripping in front of him and making herself completely at home in a stranger's bedroom as odd. In fact, he suspected she didn't see them as strangers at all.

As he stood, concealing his surprise, she untied the fastening of her silky skirt at her hip, and it too fell to the ground.

A fine gold chain around her tiny waist caught his attention. It was unusual, the design appearing very old, but it glinted like new when she moved. Once he could take his eyes from it, he found her in only that wispy bra and scanty, black underwear so intricate he was shocked anew. They were like a work of art—or a like a ribbon decorating one.

She gave him a teasing smile. *"Vampire like?"* she purred, unclasping the front of her bra to toss it with her other clothes. He scowled because he did like. Very much. He ran a hand over his mouth, wondering if her high, plump breasts could be any more beautiful. She had coral pink nipples that he could spend hours tonguing and alabaster flesh he wanted to cup and palm. He began to speak, then had to cough in his fist to continue. "You'll strip in front of a vampire when you don't even know his name?"

She gasped with mock horror and covered her breasts with her hands. "You're right! So what's your name?"

"My answer will be as forthcoming as yours. What do you want it to be?"

She smiled at that but then replied to the question, "Some kind of name that fits a battle-scarred, overgrown vampire warlord."

Battle-scarred? Overgrown? He wondered why in the hell he cared how she saw him. She was divinely wrought, but mad. He'd take his scars with his sanity. "Nikolai Wroth," he grated.

For the briefest second he thought he saw recognition flicker. But then she eyed him archly and breathed, "Oh, you are *good*. Wroth, the old word for rage? That's a bingo idea for a name." Her hands dropped. "I'll just call you by that," she said, then gave him a second look, shaking her head with a rueful smile as if she couldn't believe he was so clever.

. . . as a hatter.

She leaned back against the doorway, raising her bent arms above her head to grasp her elbows. Displaying her mouthwatering breasts and flashing a flirtatious smile that would've dropped most men to their knees, she asked in her whiskey voice, "Care to join me, *Wroth*?" She winked when she said his name and rolled her hips up off the doorframe.

"No," he bit out the word with difficulty. He didn't want her to know how his body didn't respond to her. His mind did, his vague memories of being human did. But not his body. He was the walking dead. No respiration, no heartbeat, no sexual need—or *ability*. Not until he found his pre-destined Bride and she *"blooded"* him fully. With his blooding, something inside him, some essence—maybe even his soul—would recognize her as *his*. He would see her as the one he was meant to spend eternity with, the woman he could love without measure, if one believed in that, and his body would wake for her.

In the past he'd yearned for his Bride because of the power she would bring him—he would finally be as strong as blooded vampires, his senses as acute as theirs—but he'd never missed the sex before this. And Wroth knew after this display that she was not his. For this should've blooded any vampire.

She shrugged, the simple movement a sight to behold, then turned the corner to the bathroom. When she emerged fifteen minutes later clad in a towel, she crossed to his closet. He was almost certain she'd used his toothbrush.

Which . . . charmed him for some reason—

The towel dropped, leaving her with only her chain and him with a view of her perfect ass.

He swallowed. "Have you no modesty?" Never in his life had he encountered a female so quick to be naked. Of course, he'd never in his life encountered a female who should so utterly be naked at any chance.

"Not at my age," she said as she began exploring his recently unpacked clothing. How strange to hear her say that when she looked so young. He found his head tilting to keep his gaze on her as she moved and bent. The chain swayed at her waist, and her long, damp hair cascaded down over her breasts. He stifled a groan at a particularly fruitful glance. *A true redhead.* He closed his eyes. And he couldn't have her.

"How old are you?" he grated, opening his eyes.

"Physiologically, I'm twenty-five. Chronologically, I'm . . . not."

"So you are an immortal?"

An amused smile played about her lips. "I am." She pulled on one of his shirts though it fell far off one shoulder and well down her legs.

"Why did you stop aging at twenty-five?"

"When I was strongest. Not for the same reason you were frozen at . . ."—she trailed off, eyeing him—"thirty-four?"

"Thirty-five. And why do you think I stopped aging then?"

She ignored him to continue digging. After a few moments, she plucked out an old bejeweled cross from his bag. She pinched the relic, holding it away from her, keeping her gaze from it. "You're Catholic?"

"Yes. It was a gift from my father." To help keep him alive in wartime. Wroth shook his head at the irony of just how well it had worked. "I thought I was the one who should be repelled by it."

"Only a turned human would say that. Besides I'm in no way *repelled*. With jewels like that? If I look at it, I'll want it."

"So you wouldn't want it because you're Catholic, I take it?"

"My family was very orthodox pagan. Can I have?" She held it forward, still not looking at it. "Can I, can I, Wroth?"

"Put it back," he said, fighting the unfamiliar urge to

grin. With a pouty expression, she returned it, mumbling something about tightfisted vampires, then dipped her feet into his boots. When she turned to him with her hands on her hips, his lips almost curled at the sight of her, a mad pagan immortal swallowed by his boots.

"What did your mother feed you?" she teased. "Renaissance anabolics?"

His urge to smile faded. "My mother died young."

"So did mine." He thought he heard her murmur, *"The first time."*

"And I was born after the Renaissance."

She drew her feet from his boots and sauntered past him. "But not by much."

"That's true. And why do you think I stopped aging at thirty-five?" he asked again.

She frowned as if she didn't know where his question had come from, then said, "Because naughty Kristoff found you dying on a battlefield, decided you'd make a fine recruit, then made you drink his blood. Bit a wrist open, perhaps? Then with his vampiric hoo-doo blood in your veins, he let you die. Unless he was in a hurry, then he would've killed you. One to three nights later and voilà, you rise from the dead—most likely with a frown on your face as you think 'Holy shite, it worked!'"

He ignored the last and asked, "How do you know the blood ritual?" He'd thought that only vampires knew the true way to turn a human. In movies and books, the change always came as a consequence of a vampire's bite, when in fact a human had more chance of turning if he bit a vampire.

"Like I said, I know everything."

Yes, but he *was* learning, if sporadically. She was an immortal, who'd been frozen physiologically at twenty-five. If she was pagan she was at least a few hundred years old. She knew of the blood ritual and that Kristoff "recruited" his soldiers straight from the battlefield.

When she scooped up her clothes, opened his door, then snapped her fingers for a guard down the hall, Wroth merely watched like a bystander.

"Pssst. Minion. I need these laundered. Very little starch. Don't just stand there gawking or you'll anger my good frenemy General Wroth. We're like *this.*"

He couldn't see her but knew she was twining two fingers together.

Once she'd foisted her laundry, she closed the door by dramatically leaning back against it—as if to say he couldn't get away from her now—then glided over to him. As a rule, he observed, he calculated and he waited, but he'd never quite enjoyed sitting back and watching events unfurl as much as with her. Unpredictable didn't begin to describe—

She clutched his shoulders and straddled him.

Nothing between them but his pants and a few inches. He could even feel her heat as she knelt over him. She was definitely not his Bride or he would've ripped through his zipper to get inside her. His heart would beat, he would take his first breath in three hundred years, and in the space of one of those breaths he would be buried so deep in her tightness, wrenching her down on him. . . . But nothing approaching that happened.

"Now, Wroth, we need to work some logistics out. When I'm kept as a pet, my care is very involved."

His brows drew together. "I have no wish to keep you as a pet."

"You hold me prisoner. You think to order me. How does this differ?"

"You're not a pet," he insisted. He couldn't think—her eyes were mesmerizing, her sex was inches away from his, and her pleasing accent was lulling.

She leaned in by his ear and murmured, "What if I want to be your pet? Would you like that, vampire?" Her fingers brushed their way over his chest, unbuttoning his shirt. She picked up his hands one at a time and set them on the armrests, giving each a squeeze as if to let him know she wanted them to stay that way.

With raised eyebrows, he let her. He wasn't about to move, and couldn't imagine what she would do next.

"If I was your pet, you could keep me for your pleasure, and I would serve you in *every* way you desire." She pulled his shirt open, clearly admiring his chest. "Hard." Her voice was breathy. "Scars." She moistened her lips. "I'd *endeavor* to blood you so you could wake at sunset with my mouth greedy on you while you clutched my thighs to drink from. You would go to sleep at sunrise still deep inside my body." Her hand was trailing down, her eyes raptly following the jagged scar that had been his deathblow. "I am here for the taking and ache for your touch."

She reached down and cupped him beneath her before he could grip her wrist. In an instant her seductive look vanished, though she showed no surprise that he wasn't hard. She felt around his cock, then arched an eyebrow to say, "Well, my word, Wroth. If you were hard, I wouldn't know whether to be tantalized or terrified."

Then with blurring speed she was off him, and in the bed, lying on her stomach, chin propped on her hands. She was utterly unaffected by what had just occurred, while he was angered and . . . shamed that she'd felt him like this. He wanted to show her hard. . . .

"How do you plan to keep me here during the day? An unblooded Forbearer shouldn't be so hard to vanquish."

Vanquished by her? Amusing. "I'll send you back to the cell. You want to be my pet? I'll take you out and put you back in your cage at my pleasure."

She blinked at him. "You don't want to send me back. Who will entertain you? I can deal poker *and* make shadow animals."

He shook himself. This was just another instance of the Lore playing with them. She was not *normal*. He knew that anything he'd learned about females was inapplicable with her.

If she could be unaffected, he could pretend it. "I need you to answer some questions. I need to know what you are and what your name is."

"I'll answer your questions if you answer mine."

"Done," he said quickly. "Ask."

"Were you afraid when Kristoff stood over you?"

"I was . . . tired." Strange question.

"Most mortals would have been terrified to see the Gravewalker."

"Is that what he's called?" Kristoff would find that amusing. At her nod, he said, "Well, I'd seen a lot by that time."

"What's his agenda? Does he want to replace Demestriu?"

Wroth hesitated, then answered honestly, hoping that she would do the same. "He wants his crown back, but he doesn't want to rule over any faction but our own."

"Uh-huh." She raised an eyebrow as if she didn't believe him, then asked, "That was your brother in the dungeon?"

"Murdoch, yes."

"Turned vampires don't usually have *family* within the Horde."

"Murdoch died in the same battle. I've two other brothers turned later as well."

"You're young. Yet you're a general. How'd you swing that?"

He was over three hundred years old. Young compared to her? "I refused the dark gift if certain conditions weren't met."

Her eyes grew bright with new interest, and she patted the bed for him to come sit with her. He felt he was on the verge of learning something, so he complied, resting against the headboard to face her, stretching his legs out. He almost laughed. The first time he'd been in bed with a woman in centuries, and she was easily the most beautiful of any before—and he could do nothing with her. He couldn't even drink her, though his fangs ached to pierce the pale column of her neck. Thank God he'd fed before she'd been brought up.

"Wroth, you *countered* with Kristoff as you lay dying?"

When she put it like that it sounded more reckless than it had been. As Wroth had lain in his own cooling blood, nearly freed of the constant struggle, the ongoing war and famine and plague, he'd told Kristoff, "You need me more than I need to live."

Kristoff had seen him in many battles and agreed. "I did counter. I was used to giving orders and would take them from no one but a powerful king. I wanted my brother turned if he was dying, and trusted compatriots as well. Kristoff complied." That wasn't all. Wroth had asked for sixty years so he and Murdoch could watch over the rest of their living family—their father, four sisters and two other brothers.

They'd needed only three months.

"You know, I'd heard of you when you were a human. Weren't you called the Overlord?"

This surprised him. "On kinder tongues. How could you have heard of me? Your accent isn't from the northlands."

She sighed. "Not anymore. I'd heard of you because I'm interested in all things martial. You were quite the vicious leader."

He felt his expression grow cold. "We were defending. I was anything I needed to be to see it done." He could tell by her reaction that she liked his answer. Her lips parted as she tilted her head at him. Then she sidled closer to him on the bed as if she couldn't help herself.

Her voice more gentle, she said, "But in the end you lost."

He stared past her. "Everything." The battle had only

been like the final blow on a dying man. Prior to that, the enemy had scorched and salted their lands. Famine followed and there'd been no defending when plague erupted.

"Wroth," she said softly. He turned his gaze to her. Her eyes were so captivating in her elven-like face, so clear and lucid at this moment. "Let's make a pact, you and I." She eased open his legs to kneel between them. "Let's vow that we won't harm the other in this room." She pressed him back until he lay fully on the rolled pillow. *What would she do next?*

When he gave her one quick nod, she flashed him a warm smile that made him feel praised in some way. Her damp hair was spilling down over his legs, and with the back of her hand, she swung it to one side, baring her tantalizing neck. A rush of the innate scent of her hair swept him up, like a drug. Sweet and subtle, just like her skin. If she smelled like this, he couldn't imagine what she would taste like. He wished she'd bared her flesh in offer to him.

"Wroth, this is embarrassing," she murmured in a sensual voice, "but I think I've caught you staring at my neck."

"You did," he admitted, oddly feeling no shame to be contemplating his order's most reviled crime.

She brushed her fingertips over her skin. "Are you tempted to take a drink from me?"

In the worst way.

He wondered how many times Ivo had taken her and felt a spike of some unfamiliar feeling claw in his gut. "We don't drink from living beings. It's how we got our name." It was this order's pledge, their pact. Wroth had never tasted flesh as he drank. But then he'd never felt the smallest stir of temptation to before her.

"Why?"

"So we are never tempted to kill," he said, giving her the official line, which was true, but the whole truth was more complicated, and they kept the details they'd managed to learn secret. Living blood, blood not separated from its source, brought side effects with it. A vampire would suffer torments from it, such as his victim's memories. Kristoff believed these memories were what drove natural born vampires insane and made their eyes turn permanently red. As far as they could determine, the only way not to harvest them was to drink blood that had died, avoiding the evils— and the benefits.

"What if you drank from an immortal that couldn't be killed from that?" she asked, her words lulling again. He couldn't seem to take his eyes from hers.

A tricky question to answer without saying that the immortal would have far too many plaguing memories, multiple in number to a mortal. He answered her question with one of his own. "Do you want me to take your flesh, creature?" The mere idea of it made his words rough, his fangs ache.

At her titillated look, he feared she'd say yes, calling his bluff. What would he do then?

"Rain check," she answered brightly. Then, to his shock, she curled up between his legs, face nuzzling against his uncovered torso, and wrapped her pale, delicate arms and hands around his thigh.

"I never asked my questions," he said, staring at the ceiling, trying to sound casual about what was occurring. He'd seen a great many things in his life, but this female was throwing him.

"We have all the time in the world for that, do we not?"

He thought she kissed the scar on his lower stomach with her lips—and a slow little lick. He lay tensed, rasping, "At least tell me your name, creature."

"Myst," she whispered, then she fell asleep.

Myst. How fitting that she was named after something intangible and capricious.

Long after, he was still roiling. In sleep, his little pagan clutched his leg with her pink claws. And they were claws, sharp and curling, though somehow elegant. He ignored the pain, for it was little compared to the odd satisfaction of thinking that she clutched him for comfort.

He savored simply resting with her, doing nothing but watching as her hair dried into big, glossy red curls that spread out over his chest. For centuries their army had been constantly on the move, hiding in the shadows of the northlands in often grueling conditions, keeping their growing numbers secret. Everything had been about the war, all adding up to this attack, to furthering their cause.

He brought a curl up to his face to brush it over his lips. So soft, like her flawless skin. Tomorrow night, if she hadn't given him information—and he somehow knew she wouldn't voluntarily—could he lash her skin to get at her secrets? After Myst had cleaved to him so trustingly? Could he break any of her delicate bones and have her gaze at him with pain in those green eyes? If she'd been his Bride he wouldn't have to hurt her, would be forbidden from ever harming her—his life given over to protecting her.

He ran the backs of his fingers down her silken cheek, feeling her light, quick breaths warm on his stomach. He'd never truly felt the sting of envy in his life, had never envied other men except those who enjoyed peace in their land. He'd been born affluent, his family aristocratic, and fortune had followed him until the latter years of his mortality. To envy was to lack.

So why did he want to destroy any vampire who might be blooded by her?

CHAPTER THREE

Where the hell is my freaking warlord?

Myst jerked upright, waking from the first real sleep she'd enjoyed since she'd been taken by the Horde four nights ago. She was alone in his bed, her clothes washed and folded at the foot. She smiled to realize he'd drawn a blanket over her.

She needed to keep up with Wroth until her sisters broke her out of this pokey. She swore again that this was the last time she would be bait—and this time she meant it. Rumor was rife in the Lore, but tales of Ivo the Cruel making dark alliances proved worrisome enough for them to "reconnoiter," or undertake Operation: Myst Gets Nabbed. Yet she'd learned little about Ivo for her troubles—the acting, the getting too close and then letting herself get caught, etc.—only that he was definitely planning something major.

She chuckled—that is, until General Wroth punked his ass out of a castle.

No, she hadn't learned much about Ivo, but this Kristoff and the general would make good dish. What if this king really wanted to kill Demestriu and stop vampires from terrorizing everyone else? Was it possible that not all vampires had a predisposition toward sociopathic evil? What if the Valkyrie didn't have to war with these Forbearers? However, it was doubtful. Her sisters wouldn't discriminate between the two vampire factions. Kill first and then say, "Gosh, were you actually good? My duh!" Vampires as a species were simply too powerful to go unchecked.

Demestriu and his vampire Horde had been brutal to all the Lore, but especially the Valkyrie. Fifty years ago, Furie, their queen, the strongest and fiercest of them all, had tried to assassinate him. She had never returned. Tales abounded that he'd chained Furie to the bottom of the sea to drown again and again only to have her dogged immortality surge her to life for more torment. When the covens finally found her and freed her, Furie would be as none other on earth, awash in rage. She wouldn't check for vampire affiliation before she slaughtered and would expect her covens to follow her example.

So, until Myst's covens decided on their plan of action with this new power, she'd go about business as usual, which meant she needed to find Wroth. Before he'd come, Myst had been powerless here. She could handle weapons as well as most in the coven, though a sword and bow were not her strengths.

Her preferred weapon was men. And now she had one—a big, scarred one with gorgeous eyes, and with skin that she wanted to lick until her tongue got tired—in her clutches.

Or she'd had him.

Manipulating them, playing them, making them believe she lived for them alone in order to have them do her bidding were her m.o. Furie had once asked her, "Why would you ever send a man to do a woman's job?"

Confused, Myst had answered, "Because I can."

The problem with Oblak's vampires was that they had no appreciation for her whatsoever. At least Wroth liked to look at her.

For them, the blood superseded all, and she could neither withhold it nor capitalize on it. Though the eyes of every creature in the Lore turned a certain species-related color with intense emotion, theirs were permanently, wholly red from sucking the life from their victims to the very marrow—not from merely *drinking* as these Forbearers feared. One kill put them in a downward spiral, because with the kill came the bloodlust riding them to do it again and again. Then the subsequent accumulation of their victim's memories over the years drove many of them mad.

Yet for the last four nights, Ivo and his men had never drunk from her, vacillating, examining her as she had yawned with boredom. She'd snapped to Ivo, "Get dental with me or don't, but make a damned decision." His eyes had slitted with menace, his red gaze a contrast to his pale face and shaven head, but in the end he'd avoided her blood, thinking *her* madness might be catching. Worked for her. In fact, she'd never in her life been bitten.

She wondered what it would have been like to have Wroth take her neck last night when his pupils had flickered black with want. She was an awful person, she knew it, weak with perversion to even entertain these thoughts. Probably the only Valkyrie on earth who'd ever fantasized about a vampire. She frowned. No. There'd been one other. . . .

Myst tapped her chin, wondering if she should tell the Forbearers that they forwent for really no reason.

Neh.

Maybe if the scrumptious general continued to be nice to her she'd hint a little. She *had* heard of him back in the day. Of course they'd had a correspondent in the field following that war and she'd reported back that Wroth had been big and brave and deliciously ruthless to his enemies. Though the Overlord had lost in the end against a much larger force, he'd bought his people at least a decade of protection.

Myst and her sisters had sat by the hearth, sighing over tales of his deeds as though ogling an issue of *Tiger Beat*. Myst remembered that she had felt loss at the news of his defeat because she'd known it meant the death of a great man. But he'd made a comeback, and, in person, he hadn't disappointed. Except for the fact that he was now a mortal enemy—or rather, an immortal mortal enemy. Oh, and a leech.

She tried the door to his room, just in case he'd decided to trust her, but it was locked—though not mystically reinforced like her cell was. She could easily have broken it down, but she didn't have to be back in the dungeon until dawn. So she took her time dressing and piling her hair up in a way she thought he'd like, and still had time to root through all his things. Though she kept her eyes from the shiny jeweled cross, lest she get sticky-fingered with it.

Digging through his clothes, she realized she liked how he dressed, his style modern but still aristocratic somehow. And she loved his scent and his careless but sexy hair. She'd rolled in the bed with one of his big cable-knit sweaters, her face buried in it, uncaring if he returned and found her like that. But he never showed, and instead two guards had arrived to escort her back down as per *his* orders.

They wouldn't meet her eyes.

Well, shite, they knew something she didn't. Wroth hadn't kept her as she'd hoped. She was in trouble, and she suspected she knew why. *If you do happen to have information, I can get it from you,* he'd said.

When they closed the cell door behind her, and she realized she was the only one in the dungeon, her fears were confirmed. The low beings here—those who made up the Saturday night creature-feature underbelly of the Lore— had been taken away, no doubt to be tortured and killed.

She was the only girl left on the dance floor, but not for long, she knew, because none of the others would've talked. Of course, she'd threatened to peel them, and their families, for revealing any information, and there was a reason that *"And may you never feel a Valkyrie's breath at your back"* was a drinking toast among the Lore. The vampires might come and take one's village, but the Valkyrie would creep in, hiding under a bed to take one's head from one's pillow. Their word was law.

Which left her . . . She looked up when she heard boots clicking over the stone.

"Listen carefully, Myst," Wroth said as a guard opened her cell before leaving them. "I'm going to ask you questions about your kind and about the different factions in the Lore. You must answer them or I've been ordered to get the information from you by force."

"Torture? Ordered? Can't disobey Kristoff for me?"

"Myst, you know I'd be dead if not for him. My brothers and friends as well. My life has not been my own since that night."

He was actually serious about this. But then Myst hadn't been kidding either when she'd said that torture really pissed her off. She'd been giving Wroth preferential treatment because he was, like, a *celebrity* in martial circles, but now he'd taken a plunge into vampirism—and she needed to remember that. She'd push and cajole to the end but after that . . . *Bring it, leech.* Still bubbly friendly, she said, "Wroth, you could help me escape—"

"I swore my fealty and I'll see my order through. Answer or you'll face the consequences," he said. "I'll begin with the most basic. *What* are you?"

"Pussy Cat Doll?" she asked, immediately doing a slow headshake at his look. "Judge, jury and executioner." He scowled. Her eyes lit up. "Transient! What? Really. No? Babe in Toyland?"

"Damn it, Myst, just answer the questions. Then you can come back up to my room." He lowered his voice and curled his finger under her chin. "We can sleep together again as we did today—"

"But you don't understand that torture would be easier for me than to go back to the Lore as an *informant*." She'd no longer be an A-lister, an "avoid at all costs" enemy. She'd lose her status as a *creature with which one did not fuck.*

"My brother has tried to get information from the others—"

"But they didn't talk either, huh?" Did she sound smug?

He seemed to shake himself, hardening his resolve. "You're leaving me little choice."

Well. She was about to experience first-hand the Overlord's ruthlessness she'd admired, because apparently he'd decided she was an enemy just when she'd thought they were getting kinda cozy.

Way to hurt my feelings, Wroth. She sniffled. *Now I'll really have to kill you.*

With his thoughts constantly on her throughout the night, he'd stalled for hours, as much as he could, waiting till nearly dawn, ensuring it would at least be brief.

"You're really going to do this?" she asked as she turned from him, moving into the back corner.

Her shoulders were shaking, and he suspected she was laughing. When he crossed to her, taking her arm and turning her, he was shocked to find genuine tears streaming down her heartbreakingly beautiful face. "Wroth, I thought we had an *arrangement*." She cast him a brows-drawn look of betrayal.

She wasn't feigning this. In her wild, mixed-up mind, she had thought they were . . . friends?

The cell wobbled and he braced himself, frowning that she seemed not to notice. *Just aftershocks from last night.*

He didn't want her to hurt. But her eyes blazed with it, raw and true and bare. He was actually seeing *her*—Myst with her false swagger and play peeled back. This was a facet of her, but it *was* finally Myst, and suddenly he found it unbearable as each tear fell. He flinched when one dropped to her cheek, flinched as if he'd been hit. Another shake all around him.

She turned from him and appeared to wipe her face. When she turned back, she was blatantly sexual, as though she'd donned a mask once more.

"Myst, I don't want to hurt you, but you must answer my questions. This isn't a game."

She gave him a look of utter disbelief. "That's *exactly* what this is. You want to know about the Lore? Learn this lesson well—*we are all pawns.*"

The castle shook around him, and while he glanced around wildly, she remained undaunted. No, it was not the outside shaking.

The sound booming in his ears like an earthquake was coming from . . . *within him. "What are you?"* he demanded again.

Her face never lost its expression of vague distaste even when her hand pressed gently against his chest—to feel his heart stutter then thunder to life. Because he'd finally *seen* her and recognized her for what she was. . . .

"Apparently, I'm your Bride."

"I was wondering if I could get you to turn for me," Myst purred to him, as he struggled to hide his shock.

She'd found him to be a cool, disciplined man, but she'd heard a new heartbeat was deafening for these unblooded vampires, the sudden rush of sexual desire overwhelming, their breaths unpracticed and rough at first. With soft touches, she eased him against the wall. His eyes were half-lidded as she rubbed up and down his chest. "How does the air in your lungs feel?"

He inhaled deeply. "Cold. Pressure, but it feels good." He looked at her with such gratitude for blooding him.

They always did.

"How does your blood feel, heating and moving?"

"Stronger. It's . . . searing."

She palmed his erection through his pants, and his entire body jerked as he threw back his head to yell out. She was almost as shocked. She'd known Wroth was very well endowed, but hard, he was *overly* so.

Like Demon or Lykae endowed.

He held her hand in place over his shaft, making her fingers curve around it as he slowly thrust against her palm. Her body softened when she imagined the onslaught of need clawing at him. In a sensual whisper, she asked, "And how does this feel when it hardens and distends?"

"*Good,*" he grated with a shudder. "So damn good."

"It's been three centuries? Well, you are due I suppose." She unzipped his pants just enough to wiggle her thumb inside and rub the broad tip of his penis, making it grow slick. His eyes rolled back in his head. "I can only imagine how heavy and tight this feels, throbbing with pressure, close to exploding."

"Why are you doing this to me?"

Because I can.

Soon he would have no more thought than an animal. His eyes were growing black. She stroked his length through his pants, relieved she would never have to take his uncomfortable size within her body. Five, four, three, two . . .

Wroth attacked, groaning, and he was surprisingly strong as he pinned her arms over her head. He kissed her, deeply, *possessively,* seeming to brand her with his kiss. He left her panting when he bent down to lick her nipples, sucking at them through her blouse. His other hand cupped her sex.

With a growl, he yanked himself from her, and took her elbow. "Come with me."

Damn it, dawn neared. Where were they? She had to keep him here. "No, Wroth," she said.

"Won't claim my Bride in a dungeon."

"But I can't wait," she cried. "Tell the guard to leave."

"No—"

"*Wroth,*" she gripped his shaft hard while whispering in his ear, *"my body weeps for this thrusting inside me."*

He bellowed out that order, then tore open her blouse and bra, suckling and tonguing her nipples roughly. Involuntarily her back arched, pressing her breasts into his gorgeous lips. When had she begun undulating her hips for him?

"I've waited for you," he bit out. "So long I've waited."

One hand pinned her wrists above her, the other shot up her skirt and ripped her panties completely from her. His fingers roved, hot and slow over her, teasing. He knew exactly how to set her on fire, using the moisture from her own body to slide his thumb around her clitoris in slow, slick, mind-numbing circles.

"*So wet,*" he rasped against her breast. "As soon as I saw

217

you, I wanted it to be you." His lips took her hardened nipple, sucking on it till it throbbed. He turned to the other one for the same attention.

Myst made a decision then. There was simply no way she was going to miss this.

She moaned in truth, unable to control herself as lightning fired outside in conjunction with the emotion inside her. When he plunged one finger into her, withdrew, then thrust two deep within her, she wanted to come around them. He slid them into her unhurriedly but with enough force that she was rocked to her toes each time.

She arched her back more, wanting to offer up her breasts. She spread her legs, taking his fierce touch. "Don't stop," she panted, so close, aching to reach for his shaft. But he'd captured her hands above her.

"Never." He thrust harder, until she didn't know if her toes even touched the ground, then he spread his fingers inside her as if preparing her for his size. Her head fell back and she moaned at the overwhelming feeling of fullness.

She raised her leg to lay it over the knee he'd placed against the wall as if just for that purpose. Spread to him, she ground her hips wildly.

At her ear, he rumbled the words, "Come for me, *milaya.*"

"Ah, yes . . . *Wroth,*" she moaned again, about to succumb to his stroking. She gave a strangled cry and climaxed with a fiery, wet pulsing that staggered her and made him groan as if he had as well.

"*I can feel you come,*" he grated while she clutched him, rolling her hips against his masterful touch until she was too sensitive to continue. But he didn't stop until she was mind-lessly moaning his name in his capturing arms.

When she was spent, she sagged against him, still weakly undulating for him. Her nipples were wet and achy from his tongue.

He cupped the back of her neck and yanked her up to face him, gazing down at her with lust, but his words were more. "I will be good to you, Myst. I will protect you. *You are mine.*"

He was saying these things because he was about to shove into her with that huge shaft, to *claim* her. A true vampire's Bride. He took her leg and clutched it to his hip, about to free himself.

Her half-lidded eyes had just widened with true alarm when she heard the merest whisper at the gateway to the dungeon.

Before he could react, Myst flung herself away. Why would she do that? His hand shot out to pull her back, but she shrank from him. Why wasn't he inside her right now? He'd made sure she was wet, ready to receive him—

He heard movement and jerked his head around, fangs sharpening in fury.

"Look at the lovebirds." A creature similar to Myst was standing at the entry to the cell, a bow at the ready.

A second one with bright, glowing skin joined the first, happily chewing gum and flipping a dagger in the air. "Don't make me look—I think I'll be sick. Myst, cavorting with a vampire is a new low even for you."

"What is this?" Wroth demanded, stalking toward them.

The archer nocked an arrow with supernatural speed and let it sing without hesitation. He lunged to dodge it, but she'd anticipated his move and the arrow pinned him to the wall. A second took his other shoulder, drilling its tip half a foot into the stone. He cast her a killing look, then lurched forward to simply let the arrows tear through him, but the shafts were ringed like shank nails.

When he realized he wouldn't be moving, he bellowed with rage.

He saw Myst pulling her clothing together, turning for the door. *"Don't you walk away from me."*

"So sorry to interrupt your plans for tonight." She cast him that hurt look. "You almost made me forget that you'd come down here to *torture* me. You want to learn? Know that we *hate* torture. It starts to add up over the years—"

"That was before I knew you were my Bride."

Her face went cold in an instant. "Before you knew you could finally screw me? Now that your body's in working order, I don't feel the skin flayed from mine?"

"You're my Bride. *Mine.* You belong *to me.*"

She flew back at him, enraged. The bright one tossed her a dagger and Myst caught it behind her without looking. Again his mind demanded to know what she was.

She pressed the blade to his jugular. Her pupils were silver and lightning bombarded the castle. "If I *belonged* to every man who wanted it so or to every vampire I've blooded there'd be *nothing left of me.* But no one cares about that."

"You've not blooded others. They would be here protecting you, fighting for you."

"Not"—she leaned in closer, tilting her head like an animal—"if I killed them all."

Then she grabbed the back of his head and pulled him to her, pressing her lips against his. She kissed him hard. Yet he soon tasted . . . *her blood?* Just as he groaned, she drew back with an inscrutable expression on her face.

Unimaginably warm and rich, her blood was as exquisite as everything else about her, and he shuddered in ecstasy at the luscious taste. "You know I'll want nothing else now," he rasped.

In response, she snapped her teeth at him. To the others she commanded, "Leave him," then exited the cell.

The archer and the bright one exchanged a confused glance. "And by 'leave him' you clearly mean leave him beheaded, disemboweled, and chock full of quills like a pincushion."

"You heard him—I'm his Bride."

"Ohhh," the bright one said, blowing a bubble. "You mean he hasn't, uh, you know, *released,* the first time since his blooding?" Then with a quick glance at his crotch, she said, "And he stays like *that* without you, right?" She chuckled. "I'm cool with the plan."

The archer wasn't convinced. "Don't get me wrong, I enjoy condemning vampires to unending sexual torture as much as the next fabulously talented huntress . . ." When Wroth heard a guard charging in, she leisurely shot an arrow in that direction, tilted her head at the result, then sighed to

Myst, "But *Vampire Bride* just sounds so B-movie. He just dragged you down to B-moviedom."

The bright one made her voice overly dramatic, saying, "For that alone . . . *he must die.* Seriously, Myst. Your 'husband' has irrevocably damaged your street cred unless you kill him like the others."

They were *all* mad.

And still he was hard, aching for her body, for the blood she'd given him just to torture him. "You evil, teasing bitch. Kill me then."

For just the merest second he imagined he saw compassion in her eyes, but when she shrugged, his hazy mind finally grasped that she was going to leave him here with nothing but a body knotted with lust for her and a taste of blood that he would go to his knees for. "You're the most malicious bitch I've ever known."

"Flatterer," she chirped.

Across the corridor, she easily leapt to the window forty feet above, opening the shutters to draw the unfortified bars from the space as though she might pluck back a curtain. She held a hand down for the others.

"I will find you," he bit out. "I will find you and make you pay for this a thousand times."

The bright one leapt up and caught Myst's forefinger with her own. "Sounds like he's setting up a date," she said as she dangled.

"Oooom," Myst purred, her gaze flickering over him. "Dress casual."

CHAPTER FOUR

Present Day

*N*ever-ending sexual desire that could never be slaked.

She'd knowingly—delightedly—surrendered him to this torment. His Bride had blooded him, giving him his first need as a vampire, then stoked it to a fever pitch—and only his Bride could work his body free to release the first time. If she had only stayed long enough for him to take her just once, or to merely touch her skin as he'd taken his own ease, she could've spared him this. But then she'd clearly said that that was the plan.

And for the last five years, Wroth had been cursed with more than that. He was cursed with her memories as well.

The minuscule drop of blood taken directly from her body did more than make any other blood taste like tar to him—it did just what the Forbearers feared. With her living blood came dreams where her memories unfolded, so realistic they were as if he was there to experience scents she'd smelled and textures she'd felt. Sometimes he could even feel her hands clench in anger. But he'd told no one, keeping his secrets because he didn't want to lose his power within their army—or be killed.

Each sunset he rose and checked his eyes for the telltale red, and every day if he could manage to sleep, he was subjected to the same series of memories that subtly grew in detail each time.

The first found her atop a hill, sun bright, with snow still on the ground. "I've cursed you to your hell," Myst hissed at the site of a rough gravestone. She was roiling with so much hostility that Wroth knew she must have killed whatever being lay there. She spoke an ancient language that Wroth shouldn't understand, but he did. He felt the sensations she'd felt, the constant sway of her chain around her waist, the smell of the ocean just below her, brine on a cold day.

Another familiar dream. A drunken Roman senator kneeling at her feet. "At long last, I'm about to have Myst the Coveted. And you'll no longer be coveted, you'll be possessed." He laughed. "You'll make me twist on your little hook no longer."

Wroth had discovered the full name of his tormenter. Myst the Coveted.

With disgust, Wroth saw the Roman take Myst's dainty foot in his mouth, sucking greedily, stroking himself, as she slowly lifted her skirt up her silken thighs for him. As ever, Wroth fought not to see this, fought to wake. His violent revulsion never diminished over time.

The first time he'd had that dream, he'd been relieved

when another scene unfolded before that one came to some kind of sick conclusion. But never again . . .

Myst was running past a Viking raiding party on the coast of some northern land. Purposely. She wanted them to hunt her. To catch her and throw her to the ground in the hard snow. What kind of twisted need did she have? She was excited, her blood pumping. Her skin felt like it was sizzling with electricity, and lightning was generated from her excitement. She stifled a smile, when with bellows and cheers, the men gave chase. . . .

As ever, Wroth fought to force his mind away before he saw a dozen Vikings rutting on his Bride. To her delight.

Tonight a new dream. Finally. Snow outside, packed so high it covered half the window. Women, or other creatures like her, met around a great hearth. They were sisters and Wroth saw their faces as though familiar and knew their names and who they were as well as Myst did. He recognized the archer as Lucia, and the bright one he now knew was Regin the Radiant. A vacant-eyed one was called Nïx, the oldest of her sisters and believed to be a soothsayer. Their clothing indicated early twentieth century.

They were meeting over the fate of a baby that their leader, a somber creature named Annika, wished to keep. Myst frowned at the little girl in Annika's arms, confused to feel some stirring of feeling for it.

"How are we to care for her, Annika?" Lucia murmured.

Regin snapped, "How can you bring a vampire among us when they slaughtered my people?"

One named Daniela the Ice Maiden knelt beside Annika, gazing up at her, briefly touching her with a pale hand. Myst shivered to think of the pain Danii had just felt to offer that cold touch. Daniela's mother's people had been the ice fey and she couldn't be touched by anyone but one of them without extreme pain. *"She needs to be with her own kind. I know this well."*

Annika shook her head determinedly. "Her ears. Her eyes. She's Valkyrie as much as vampire."

Valkyrie . . . ? Impossible.

"She'll grow to be evil," Regin insisted. "She's already snapped at me with her baby fangs. By Freya, she drinks blood!"

"Trifling," Myst interjected in a casual tone. "We eat electricity."

The vacant-eyed Nix laughed.

A vampire child? Eating electricity? His heart was racing. . . .

Annika said, "I will keep Emmaline from the Horde and guide her to be all that was good and honorable about the Valkyrie before time eroded us." Her words were laced with sadness and triggered a memory that Myst hated.

Wroth wanted to see it but couldn't.

Annika rubbed noses with the baby and asked her, "Now where's the best place to hide the most beautiful little vampire in the world?"

Nix laughed delightedly. "Laissez les bon temps roulez . . ."

New Orleans.

Wroth shot up in bed, body drenched with sweat.

My Bride's a Valkyrie? he thought with a choking cough. His mind couldn't wrap around the idea of it.

He hadn't known they even existed. A character from legends told around campfires was linked to him for eternity. From the dreams, he knew she was a millennias-old mystical being born of a fierce Pictish princess—who'd plunged a dagger into her heart rather than be taken alive by an enemy—and of *gods*.

She didn't eat because she took electrical energy from the earth and gave it back with her emotions in the form of lightning. She was a killer and had been a Roman senator's whore. She despised men and enjoyed tormenting them, just as she'd done with him.

He glanced down at his throbbing erection. Even his hatred couldn't battle his relentless need for her. The impulse to take his cock in his fist was there, but he fought it, knowing he could never bring himself to come, knowing it would only increase his pain.

For five years she'd sentenced him to suffering from this constant, grueling ache. Before he'd learned there was no relief without her, he would've futilely stroked himself or thrust against the bed, imagining it was Myst clutched beneath him, but he never took release.

Other females repelled him—because they weren't *her*. Even if he believed he could find ease with another woman, he would never demean himself with another. He'd felt his Myst's incredible softness, felt her wet with desire for him, her body squeezing around his fingers as she'd climaxed from *his* touch.

He shuddered and his cock pulsed hungrily. Linked for eternity. To *Myst the Coveted,* a mythological being who despised him. The only way he'd keep her for eternity would be to punish her for that long.

He knew he coveted her as none other had. And now he knew where to find her.

CHAPTER FIVE

*T*he fumes of swamp, steamed hot dogs and soured beer wafted up to Myst and her sisters as they perched on a roof above the chaos that was Bourbon Street.

There were rumors of vampires running about in New Orleans.

Vampires in Louisiana? Unheard of.

If there'd been only one account of leeches, then she and Regin and Nïx would still be back at Val Hall, their bayou manor, playing video games. But a demon friend had sworn he'd seen one—and a phantom had whispered that there was not just one faction of vampires, but *two*.

Myst's eyes darted over the scene, trying to remain focused and not notice the couples frantically grinding against each other in dark alleys. If Daniela was here she would blow them a kiss and cool them off, freezing hands to asses in mid-grope and making her sisters chortle and roll along the roof. Myst supposed that the Valkyrie were easily amused.

But focus was proving futile ever since her heart had sped

up at the idea of vampires here. If for some reason they had come to the New World—which the Horde historically found vulgar and beneath them—that still didn't mean *him*.

Wroth. One of her true regrets in her life.

Every day, she mused that she shouldn't have left that vampire to suffer—she should have killed him.

Regin tossed her blade up, caught the point into her claw, then flicked it up once more. "You know, not that I believe there are actual vampires here—cause that's just whacky speak—but if there were, they should know that this is our turf."

"Should we ask them to rumble? Or maybe *mash?*" Nïx asked as she swiftly braided her waist-length black hair. "I've heard those can be a graveyard smash." Even sporting the old-fashioned hairstyle and an occasionally confused glance—she saw the future more clearly than the present—Nïx still looked like a supermodel.

"I'm serious," Regin said. "New Orleans may have once been the mystical melting pot of the world, but we control this place now."

"We can always send Mysty the Vampire Layer to battle them," Nïx said thoughtfully. "Oh *wait,* she'd run off with them."

Regin added, "Or use her famed tongue assault to flail the skin from their bodies as they inexplicably line up to sacrifice themselves."

"Har-de-har-har," Myst mumbled, half-listening. She'd been razzed about this continually. And she deserved it. She might as well have been caught free-basing with the ghost of

Bundy. Of course others had overheard the jokes in the coven and the word spread. Even other factions of the Lore—like the nymphs, those little hookers—whispered about her unsavory predilection toward vampires. But it wasn't vampires plural, it was only one.

Wroth. She shivered. With his slow, hot fingers . . .

In her bed late at night, when she touched herself, she always fantasized about him, remembering his hard chest and harder shaft, imagining his ferocity, his intensity, if he ever found her again.

Truthfully, she thought he might have found her by now. She'd—*accidentally?*—given him her blood, possibly giving him her memories, which could lead him straight here. She often pondered that reckless kiss. She'd had no discernible intention of giving him blood, but hadn't she known in the back of her mind that his fangs would be razor sharp with her sisters' arrival? Had she *wanted* him to find her?

She shook her head, needing to stay sharp. Annika, Daniela and Lucia were down there somewhere.

"Lookit," Regin said, pointing down. "Men that big shouldn't get schnockered."

Myst turned her attention to a tall man who reminded her of Wroth from the back—*why couldn't she get that vampire off the brain?*—though this one was much rangier in build. The man leaned against another massive male, hanging on to him for balance as they walked. She noticed her claws were curling.

"Myst, can't you control that?" Regin asked with a fleeting glance at her claws. "It's embarrassing."

"Listen, I can't help it, I like big males with broad shoulders. And I bet under that trench coat he has an ass that begs to be clutched."

Nïx offered, "And it's not like she can put Band-Aids over them—"

"Holy shite," Regin exclaimed. "I see a glow. Ghouls, down by Ursilines Avenue."

"Damn it," Myst muttered. "In public again? They are hard-up recruiting then." Ghouls were maniacal fighters out to increase their numbers by turning humans with their contagious bites and scratches. They had green, gelatinous blood, and the parish of Orleans went gooey every time the coven fought them.

"Again." Nïx sighed. "And there's only so many times we can convince drunken tourists they're extras in a sci-fi flick."

Regin slid her blade into her forearm sheath. *"Stargate* part twelve is officially on location." She rose. "We'll go canoodle the ghouls. You keep a watch out for *vampires."* She made a ghostly wooo-wooo sound. "And try not to lift tail for any of them, 'kay?"

As Myst rolled her eyes, her sisters linked arms and leapt down, moving so quickly they were like a blur. As usual, no one could see them, and if they did in this Lore-rich city no one registered it.

Myst surveyed the glow from afar. It wasn't that extensive, so she knew they could handle it. As eldest, Nïx was strong and Regin was wily. Besides, Myst had new boots on and she'd be damned if she'd lose another pair to the epic battle between buttery soft Italian leather and goo. Too many casualties already. It was terribly saddening. Really.

Her attention easily fell once more to the man on the street, and she raised an eyebrow. If his front matched his back, she'd be tempted. It had been ages, literally, since she'd had a little some-some, and she deserved—

She sucked in a breath, springing back against the dormer. The drunk was no drunk at all she saw when he peered down an alley, giving her his profile. The body she'd been ogling was that of her "estranged husband," as the coven liked to tease her.

He stumbled not from drink but from weakness, his build different because he'd lost weight. And that was his brother Murdoch helping him—helping Wroth *find her.*

Shaking, she crept along the roof, pressing herself around the dormers, hoping to get away before he saw her. He stopped, lifting his head above the milling crowd, then swung around to her direction.

His gaze fell directly on her, his eyes black, feral and riveted to her with a look of utter possession. When Murdoch's gaze followed Wroth's, he gave her an almost pitying expression, then he slapped Wroth on the back before tracing away.

The blood left her face. She leapt to the roof of the adjoining building, gaining speed for the next—

She screamed as Wroth's gaunt visage appeared directly in front of her. Traced. She sprinted in the other direction, but he snatched her around her chest, pinning her to him, making her feel his erection thick against her. She elbowed his throat, dropped from his arms, and dove over the edge of the roof. She tumbled into a high-walled courtyard, landing on hands and feet, then scrambled up to leap out of the darkened space. But her speed was no match for his tracing.

He snagged her again, and though she fought, he was somehow stronger even in his condition—maybe *because* of his condition. One of his hands yanked up her short skirt.

"Wroth! Don't do this!"

"Five years of hell," he sneered, palming her ass roughly. "You deserve to be fucked till you can't walk."

She gasped, trembling. "So the warlord claims his prize? It figures that you'd take your Bride whether she wants it or not. You'd make me remember being forced?"

After a pause he bit out, "No. God, no." She heard him freeing himself. "Myst," he groaned, "just feel me." He took her hand and made her cup his heavy sack, then grip his shaft. Never had she felt such hardness. "Rub the head," he rasped in her ear, making her shiver as she felt the moisture. "That's as close as I can get without you. I need to fuck you so bad I'm sick with it."

"Wroth, don't . . ."

With a bitter curse, he lowered his head, forehead against her neck, but he only thrust against her ass. "Can't stop," he grated, and she knew then that he wasn't going to take her body, just touch it, use it. Why would he refrain for her . . . ?

His fingers strummed her nipple. Lightning. No, she couldn't *want* this.

His breath was hot on her and made her body go liquid. She *could* want it, just as she did every night in her lonely bed. The air was sultry, redolent with the scent of jasmine and even more moist than usual from the pounding fountain in the corner. No one was home. He wouldn't take her, so why not enjoy this for mere moments?

When she went soft in his grasp, lacing her arms back to lock behind his head, he growled and kicked his feet against hers, making her spread her legs. Shuddering, he ruthlessly shoved against her flesh, then threw back his head and yelled out just before he came. At the last minute he turned from her and began to spill his seed onto the ground.

She was frozen, unable to see, and for some reason it affected her more to only hear his reactions, the guttural groans erupting from deep in his chest. She felt the violent shaking, the strength in his wracked body as he clenched her through waves of pleasure.

It went on and on, each second that passed reminding her of how badly he'd *needed* this. Then he put his lips to her neck, clutched her ass and she knew he was stroking himself directly to ejaculate again. When she thought about how many nights he would have envisioned this, her head fell back against his shoulder.

The second time was impossibly even more powerful as he desperately kissed and licked her skin, squeezing one breast then the other, reminding her keenly of when he'd brought her to come that night in the dungeon. She wanted to join him—she wanted him to work those fingers on her next.

When he was done, he lifted her hair and brushed his lips to her neck, shuddering and breathing heavily. Her eyes closed and she was just about to say, "My turn," when he did the most bizarre thing.

He arranged his clothing again and pulled down her

skirt, then he turned her to him to stare down into her eyes. He cupped the back of her neck hard to yank her to face him, but instead of drinking her, or hitting her, he squeezed her into his broad chest, his hand moving to the back of her head, tucking her into him with those powerful arms. Which was disconcertingly pleasant.

Curious, she let him embrace her, relaxing a fraction, and in return, he lowered his head to kiss her hair. Finally he set her back to face him. His expression was not as wild, but grim. "I've searched for you, Bride."

"Been right here."

"You've treated me ill, leaving me in that state."

"My sisters were going to kill you, but I saved your life. And you were about to treat me far worse."

"And licking my fang?"

That had been an accident! Still she raised her chin and said, "The least I could do since you were about to *torture* me. Consider it a memento."

His face hardened at that, but then he seemed to get his temper under control. "For five years I've envisioned the retribution I would mete out, constantly imagining making you pay for what you did to me." He exhaled a long breath. "But I'm weary of it, Myst, weary of carrying this. I want to look forward and get on with our life."

Our life?

"From here I'm willing to start with a clean slate. We are even for our misdeeds against the other and we will forget about any past . . . *indiscretions* that might have gone on before we met."

"Indiscretions?" How magnanimous of the vampire to give her an empty score card. To fill back up.

"Your blood gave me more than a mere taste. How do you think I found you?"

"So you collected my memories?" Lovely. Did he now know she'd been utterly infatuated with him? Had he harvested all her knowledge about the Lore? "Did you enjoy telling your brother and your friends all about my life—my private thoughts and private . . . deeds?"

"I have never told anyone anything I've seen. Believe me," he added in an odd tone. "And I vow I never will. That is between us."

"Can you vow you'll never use information about my family to harm them?"

He scowled.

"Forget it, then. Doesn't matter anyway," she said, trying to wrench away from him. "There's no starting *our* life— even if you hadn't been about to do what that night? Break my fingers, my legs?"

He didn't deny these things. "That is in the past and you've paid me for that in kind. If it is consolation you want, know that I've suffered far worse than I could ever have dreamed to inflict on you. For these years, I couldn't sleep, I couldn't drink. The only thing I could do was fantasize about fucking you, with no relief."

Warmth bloomed in her belly, but then she frowned. "It doesn't console me. I just want you to let go of my arms and allow me to walk away. My kind *abhors* yours. And even if I liked you and you were decent to me, my sisters would kill you, and I'd be ostracized by every being in the Lore. There's no way I'd choose pariah-hood with you over my current life—which I happen to enjoy the hell out of—so back off. I don't want to have to hurt you again."

He raised a patronizing eyebrow at that, which made her bristle, then said, "I can't let you go. I'll never do that. Not until I die."

"I've given you a warning and I'll say only once more—release me."

"It will never happen. So what will make you accept this? A vow? Done. I vow to you that I will never use what I've learned to harm your family. As your husband I could never hurt them anyway because the end would be hurting you."

When she saw he was deadly serious about this, she realized playing with him was over. He was going to try to force her to live with him. Because he felt that was his right over hers.

No different from all the others. Her name should be Myst the Possession.

She wondered if she'd keel over dead if someone finally *asked* her to be with them.

"Wroth," she whispered, snaking her arms up his chest to twine her fingers behind his neck. He leaned down to hear her. "Do you know what it would take to make me your Bride in truth?"

"Tell me," he said quickly.

"The life leaving my cold, dead body." She kneed him, deciding at the last minute not to break his tailbone with her blow. When he fell to his knees, she backhanded him, sending him flying twenty feet into the courtyard wall.

He bellowed in fury, slow to rise as she sprinted down a breezeway nearing the wrought iron gates at the street. But he traced forward, snatching at her, brushing down her back with his fingertips, then snagging the chain. She screamed in pain when it broke from her.

Great Freya, not the chain. If he figured out its power over her, it wouldn't matter how strong she was as a Valkyrie or how well she fought. She ran for her life, busting through the locked gates, blowing them off their hinges to clatter and spark across the street. For two thousand years it had been unbreakable.

Don't hear, don't hear, run, escape from his voice . . .

"Myst, stop!" he roared, frustration choking him when he found only the fine, gold strand from her waist.

Yet she froze, nearly falling forward her feet planted so quickly.

She turned to him, sauntering back down the corridor to rejoin him in the courtyard. Licking her lips and smoothing her hair, she said, "That's mine and I want it back."

She reached for it, but he held it high from her. He was not magically inclined—he hadn't believed in the Lore until he was turned—but even he felt the power in the strand of gold. The power of what?

"How badly?"

Lightning streaked the sky behind her. *She must want it very badly indeed.*

"Would you steal from me?"

"You've stolen from me. *Years*—you've taken years from me."

"I thought we were even."

"That was until you tried to unman me."

"I will be kinder to you if you give it back."

Her eyes were mesmerizing, and he had to shake himself. "We're past that point. All I wanted was to make my life with yours. And you left me in pain." Earlier, when he'd finally been released from endless nights of torture, he'd felt overwhelming gratitude to her—irrational, since she'd consigned him to it—but he'd known a measure of contentment for the first time in years. Then she'd lashed out again. "After tonight, I understand that you'll never be brought to heel." He clutched the chain, recalling earlier how she'd stopped so suddenly. "Unless . . ." He trailed off, staring down into her eyes, riveted to his. "Kneel."

Her knees met the stone as if she'd been shoved down.

His eyebrows drew together in shock, his breaths coming fast. "Shiver," he commanded, not quite believing . . .

She did, and her skin pricked as if with cold. Her nipples hardened and she hugged her arms around herself.

He knew his grin was wicked. Five years of imagining had never prepared him for this. "Grasp my belt."

She looked up with dread, was staring into his eyes pleadingly when he said, "Come."

CHAPTER SIX

*A*s soon as her mind registered the command, her body rushed to obey with a swift, fiery clenching that left her sagging against him, her grasp on his belt the only thing that kept her from falling—as he'd anticipated.

When the bliss finally ended and she could catch her breath, she raised her face, parting her lips to ask—

"Again."

She moaned, unable to release his belt as she twitched and swayed on her knees, brushing her breasts frantically against his legs. *"Stop, please . . ."* She pressed her face against his huge shaft, needing it, her body squeezing only emptiness. She ran her mouth over it even as she begged him to stop. Though she'd hurt him, he was recovering right beneath her lips.

"Come harder."

To her shame, she did, arching her back and crying out, opening her knees and undulating her hips for him to come fill her.

As the waves of pleasure relented, she dimly perceived

him scooping her up into his arms. She was limp, disbelieving, yet every nerve was on fire. There was blackness, dizziness, and then she was in a new place, in a dark paneled study.

He set her to her feet, but she'd gone boneless from his orders and from . . . *tracing?*

In a tremulous voice, she asked, "Where am I?"

He held her until she was steady, then crossed to open a small wall safe. He tossed the chain in and shut the door. "You're at Blachmount, my manor in Eesti. This, Myst, is your new home."

Her lips parted in shock. "You can't just keep me here—"

"Apparently I can do anything I want where you're concerned. This is where you'll stay and where I'm going to show you all the mercy you showed me."

Her eyes went wide.

"Listen carefully. This safe is unbreakable and you will never, never touch the lock. You'll never try to deduce the combination or garner it from me. Do you understand? Answer me."

"Y-yes."

He strode to her, clutched her arm and traced them into what looked like a bedroom. A vampire's lair. With the bed in the corner on the floor as they preferred. She shivered, knowing she was well and truly screwed in every possible sense.

"Undress," Nikolai ordered from the shower.

Her shock had been quickly replaced by rancor, and she

glared before obeying. He didn't care. Watching her yanking her clothes off in the steamy bathroom was like witnessing a gift unwrapped.

He stood under the pounding water, his body healing at a rate he'd never imagined. He'd taken a blow from her that would've crippled him for days in the past, and yet he was already hard for her again. In fact, his pain had been the only thing that had kept him from covering her in the courtyard and plunging into her as she writhed from her orgasm, her eyes firing silver with pleasure. Now nothing would spare her.

When she was completely naked, he stared at those plump breasts that had haunted him, his mouth watering at the thatch of auburn curls between her legs. What to make her do? The possibilities were endless. He could tell her to take him into her mouth and see how many times she could make his cock rise under her tongue. He could force her to *beg* to do it, to beg for him shoved inside her. After these last long years of agony, and now to have such a gift as this chain . . .

If Wroth had a sense of humor, he might have laughed.

He didn't understand the chain's power, only knew that it was absolute over her. He wasn't one to mull over its origin. If he spent time questioning every new development in his life for the last centuries, he'd have gone mad. It was a tool he needed. Simple enough.

He'd decided to bury the past, but tonight he'd realized she was too wild and too vicious to accept him. She'd proven she was just as his dreams told him. With this mysterious chain, could he make her a biddable wife, in his life—and in his bed?

Earlier, he'd been very conscious of her reaction as she came. She'd rubbed her face against his cock, wanting it. In an alley, with his clothes on, having just had his manhood battered, he hadn't been able to fully capitalize on her need. But in the shower . . . ?

"Join me, Bride."

She was compelled to, though she had an expression of disgust on her face. "You keep calling me that, but you don't have that right. I've given no consent, so I think the term you're looking for is *slave.*"

His eyes narrowed as he took her tiny waist and pulled her into the water with him. "Semantics. The end's the same. You forget that I'm from a time when men needed no consent to take what they wanted."

"And you forget that I lived in those times as well and was glad to get past them. I'd almost forgotten what it was like having to kill all the leeches like you when your pesky little hearts would beat for me." She cast him a look of pure venom. "But it's coming back to me."

When she bent down to wash off her knees, he crossed to sit on the marble bench at the end of the shower, watching her move. "If I weren't a vampire and we had no history, would your body be aroused by mine?"

She'd just stood fully to lift her face to the water. At his words, she clenched her jaw.

"Answer me."

"*Yes,*" she grated.

"Good. Come here. Closer." When she'd finally sidled over, he commanded, "Kneel once more."

"You can't make me do this," she hissed even as she obeyed.

"I'm not going to *make* you do anything. I will never force you to touch me or force myself upon you," he explained while her expression turned disbelieving. "No matter how badly you've treated me. In fact, just to make this harder on you, I will never touch you or kiss you unless you *ask me* for it. This will be that much sweeter when you reach to put your hands on my cock or beg me to fuck you."

"Never."

He ignored her protest. "If at anytime in anything we do, you want to deepen the experience, for instance by climbing up here to straddle me, I give you leave."

"Are you off your meds?" she snapped, but he could tell she was nervous.

He gently cupped her face with both hands, thumbing her glistening bottom lip. "Touch yourself."

She gasped, her hand flying to her skin as though magnetized. She stroked up and down between her breasts.

"Lower," he commanded. Her fingers snaked down her flat stomach though she clearly resisted the order. *"Lower."*

She twitched from the fight, but she obeyed, her fingers descending to her sex.

"Open your knees wide and pleasure yourself as if I wasn't here."

"Don't," she whispered, even as she spread her knees to run her delicate finger against her flesh. His cock pulsed and the head grew slick. After long moments of simply staring in awe as she began trembling and her eyes grew silver, he rasped, "Are you wet?"

"Yes," she moaned.

He felt electricity rolling from her, pricking at his skin, revealing how much pleasure she was experiencing, and it quickened his own need. He bit out, "Inside. Put your finger inside."

When her finger slipped inside her sex, she threw her head back, crying out.

"Two fingers. Deeper." He clenched the edge of the bench, and the marble cracked under his grip. "Harder."

She obeyed, this time throwing her head forward, hair cascading over his torso as she moaned against his cock. Her tongue flicked out while she panted against him.

"Ah, deeper. Faster . . ."

She moaned around him this time, because she'd taken the head into her mouth. She continued to work her body with one of her hands, her fingers sliding in and out of her heat. Her other hand was all over him, wickedly seeking, her lips so moist and plump and hungry, behaving just as he'd suspected she would. . . .

His Bride was on her knees, her fingers deep inside her body at his command, sucking greedily at his cock. He bit out, "Do you want me to touch your breasts?"

When she nodded eagerly, he grated, "You have to ask me for it."

Her fingers slowed, and she released him from her lips, though her head was still bowed. He didn't want her to stop, knew he'd pushed too far.

"I want to, Myst. I want to have my hands on your beautiful breasts. I've dreamed of this for so long," he admitted.

She hesitated, her body quivering. "Will you touch them?" she breathed, then set right back to her ministrations. He choked out a groan when she kissed all around the head wetly with her tongue, as she might his mouth. She took him with such abandon that he knew she was on the verge again. He reached down and covered her breasts with his hands, closing his eyes at the feel, squeezing, stopping only to pluck and thumb her nipples.

The pressure was building inside him. His body tightened, knees opening and heels planting on the ground as he tensed to spend. He didn't know how he'd lived so long without this blinding pleasure.

"Watch me come," he growled.

She raised her face, and somehow she knew he wanted her to meet his eyes, not watch the actual spilling of his seed. Silvery eyes riveted to his, she worked her fist on his cock, pumping it in time with her finger dipping inside her—as if she yearned for him to fill her.

That thought sent him over the edge. The unbearable pressure exploded as he ejaculated, mindlessly thrusting against her hand, arms shooting straight out to cup her face with both hands. When she saw him spend, her eyes grew wide before fluttering shut and she cried out, jerking against her fingers as she came all on her own.

She collapsed against his knees, still shuddering, clutching his leg as she had that night in Oblak. *Before she'd left him, bleeding and in pain.* The need dampened, the familiar resentment flared.

He brushed her aside and stood, rinsing his seed away, staring at the stunning, evil creature still on her spread knees, hands on her thighs as she panted. The sight of her perfect, generous ass and her wet hair whipped all along her slim back had him stirring yet again.

But she was breathing hard and he knew he'd worked her pitilessly for their first night together. "Rise and come to me."

When she faced him, her eyes were stark, flickering in color, showing how shocked and uncomprehending she was as she stumbled to obey. He felt a stab of guilt, but made himself remember all the aching days he'd spent rolling in pain. The nights he'd sweated from fucking desperately at the very sheets to take relief. She'd reduced him to that.

She was wary, nearing him slowly, and when she was at arm's length, he said, "Sleep," then caught her as she fell limp. He rinsed and dried her body and his own, then carried her to his bed.

This should have been a time of satisfaction—by Christ, he had a living, breathing Valkyrie in his bed, and she was *his* Bride—yet there was little. She was utterly under his control, but he wished she didn't *have* to be.

Like a natural born vampire, he hunched over her, dragging the beauty into the shadows with him as he bedded them down in a corner.

Rise.

Myst hazily heard the command, knew she must still be dreaming because her skin was touching another's, though she hadn't slept with a lover in memory. She frowned, disconcerted because her body was so pliant, every muscle released of the tension she normally carried. But why was her face pressed against the naked, broad chest of a man? She was surrounded by his delicious scent that made her go warm and liquid. Snuggling closer, she dragged a leg up over his.

She heard a male rumbling sound of pleasure, and her eyes went wide. She shot up, drawing the sheet to her neck. Dread settled over her as the events of the night came back to her mind. She was in a vampire's bed, here as a slave to his every whim. Or as she figured it, she was in hell.

"Were you dreaming about last night?"

"No," she answered honestly. She'd been thinking about licking every inch of the hard male beneath her.

"How do feel about what we did?"

"We? What *you* did."

"I only commanded you to take your pleasure. Of your own volition you took me into your mouth." He raised an eyebrow. "Greedily."

She turned away sharply. "Then I feel shame."

"And?" When she frowned at him, he said in his deep voice, "There's rarely an instance where emotions do not conflict. What else do you feel when you think of last night?"

She recalled being *mindless* with lust as she had never been before, hungry for his huge shaft. She had wanted to straddle him and slowly work him within her. Shivering at the delicious image, she struggled to keep from admitting her desire. "A-aroused," she bit out.

"Are you aroused now?"

She felt herself blushing deeply. Myst *never* blushed. "Yes."

"Do you need to come?"

Oh, God, no, how could he ask her this just when she was reliving last night? "Y-yes." She turned from him, curling her knees to her chest. "But I won't ask you."

"Even when I can give you what you need?"

"The only thing I'll ask you for is to give me my chain back."

"You'll get it back when I am convinced you will stay with me," he said. "Explain to me what it is." When she didn't reply, he grated, "Answer me."

"It's called the Brisingamen."

"Why do you wear it?"

"Punishment and to protect it."

"Punishment for what?"

She placed a hand out to her side and turned back to him, her green eyes taunting. "When I was only seventeen, I was caught in a compromising position with a demigod of no importance or standing other than his mind-shattering talent at kissing. My family was unamused."

A muscle ticked in his jaw. *Demigod?* Wroth was a battle-scarred vampire who would never walk in the sun with her.

She studied his expression. "Jealous, vampire? Or do you realize I'm out of your league?"

He ignored her words. "So your family punished you with a vulnerability that gave men control of your body? How many have had it, commanding you to fuck them for your very life?" When she glared at him, he calmly said, "Answer. Fully."

"There was no vulnerability. It has never been broken. I've been tossed by it, caught by it, even held above a pit of boiling tar by it. I'd tried to have it smelted from me in the olden days and then lasered recently. Nothing could touch the integrity of the chain before . . ."

"Before I pulled it free like a thread? So I'm the first." This pleased him and he exhaled in relief, only to immediately frown. "You don't think it's more than coincidental that you were given to me over all other females in any time and place to be my Bride, just as I've freed you from something that no man has been able to before?"

She clenched her jaw.

"How do you find those facts? Answer honestly. Now."

"I find them. . . . They might be. . . . It might be fated," she bit out.

"*We* might be fated." He'd already known this without doubt. He couldn't believe his heart would beat for a woman that could never love him back. Of course, she'd said there'd been others she'd blooded—then killed.

"Yes, but just because we've been set up by a fate with a sick sense of humor doesn't mean my feelings about you will change. Are you going to keep me prisoner for eternity?"

"Before I let you go philander with your *demigods?* Yes."

Her slim shoulders stiffened and she stood.

He lay back, proudly ogling his Bride's ass as she sauntered around the room, studying her new surroundings. Myst couldn't merely *walk,* he'd discovered—her every movement was the stuff of fantasy, her every touch as well. He hadn't even gotten the chance to claim her last night because he'd been so enthralled with her wet kiss, but he was hard yet again and would remedy that soon.

"So what miraculous feat of engineering brought modern plumbing to this schwag place?"

Schwag? He frowned at her question, watching as she ran her hand along an old papered wall. She opened a rusted shutter and gazed out the window into the night, seeing, he knew, tangled gardens blighted with neglect. He had a sudden urge to make an excuse as to why his home was in this condition.

"You're actually going to keep me *here?* Your torture is fiendish and boundless, Wroth."

He clenched his jaw, then said, "As I told you, *here* is called Blachmount and it used to be awing and will be so again, but the estate's been abandoned for many years. While I searched for you, I lived in New Orleans, and in Oblak before that. I only come here on occasion." When he missed his family.

She sighed, meandering to her pile of clothes, ripped and dirty on the floor. She stared at them then blinked up at him, clearly wondering what his next move would be. It hit him full force that no matter how he felt about her, it was his responsibility to take care of her. His stunning wife, with her wild red hair and her soft, pale skin, who was so utterly out of place here, would be living with him under his roof—he'd best get this ancient shell of a keep back to its former glory and give her a home as befitted her.

He knew there would be things she would require that he couldn't anticipate, because he was beyond unknowing when it came to female needs. Did he dare take her to get her things?

As soon as he'd realized where she lived, he'd left Oblak behind and had had Murdoch purchase a property far from the crowds of New Orleans where they could live during the search. Wroth could've traced back and forth, but the time change meant each night he'd face dawn back in Oblak. Plus he'd been weak, and tracing the shorter distance to the renovated mill on the outskirts of town had been less demanding.

Now he needed to return to the mill for the large supply of blood he'd left there. He was thirstier than usual, and claiming her in this condition would not be wise. He assured himself it was only because his appetite had been reawakened and not because throughout the day, he'd dreamed of drinking from her white thighs.

He could check in with Murdoch, send word to Kristoff that he'd found his Bride, and drink in preparation of finally claiming her. While in New Orleans, he might as well visit a Valkyrie den.

"We go for your belongings tonight."

CHAPTER SEVEN

*H*ow are we going to do that?" she asked. "You can only trace to places you've been to at least once."

"But I can drive anywhere," Wroth replied casually, every inch a modern warlord.

So she was to return to her home in ripped clothing, with her skin still flushed from last night, her body still singing for a vampire's touch.

Lovely.

She would never live this down. And for an immortal, *never* was a particularly woeful proposition.

Yes, going back to Val Hall would mean a possibility for escape, but he could kill one of her sisters if they tried to free her. When he rose and strode to his closet, she studied his body, noting yet again how incredibly strong he was.

He turned and tossed her a button-down, catching her gaze just as it drifted south to his hard shaft. She almost missed the shirt and he smirked, making her jerk her face away. "Come here," he ordered and she dragged her feet over. His hands reached out to pile her hair up, just so he could lean down and breathe along her neck, then murmur in her ear, *"Bride, this is embarrassing. I think I've caught you staring at my cock,"* making her quiver. She'd teased him the same way when his eyes had been riveted to her neck so many years ago. He added in a sensual rumble, "You like it, don't you?"

When the question sunk in, her eyes went wide with disbelief, the spell broken. How could he ask her that? When she would be forced to answer? His lips hovering over her shoulder, he said, "Answer me honestly."

I want to curl up between your legs, rest my head at your hip, and draw you over into my mouth to taste you for hours, she almost said, then negotiated her mind into another honest answer: "It's too big."

He dropped her hair, smirking again. "So it terrifies you more than tantalizes?" he asked using the words she remembered well.

Knowing he was getting his revenge little by little, she gritted her teeth against her answer but lost. "Both."

He clucked her under the chin. "I'll be sure to break you in slowly, ride you easy the first few times."

Myst of the witty banter and dripping sexual innuendo was speechless. Break her in? Arrogant! When he turned for the shower, she tried not to stare at his back and how it tapered to his narrow hips and his muscled ass with the hard hollows on the sides. She'd been right, it did beg to be clutched.

Damn her claws for curling—

"I believe you like everything about me," he rumbled from inside the bathroom.

She gazed at the ceiling, embarrassed as she couldn't remember ever being before. Of course he'd known she was staring, probably by the holes she was burning into his skin. As she dressed, she thought that he was right—she was *tantalized,* and she did like *everything* about him physically. The way he'd made her feel last night left no doubt in her mind that he could not only get her to ask for him inside her, but *beg.*

She needed to escape before then, before he "claimed" her. He hadn't drunk from her and they hadn't had sex. As long as those two things stayed sacred she could get past this patch in her life.

When he returned to the room, dressed like a male dream, she felt like shuffling her feet for her ridiculous getup, draped in his shirt that fell to her knees. She had *never* felt insecure before. But she didn't have long to ponder it, because he put his hands on her waist. "Are you ready?" he asked, staring down at her. Ready? To kiss him, hug him, go to her knees? What?

He pulled her to his body, wrapping his arms around her. "Close your eyes," he commanded. She did. "Open them."

Suddenly, they were in a garage. This was the first time she'd traced and been able to think about the process. She'd dropped an intoxispell or two in her day and found tracing on par with that. She was unsteady at first, but the air smelled like bayou at high tide, which she liked, and was heavy with humidity. New Orleans, but where? "What is this place?" she asked, breaking away from him to look around.

"An old restored mill north of the city," Wroth answered. "Where I stayed while scouring the streets for you for as long as I could manage every night. Before collapsing in agony and weakness."

She looked away quickly, fighting a flare of guilt—and spotted his cars. She tried to be cool, but of course, Wroth caught her eyeing them—especially the Maserati Spyder—and she knew he'd seen her flicker of appreciation. The Valkyrie prized fine things. They were acquisitive to a fault—it simply couldn't be helped. Her own mother had told her that Myst's first word was, roughly translated, *gimme*.

He opened her door to the Spyder, and once she was inside, she curled up on the soft leather, loving it. Joining her, he cast her an inscrutable expression. "We are fortunate, Myst. You'll want for nothing as my wife."

She'd already been fortunate. She already wanted for nothing. The coven divvied their collective earnings from investments, and the take was always incredibly generous. She had enough money to buy any clothing that struck her fancy, to purchase two thousand dollar hand-painted lingerie sets to placate her obsession. In a deadened tone, she mumbled, "Oh joy. I'm rich."

He commanded her to direct him to her home, not in itself an unforgivable crime. They didn't hide their address like the Bat Cave, yet they didn't often have trespassers at Val Hall. When his breath hissed in at the sight of the manor, she was reminded why.

"This is where you live?" he bit out, forearms resting on the steering wheel, his tone incredulous.

She tried to see it from his eyes. Fog shrouded the property, and bolts of light illuminated it in a staccato rhythm. There were lightning rods everywhere, but sometimes they didn't catch all the lightning, as evidenced by the massive oaks in the yard still lazily giving up smoke. And the wood nymphs—those little hookers—were way behind on repairing the trees. If Myst heard them whine, "But Mysty baby, there was this orgy," as an excuse one more time—

"Hellish," Wroth said.

She tilted her head. In the olden days they used to stick a sword into the ground to mark a grave, and she'd always fancied that the rods made this place look like one of those mass burial sites. Even at this distance, shrieks could be heard coming from within. The Valkyrie often screamed. If Annika got angry enough, car alarms in three parishes would blare.

Okay, it might be a *bit* hellish.

"It's time you had someone take you from here," he bit out as he continued closer.

She frowned at him. "You forget. This is where I belong. I'm as much monster as what lies within."

"You're a lot of things, Bride. But you're not a monster."

"You're right. I'm what monsters like you fear beneath their beds."

"But now you're *in* my bed where you belong."

"So in this life of ours that your crazed mind envisions, I'm not going to fight?"

He shook his head as he parked down the gravel drive. "No. I'm well aware that you're deceptively strong. I know that other beings would rather die than risk your wrath. But I won't ever allow you to put yourself in danger again."

She batted her eyelashes at him and in a syrupy voice said, "Because I'm just so darn precious to you?"

"Yes," he answered simply, making her roll her eyes. He got out of the car, and she followed, but he quickly traced to open it for her, looking at her as if she was crazy not to wait for him to assist her.

Perfect. A gentleman warrior. Which she was discovering she might have a weakness for.

As they walked the drive, he said, "Hold my hand."

"Big vampire scared the wittle Valkyrie will get away?"

He turned to her with his brows drawn. "I just want to hold your hand."

What was that flutter in her stomach? And why didn't she mind that her hand was slipping into his big, rough one to be completely enveloped and secured? They walked like this to the side of the cavernous thirty-room mansion.

He was tense here, ready to trace them away in a split second, and she almost felt sorry for him when she realized he'd never seen anything like her home before. He was of the Lore, and yet in so many ways he was as human as he'd once been.

When he made her point out the window to her room, showing him a destination, he was able to trace them again. Inside, he scanned the lace and silk filled space with those discerning eyes, studying everything within. She was the girlie-girl of the coven with her candles and silk sheets, her room and lifestyle the most human-like of any of them.

Her room was next to Cara's, which housed only a spartan sleeping mat, her ancient winged helmets, and a string of vampire fangs she'd taken as trophies. Across the gallery was the room of petite, timid Emmaline. Though she was part Valkyrie, she was a vampire through and through and made her little nest on the floor *under* her unused bed.

It could be argued that Emma proved that not all vampires were evil and that the coven could coexist with one. Yet Emma had been the daughter of a beloved Valkyrie, and that half was believed to "temper" the other. An exception had been made for her, but Myst often wondered if she was the only one who noticed Emma flinch and tremble, her big blue eyes glinting with apprehension whenever the coven shrieked and railed about killing leeches. "Present company excepted" really was a weak statement when one thought about it.

"So what do you want me to pack?" Myst asked.

He raised an eyebrow. "You should be used to this. Choose clothes as if you were going away with your lover."

Her hands clenched as she crossed to her drawers that housed her Agent Provocateur, Strumpet & Pink, and Jillian Sherry collections, and those were mass purchases from just last week. "Depends on which lover." She plucked out a red leather quarter-cup bra and a baby-doll teddy that was completely translucent, then held them up for him.

"Both," he rasped, his expression pained. She saw he was getting hard again. He noticed her noticing and his eyes darkened.

Assuming a brisk manner, she crossed to the closet to gather a weekender bag, but he picked her up bodily by the waist and set her out of the way to gather a four-foot-long moving case. He dropped it at her feet. "Fill it, because you're never coming back to this place."

At his words, she nodded, making it somehow sarcastic, and he knew she was thinking to herself how wrong he was. He exhaled wearily. If he had to battle against her for the rest of their lives, he would.

He moved to assist her, but every drawer in her room was full of thongs, hose, lace and little silk nightgowns that made his blood pound. She had a drawer for nothing but garters. It would take him months to bite all of these off her body.

He frowned. Women wore clothes like this for a lover. How many did she currently have? When he imagined them relishing her beauty, the gold chain slapping against her body as she writhed on them, he crumpled the iron post end of her bed.

Now she smirked at him, reading him so clearly. "Nikolai, if you can't control your jealousy, we're heading straight for divorce." She tapped her finger on her chin and added, "Make a note now that I'll expect the house, the kids and the hellhound. Actually, you can keep the schwag house."

He scowled before turning away, examining her belongings for more insight. Her film collection was copious. He was unfamiliar with them, as he was with most things that had to do with leisure time. "Which of these do you prefer?"

She clearly hated having to answer his questions and struggled against it each time. "I like romance and horror."

"A bit disparate."

She eyed him. "Funny, I used to think so."

He ignored that and tossed a few DVDs in the bag.

She put the inside of her forearm behind dozens of bottles of fingernail polish, pushing them over her dresser into the bag. The look she gave him dared him to say something. Nail polish was out of his realm of understanding, and he merely shrugged at her.

He crossed to her bathroom, searching the cabinets and drawers. "There are no medicines. No things . . . females need."

"I don't get ill and I don't have those types of functions. Just like you, vampire."

"None at all?" He wondered if she could get pregnant. Perhaps he didn't have to be as careful with that as he'd planned.

"None. Why, you can force me to have sex with you nonstop all month!"

"Why would I force you when I can barely keep your hands—and mouth—off me now?"

"Wroth, darling," she purred, smiling so sweetly. "I can't wait for the next time I get to put my mouth on you." In an instant the smile faded and she snapped her teeth and yanked her head back as if she was chewing something free.

He didn't even have time to cringe because she wriggled from his shirt then. At the sight of her naked body, his cock shot hard as steel. She sensually dragged her underwear up her legs and then bent over in only the thong to step into a skirt. Just as he was fighting the overwhelming urge to take her hips and feed himself into her, shrieks erupted from downstairs.

On edge in this place, he moved to peer over the landing outside her room and found ten or more Valkyrie downstairs. Some were lounging in front of a TV, bowls of popcorn in front of them—that they didn't eat. One was up and sparring with what looked like a ghost or a phantom. When the pair crossed in front of the television, the others screeched and threw popcorn at them.

A small Valkyrie stalked in the door. She was covered in blood.

"Cara!" they shouted in greeting, completely unsurprised by her appearance.

"What'd you get into tonight?" one asked from her perch on the mantle.

Cara pulled her sword sheath from her back. "My human unknowingly went into a demon bar. A demoness thought to make her lover jealous using *my* charge." She shook her head. "It was everything I could do to keep the demon from ripping Michael's throat out with his teeth."

"How'd you do it?"

Without blinking an eye, she said, "I ripped the demon's throat out with my teeth."

When they all laughed, Wroth raised an eyebrow, vowing that Myst would never see these malicious creatures again. *Never.* Without their influence, she would be kinder, gentler.

She sure as hell couldn't get worse.

"Have Myst or Daniela returned?" Cara asked.

"No. I'd expect this from Myst—"

Because she often ran off with men?

"—but certainly not from Daniela. She never returned from the Quarter."

"Well, the hits keep coming—I just saw Ivo the Cruel in the Quarter."

When they laughed again, she said, "You should know by now that I *do not* jest about vampires unless they're dead."

They sobered and one asked, "Has he returned for Myst? Somebody needs to warn her."

Wroth quickly turned back to her room—but Myst was gone.

He traced to the opened window, then to the end of the field below when he caught sight of her sprinting away. He yelled for her to stop and somehow she kept running.

She was fast and might have outrun him with her unnatural speed as she covered miles, but he traced, lunging from that momentum to snag her ankle, tripping her forward. She wore plugs in her ears from a music player. Enraged, he yanked them from her, heard the music blaring and threw the contraption into the woods beyond.

She'd almost escaped him. *Before he'd claimed her.* Thoughts grew distant. A shadow fell over his vision. He pinned her down, tossed up her skirt, then ripped the silk from between her legs, glorying in that feeling. He was finally going to take his Bride.

Hazily, he realized she was still struggling from him. Her

words echoed inside him. "Wroth, you want it? I'll fight you for it."

He would always fight for her, *always*. Would he fight *her* for the right to her body?

"Then you're *mine.*"

CHAPTER EIGHT

A nightmare was about to take her.

When his fingers dug into her skin, dragging her beneath him, she knocked her forehead against his. He bellowed with rage, until she squirmed around and drove her elbow back into his throat. As he fought for breath, she took advantage by scrambling from him enough to mule-kick his chest, sending him reeling.

Why hadn't she broken his neck with her elbow through his throat? She had before with other vampires. Why did she hesitate whenever it came to hurting him? She wouldn't again, she thought as she leapt on top of him, drilling her fist into his face so quickly it was like a blur. His lip split. Another two hits in rapid succession. She thought she broke his cheekbone.

"You'll get no mercy now," he bit out, his eyes black, his deep voice rumbling almost unrecognizably. He caught her fist when she struck again and squeezed. With her other hand she swiped her claws down his shirt, across his neck, hissing in fury. Lightning came down like a hail of bullets.

Somehow he caught her free wrist and turned over on her, pinning her hands above her head.

Just as she tensed to kick her leg straight between his and send him flying forward, he groaned as if in desperation, sinking his teeth deep into her neck. She shuddered and cried out, body going limp beneath him. Her eyes widened in shock as she stared at the lightning above. This wasn't pain he was giving her.

His bite was ecstasy.

He did it again and again lower on her neck. Each bite, each time his fangs entered her skin was like the thrust of a man inside her. Each time he released her skin was like a slow, measured withdrawal. The pleasure was dizzying. Exquisite agony.

She'd never been defeated before in a contest of two—no man had ever been strong enough. And Myst had an animal need deep inside her for a powerful male—like this one who'd pleasured her, fascinated her—to win. Her mind rebelled, reminding her of what he was. She'd killed the last three she'd blooded. Why not him? He'd planned to *torture* her in that horrid dungeon, planned to control her with the chain.

But his bite . . . It made her body demand, growing wetter, feeling empty without him shoved tightly inside her.

Please be strong enough . . . Please . . . For once in her life would a man take control?

So she could finally lose it.

When he pinned her wrists with one hand—hard—she arched her back in delight. He used his other to rip open her shirt and bra and bare her breasts. He palmed her flesh, then opened his jeans and freed himself. His huge erection jutted between them, the sack heavy beneath.

Her eyes widened and she fought anew, digging her heels into the ground to scuttle back. Too large for her. *Break her in slowly*—that's what he'd said.

His palms landed with a slap on her upper thighs, lifting her pelvis. Her hands loose, she rose up and fought him viciously—scratched, bit, hit—but it was futile. Still clasping her thighs, he used his thumbs to spread her sex, then wrenched her down on his shaft. Yelling brutally as she cried out in pain, he buried himself into her flesh until he was thick and throbbing deep within her.

He'd done it. *Myst will want the first man who can defeat her.* That's what they'd always whispered about her.

They'd been right. She'd challenged him and he'd bested her. In her mind, he deserved to claim his prize no matter the consequences.

He stilled, then bent his head to her and dragged his tongue over her nipple as if to soothe her. As if somewhere in his crazed mind, he wanted her to have pleasure.

He set to her other nipple for long moments, then sucked from her neck again. Somehow the bite turned pain to pleasure, helping her body grow slick to accept the invasion. She yanked the remains of his shirt open to sweep her fingers over his splendid chest and that helped as well.

As he slowly withdrew, he groaned, *"So wet,"* but when he thrust again, she hissed in a breath, eyes watering.

"Wroth, it really hurts," she whispered.

"Can't stop," he bit out. His neck and chest sheened with sweat, the muscles rigid from his effort already.

"T-tell me not to feel pain."

"Ah, Myst, don't hurt." His words were ragged. "I don't want you to feel pain from this." Immediately, the pain muted to only a feeling of fullness.

When he drank from her, pulled back his hips and then tentatively thrust, she cried out again. He stiffened. "No, Wroth . . . it's good! . . . Keep *going."*

He did. He timed each draw from her neck with the bucking of his hips, and she knew it was over, gave herself up to it, arched her back, arms limp overhead. The lightning whipped up the wind, and it rushed over her heated body, over her tight nipples.

He raised his chest up, positioning himself on his knees. She whimpered when she thought he would withdraw, but he dragged her up with him until she was straddling him. He spread his knees so he could thrust up inside her. He was getting too large to move within her, already hitting the end of her sex so she couldn't take him to the hilt.

His body was so big around hers, making her feel truly vulnerable. As if he read her mind he wrapped his arms tight around her, pinning hers to her sides. He completely captured her to hold her in place while he drove into her from below.

She relaxed every muscle in her body—why not? This was a position she had never allowed before, from which there was no fighting even if she'd wished to. She knew he wouldn't let her go or fall. She relaxed in the crushing tightness of his arms, her naked breasts pressed against his scarred chest.

He kept her immobile while he continued to fuck like a piston below them. Her head fell back and she watched the sky in a daze of pleasure, seeing her own lightning thrashing the earth.

Bliss welling up, strengthening, so close.

"Myst," he growled, releasing her neck.

She thought he would order her to come, thought he was tightening his arms even more as if to threaten her should she disobey, but he didn't. *"Milaya, I want you so much."*

Milaya, the endearment from years ago said in his accent, sent her over the edge. She cried out from the shattering pleasure. But it only built when he desperately wrenched her up and down on his shaft as he tensed to come.

Groaning, snarling, another bite that made her shudder in her second orgasm. Then he threw his head back, neck and chest tensed with corded muscle, to bellow from the force of his spending. She felt it inside her, searing, palpable, seeming endless as he pumped and pumped within her. She came the entire time, her body squeezing around his thickness.

Then after-shudders. Arms loosening though she didn't want them to. She didn't want this to end.

When his breaths had calmed somewhat, he drew her back to search her face. His eyes had cleared. "I didn't want to hurt you," he rasped. "I didn't—Your *neck,*" he said in a shocked tone, staring.

She brushed her fingertips over her marks. "It didn't hurt. Even before you . . . we . . . uh, worked it out." They were nothing and would be healed by tomorrow. "You've really never seen this before?"

"Never."

"I was your first bitee?" Why that would please her she couldn't know. Why she wasn't leaping away from him in disgust confused her. She was just so overwhelmed with everything. And she felt . . . *tenderness* toward him. Yes, Myst had always been the girlie-girl of the coven, but she'd never in her long, long life felt truly feminine until this male had squeezed her in his arms and *taken charge.* She had never—in all the lifetimes she'd endured—experienced that much pleasure.

"I've never taken flesh to drink because I knew what it would do to me." He rested his forehead against hers. "Myst, my eyes will go red from this. I will turn."

He looked so horrified, the words slipped out, "Your eyes will go red only when you kill as you drink living blood. The ones whose eyes turn drink to the marrow of their victims, sucking from the pit of the soul. They take all the bad, all the madness, all the sin."

His jaw slackened. "Is that why pure-blooded vampires go mad?"

She shook her head. "It's more than that. They get addicted to killing, which means they can never drink from the same source. After years and years of different victims, the memories add up."

He cupped his hand behind her head. "Every sunset I checked my eyes, not sure if I would turn from your blood. Not knowing if my brothers would have to kill me."

His tone wasn't reproaching, but hell, could she feel *more* guilty? This male was still *inside* her, inside her body that was humming as she'd never even known it could . . . and she'd tortured him. "Wroth, you're a vampire. Others might not agree, but I for one believe that you're meant to drink. To connect, to live. But never to kill like that. And it takes decades of killing every day for the memories to accumulate."

In a stunned voice, he said, "I won't turn. I'm meant to drink." His lips curled, and he stroked her hair, still supporting her with one arm. He would never let her go. *He's bested me*—she shivered.

"And you found pleasure in it."

It wasn't a question, but she answered, "Your bite was the only thing that saved you from a stiff legged kick at your groin." When he grinned, she added softly, "It was intense pleasure."

He groaned in approval and thrust into her once more, still semi-hard. To her surprise, she moaned, desire stoking again. "Did I take too much?" he asked. Still on his knees, he laid her back until she was horizontal, secure in his arms, one hand cupping her head, the other clutching under her shoulder as he pulled her along his length in a long, strong stroke.

Her eyes fluttered closed, and she answered without thought. "Immortal here. Remember?"

He stopped suddenly, brought her back into his chest, arms around her, protective once more. "I heard something."

"It's nothing." Frustrated, she kicked him in the ass with

her heels, rocking on him. He stifled a groan but didn't thrust. When she opened her eyes, she found his gaze furious and focused on . . . the sword point tucked under his chin.

Regin was pressing hard enough to bring blood trickling down. Lucia stood at her side with an arrow nocked.

"No," Myst said, her voice sounding hoarse from screaming. "Don't."

Regin stared at her in disbelief. Regin, whose entire race had been destroyed by vampires . . . and who'd secretly learned to count by her mother's bite scars. "This thing just violated you—"

"We followed the lightning here, Regin," Lucia interrupted. "Whatever he did to her she let him do."

She couldn't imagine what they looked like there in the field. They'd fought ruthlessly. They must be bruised, bloody, their clothing in shreds.

Why hadn't he traced her away? Why hadn't he thrown her out of the way and attacked Regin? She suspected the answer to the first—he wanted them to see her like this. Their relationship couldn't be made more brutally clear. She pulled away from him, though his arms tightened around her to prevent it. "Please, Wroth," she whispered in his ear, "let me face them." He finally released her.

But jealous Myst didn't want her sisters to see Wroth hard, huge and magnificent, and she pulled her skirt over them as she drew him free from her, then yanked his shirttail down. *That's mine,* she thought irrationally. She'd been acquisitive all her life but never with men. Now *she* wanted possession.

*   *   *

When Myst stumbled away, Wroth reached for her, but Regin raised her sword against him, piercing several inches into his chest muscle. He didn't fight back—he could hardly feel it—and he had vowed not to harm her family.

He was euphoric. There stood his Bride, putting her chin up as she pulled her shirt closed. Claimed. He stifled an evil grin. With witnesses. She could never go back now. She was his.

His heart pumped madly for her, his blood rushing inside him—*and her luscious blood as well*. She'd enjoyed his bite, lightning had streaked the sky each time that she came— he'd *seen* her pleasure. He could give her lightning each time he drank, without fear of turning, without fear of hurting her. No more checking his eyes each sunset.

They could sustain each other. He'd never known greater satisfaction.

Now if he could just get her witch of a sister to cease stabbing him.

"You just had sex with a vampire," Lucia said. "Myst, where is your mind? You know the repercussions. You'll be shunned by the Lore, mistrusted."

Regin added in a deadened tone, "When Furie rises . . ."

Whatever that statement meant, it made Myst's brows suddenly draw together. She appeared shocked by everything, as if her sisters' arrival had splashed ice water over her, waking her from a dream. He needed to get her home, away from them.

Suddenly Regin gasped and stared at Myst in horror. "Oh sweetheart," she whispered, "where's your chain?"

"Quickly," Wroth snapped to Myst as he reached for her, "take my hand." Myst obeyed, diving forward to take it. He traced them just as Regin leapt for Myst's legs and an arrow sang for him, hitting him in the shoulder but not staying within him as he disappeared.

Back at Blachmount, he set Myst on the edge of the bed. "Stay here," he ordered, then returned for the goddamned bag he'd gone to get in the first place. Just as he arrived in her room, Regin and Lucia bolted up the stairs. "Give her the chain back, leech!"

"I've claimed her. She's my wife now," he said simply, then traced with an ease he'd never had, covering the distance as if an afterthought.

Back home, he tossed her things to the side, then took her shoulders. "Rest, *milaya*. Take a hot bath and relax here until I return." She didn't respond, and he didn't want to leave her unsteady from tracing and reeling from the events of the night, but he needed to let Kristoff know that Ivo was in the New World. They needed to hunt him down and destroy him.

As Wroth gazed down at his Bride he wondered how Ivo could *not* be searching for her.

He brushed her hair from her face, trying to get her eyes to meet his. "Make yourself comfortable here. Your clothes are here. This is your home now."

When she nodded absently, her pupils were huge, her eyes stark, and he knew he couldn't leave her like this. He would warm her with a bath then put her in bed.

He ran water, undressed her and set her in it. She sat

silently as he scrubbed the dirt and grass from her alabaster skin and held a cloth to her neck, to the bites that marred her.

Suddenly, she turned to him and placed her hands on his face. "Wroth, you said you would vow never to hurt my family?"

"Yes. I make it again."

"I believe you. You could've traced and attacked Regin and Lucia tonight and you didn't. But please, if you take more memories from this night, don't give others our weaknesses. Don't allow others to hurt them either."

Was his first loyalty to his king or to her? She was his Bride, and as he stared into her eyes, he realized that that meant she was his family. Wroth's family had always come first, and nothing had changed except that he'd now added to it.

"If I learn of other factions I will relate that information. But never about your kind."

She pulled him to her and kissed him softly with trembling lips. "Thank you," she whispered against him, then she gave him a shaky smile that made his turned heart do things he never remembered from being a human before.

Her shoulders tensed just as he heard voices sounding from downstairs.

Trespassers in his home. His fangs sharpened. That someone would dare enter his home when he had his Bride within it . . . "Myst, finish up, then go to the bedroom and wait for me. If anyone comes in that door but me, run faster than you've ever run and escape them."

He traced downstairs, feeling his muscles tensing, his hands itching to kill. He was strong from her immortal blood, taken directly from her flesh, as powerful as he'd ever imagined, and he would use it to protect her. His fangs were sharp as razors—

"Wroth, I pity the being who wishes to harm your Bride," Kristoff intoned from his seat at a long table in the great room. Murdoch and a couple of elders sat with him and all their eyebrows rose at his appearance.

As he struggled for control, he imagined how they saw him. His clothing was filthy, his shirt stabbed and shot through, and God help him, Myst's delicious blood marked his skin and clothing. He was fairly certain that she'd gotten in a few sucker punches at his face as well.

"I would not wish to attend you in such a condition. I'll go wash and change—"

"No, we know you are eager to get back to her for the remains of the night." Kristoff appeared proud. "Congratulations, Wroth. You've now been blooded *and* claimed your Bride." He studied him. "Recently. Though it appears as if she didn't acquiesce to you."

Wroth stood, uncomfortable, reminding himself that she'd kicked him like she would spur a horse when he'd stopped.

"I'd like to meet her."

"She is resting."

"I suppose she would be. In fact, we'd wonder if she wasn't." A couple of snickers. Wroth shot them a look and they quieted. "And you drank her blood this night?"

His eyes narrowed. How had he thought this would escape Kristoff's notice?

"Did you take her flesh as you did so?"

He could do nothing but admit to the most heinous crime among their order. Shoulders back, he said, "I did."

"Take off your shirt."

Murdoch caught his glance, tensing to fight, but Kristoff waved him down, saying, "Stand down, Murdoch, no one's dying tonight."

Perhaps Kristoff would only flail his skin from his back. Wroth removed the shirt, hoping. For the first time in his life, he had his wife waiting for him and for the first time he truly cared if he lived or died.

"Toss it on the table."

Frowning, he did. The elders' eyes widened, their hands going white on the table. Kristoff had scented Myst's blood, and now the others did as well.

"And what was it like, Wroth?" Murdoch asked, his voice hoarse.

Wroth didn't answer. Then Kristoff raised his eyebrow in a silent order.

After a moment, Wroth grated, "There is no description strong enough."

"And how did she feel about your bite?" Kristoff asked.

He didn't want them to know how she reacted to that, how it had made her come with an intensity that had staggered him.

Kristoff's stare was unflinching. "You resist answering your king on the heels of confessing to our most reviled crime?"

This was his Bride they spoke of. He wanted to lie, to say he wasn't sure, didn't know, and he couldn't. Answering this wouldn't be breaking his vow to her, and if Kristoff ordered him killed, he couldn't protect Myst from Ivo. Though it disgusted him, he bit out, "She found extreme pleasure from it."

Kristoff appeared pleased. Or even relieved. "Do you think I should forgive Wroth his transgression? For which one of us could have resisted the temptation when she was our Bride and her exquisite blood called?"

Wroth hid his shocked expression. Kristoff would've normally called for him to be chained in an open field until the sun burned him to ash.

"Continue as you were, but if your eyes turn, know that we will destroy you." He was still staring at the shredded garment marked by a Valkyrie's blood.

Wroth recovered enough to say, "I was coming to Oblak tonight to tell you that Ivo was spotted in New Orleans. He's looking for someone—and I suspect it could be Myst. I need to—"

"We'll take care of it," Murdoch interrupted sharply. "For God's sake, you stay here and . . . enjoy . . . everything."

"Find out as much as you can from her." Kristoff eyed him shrewdly as he stood to leave. "And you will tell us if the memories follow the blood."

A short, quick nod. As Wroth left the room, stunned from the events, he heard Kristoff say, "Now which one of you will volunteer to accompany Murdoch to New Orleans where this coven full of Valkyrie is located?" Wroth heard every chair scrape the floor as they shot to their feet.

Like a cat licking her wounds, Myst sat in the large bath, replaying the fight.

Since she'd pulled her punches, she wondered if she could've won, wondered if she'd truly been bested. But then she flexed the fingers of the fist he'd caught. They were sore. They were *not* broken. He'd held back as well.

She sighed, unable to work up the outrage that should be exploding within her or even concern over the possible threat downstairs. Wroth would take care of it. He was strong. She shrugged, her mind easily returning to tonight's stunning developments. Now her sisters knew her chain was gone *and* that she'd been claimed by a vampire.

What they couldn't know was how much she'd *loved* it. His bite had turned her inside out, made her toes curl. Even now she shivered to think of it, knowing something was woefully wrong with her for craving it. It might be twisted, but she yearned for him to do it to her again. And again.

In addition to that, Wroth had taken her as no other had before. Though she acted as if she'd had tons of lovers, she'd actually had only a couple of steady partners. She'd dated a wonderful warlock for centuries, but it was long-distance—in those days, it took a half a year to reach each other—and they'd parted ways amicably. She'd only slept with two others, both long-term, and they'd been fun and enjoyable. But she'd seen a lot, and knew a lot, and she knew Wroth moved and used his body on hers—in hers—in a way that was nothing short of divine. And she believed it would only get better. She shivered again, unable to imagine how she could feel more pleasure without dying. Then there was a very compelling fact. . . .

He'd unchained her where none other could.

Did that mean he was *supposed* to have it? To have her? Was he supposed to possess her, to command her like a genie with a bottle? She'd always pitied the plight of genies until once when she'd freed one from a young berserker. Instead of thanks, the chit had laid into her, screaming, *"To each her own, lightning whore!"*

After Myst dried off, she dressed in an emerald-green, understated nightgown that said neither "do me" nor "don't do me." She lay back in his bed, realizing she was just so *relaxed* about everything. Strange, but she felt so at home here in this cold, bare mansion.

Less than half an hour later he returned and showered. There'd been no threat? Probably his brother visiting just in time to see Wroth looking like she'd fought him for her life. He should see when she *didn't* pull her punches.

When Wroth joined her, she wondered if he was going to make love to her again. Their time in the field had only set a fire for her—lit a pilot light, so to speak, as it had never been lit before. She was sore, but if he commanded her not to hurt again . . . yet he only clasped her into his arms to rest on his chest. She saw he was hard, but he made no advance.

Finally, he curled a finger under her chin and raised her face to his. He drew her hair back to reveal his bites. He let her hair fall, then stared at the ceiling, rumbling the words, "I regret hurting you. The number of bites, the lack of care before . . ."

She knew what he meant by the latter—he regretted not taking time to prepare her body and ease into her. When she thought about how he'd learned to do this, or thought about the first time he'd ever realized that he would even need to, she felt a scorching flare of . . . *jealousy*—so strong it rocked her. Jealous? When he could never want another but her for the rest of his life?

"I can't believe I lost control like that. I am unused to being blooded. I am unused to being a husband. But I vow to you that things will be different—I will be gentler."

That statement was the first thing to threaten her lackadaisical mood since she'd returned here. She didn't want their sex to be different. *Their sex.* Great Freya, was she thinking about keeping him? She would get used to his size, and then she would demand that he be anything but *gentle.* She couldn't have ordered up a better match for her in bed and she'd be damned if she let him hold back all that magnificent strength.

He was everything she could ever dream of physically. His scars alone . . . she stifled a moan but her claws were curling. He was a warrior, with a warrior's mentality, which she appreciated. None of her lovers before had been warriors. No, they'd been the warlock, an immortal sultan and an architect. Perhaps that was why she was so attracted to Wroth.

She and Wroth were kindred.

"Speak to me," he commanded, then immediately amended, "Will you not speak to me?"

"I want my chain back. I want to choose." If he gave it to her, she would stay awhile. Her sisters had already seen her screwing a vampire—she might as well enjoy the pleasure for a time.

He moved to his side, pressing her to hers as well. There they lay, gazes locked. Dawn was nearing and she didn't want this to end for some reason. He put his hand on her shoulder and stroked her. His palm was rough from hardships and the grip of his sword, and she relished the feel of it. "I can't lose you. The very thought makes me crazed. I can't even allow myself to imagine you leaving me." His hand squeezed her now.

"Are you so certain I would?"

"Yes. I am," he rasped. His tone wasn't blaming, but more like he was explaining something regrettable but inevitable.

She didn't deny it, because he was probably right. He called himself her husband, but she didn't recognize him as such. She didn't recognize him as the one whose arms she would forever run to get within. She might stay for a time, but in the end she would always go.

CHAPTER NINE

*T*he harsh light of day. Or night, Myst mused. The harsh light of waking was upon her.

Instead of the shame and disgust she should be feeling, she was treated to big, warm hands massaging her back until she was a boneless heap of bliss. She moaned, her mind dimly registering that vampire lovers might be vastly misunderstood. Perhaps *she* was in the know and enjoying early-adapter status.

"I have to go meet with my brother for a couple of hours. Can you content yourself here?"

"Uh-huh," she mumbled.

"Don't leave."

Huh? She wasn't going anywhere. She was too at home and relaxed here.

He bent down to murmur in her ear. "I've left clothes laid out. Will you dress for me, *milaya?*" And then he disappeared.

Strangely lazy, it took her another hour before she finally got up. She raised an eyebrow at what he'd set out for her—

a stiff satin bustier fringed with transparent lace that just covered her nipples, intricate garters, fishnet hose and thong—all in jet black. She shivered. General Wroth had a wicked streak.

He wanted her to dress for him, and she didn't have a problem with that—she was pleased that someone would finally enjoy her fabulous silks and lace. And it made a huge difference that he'd asked when he could have commanded. But as she soaked in a bath, she mused that she was still in a position where she had to *depend* that he would continue to show the same consideration. Which was intolerable for a creature like her.

She'd half-expected her sisters to have arrived already—Nix often could find her—but knew if they hadn't come by now, she would have to win her freedom with her own tools and talents. He'd said he would return the chain when he was confident she would never leave. How hard would it be to act as though she wanted to stay forever?

She dried off, tilting her head at the lingerie laid out. Why not use seduction to let him think she desired him above all others for all time? Play at love and act at surrender. As she smoothed the hose up her legs, she wondered if deception had ever sounded so delicious.

She began trembling as she donned the bustier, and the material at the top skimmed over her hard nipples so sweetly. She was already wet with anticipation.

After dressing, she lay on the bed, fantasizing about him inside her as his big hands worked her body. Would he drink her? She pictured him driving into her from behind, the length of his body stretched over hers to take her neck as well.

Her fingers found their way down her belly and into her panties. He was supposed to be back soon, but did she really care if he caught her? She'd already done it for his pleasure, and what would he do if he found her like this and didn't like it—break up with her?

A stroke on her clitoris had her back arching. Had she ever been so wet? No, not until she'd impatiently waited in a vampire's lair in tight black satin to seduce a warlord.

Her eyes closed and her legs fell wide as she ran her finger lower. When she opened her eyes, half-lidded, she found Wroth staring at her from the foot of the bed.

"Couldn't wait?" His voice was husky, his eyes dark. He was already ripping off his clothes, his shaft bulging against the material of his pants.

She shook her head.

Wroth had known his Myst was a pagan, but she'd never truly looked it until he found her pleasuring herself in his bed in black hose, garters and satin, legs spread with abandon. Her glorious red hair haloed out along the pillow and her hand was in her panties delicately stroking her sex.

She hadn't stopped at his arrival.

"I couldn't have dreamed you'd be like this. I believe I'm dreaming now."

She arched her back.

"Were you thinking of me?" *Say yes. . . .* He didn't think he'd ever wanted to hear anything so badly.

Her whiskey voice was as sexy as her body. *"Yes, Wroth."*

He groaned. "What were you thinking of?"

"Of you drinking me while you were inside me," she said, moaning the last words.

Craving his bite too? "A dream."

She licked her lips. "In your dream do you make me wait for you much longer?"

"You want this freely?" He reached to unbuckle his belt, surprised to find how difficult it had become. Finally, he just tore it apart. Her hips rolled in reaction.

"Yes."

"No games?"

"No," she panted, "just need you inside me."

"Your body wants to be fucked?"

She gasped, her fingers teasing quicker. "Yes."

"By me?"

"Yes," she moaned.

He'd anticipated it would take months of planning to wear her down, until she truly wanted him, and they wouldn't have to play at commands and power.

Yet here she was stroking herself in his bed as she awaited his return. *In his bed, waiting.* It was too impossible, and he grew suspicious. "Convince me."

Her gaze flickered over his face, her eyelids heavy as she slowly, sensuously drew her fingers away from herself. She rose, sauntered to the wall, then tugged aside the flimsy string of her wisp of underwear.

Without a word, she simply spread her legs and leaned forward until her forearms rested against the wall. When the position raised her ass and bared her lush sex, he rasped, "You make a compelling argument." He was overwhelmed by the sight of her flesh waiting to be filled and by the fact that *she* began this, had masturbated to thoughts of him fucking her. . . .

He kicked his boots off, ripping his clothing away, then stood behind her. He slipped his thumb into her tightness, briefly closing his eyes to find her so luscious and slick. Her entire body was trembling, which affected him so much. With a groan he replaced his thumb with one, then two fingers. "In my dream I do fuck you. But I start slowly, feeding my cock into you inch by inch. When you're dripping wet and ready, I fuck you with all the strength in my body."

With a little cry, she bent down more, raising her ass up higher. "What do I do?" she breathed.

"You come again and again from no command, just from pleasure."

He spread her, grasped himself, then fought not to plunge into her when the head touched her dewy heat. He shuddered violently from the battle, but wouldn't reward this gift from her by hurting her tight little sheath.

Yet the head was barely inside her when lightning exploded outside—because she was already coming, clawing furrows into the wall, gasping, *"Wroth,* now . . . please!"

"I am . . ." he groaned, clutching her hips, straining his every muscle to enter her slowly, to make this good for her—

His eyes widened when he felt her claws sink into his ass to yank him into her.

"Hard," she growled in a throaty voice.

"Don't hurt," he choked out, then with an answering growl, he thrust into her, forcing his cock through the squeezing spasms of her orgasm as though through a tightened fist. Even when he was seated deeply, she continued to climax around him. He could have stilled and let her body milk him.

But he wanted to *fuck* her. To take her so fiercely she would forget other men. To brand her as his own. He clenched her hips, withdrew, then rocked into her, hitting the end of her sex.

"Yes!" she cried.

"Can you know what that does to me?" he rasped, grinding his hips, stirring her. She moaned, hanging on to the wall. "To see you finger yourself to thoughts of me?" He withdrew completely then fell into her with another brutal thrust.

"Ah Wroth . . . yes, *oh, God . . .* " She came again suddenly, the manor shaking from the lightning. *"Drink,"* she sobbed to his disbelief. "Oh, God, please *drink from me."*

He ripped the lace to bare her breasts, then covered them with his hands, fingers pinching and tugging her nipples as he pulled her to his chest.

"You want my bite?"

"Yes," she moaned.

"As much as you want my cock?"

"Yes! Wroth, put *everything in me,* yes, yes, yes," she repeated, panting between her words, shoving and circling her hips back into him. His fangs pierced her skin just as he thrust.

She cupped his head to her neck hard so he wouldn't stop—then came again, moaning his name so that he felt her words as he bit her. He didn't stop, just snarled into her skin as he ejaculated, mindlessly grinding against her, hands squeezing her heavy breasts. Her blood scorched him inside as he pumped his come into her in wave after wave.

Afterward, when thought returned, he caught her up to his chest because she was unsteady, but then so was he. He withdrew slowly, then scooped her into his arms, crossing to the bed.

When he gazed down at her, he saw her eyes were silver and her lips were curling into a smile.

He stared, still disbelieving. "Like that, did you?"

She nodded.

"Want more?" he asked as he tossed her on the bed.

In answer, she went to her knees, pulled aside her hair and offered him the unbitten side of her neck.

His voice was ragged with lust. "That wasn't quite what I meant, but we can work something out. . . ."

The more hours toward dawn that they spent licking, fucking and both of them biting, the more overwhelming the mind-boggling pleasure—the less he could believe that this was his Bride, happily—no, aggressively—partaking.

And at the end of the night, he stared down at her in puzzlement. He didn't know which facet of her he liked better. The siren in black satin that made his cock and fangs ache or this angel with her bright red hair spread across his pillow—who made his chest ache.

She brushed the backs of her fingers along his face.

"Wroth, I want this to grow naturally between us without the chain," she whispered up to him. "Vow you'll give it back in two weeks time. Just give us a chance, give me a chance to want this freely."

He wanted to believe in her—and in himself, that he could convince her to stay. He'd already wanted to command her to close her eyes and open her palms, and then see her face once he'd poured the chain into them.

Two weeks to win her. "Yes, *milaya,* I vow it."

Nothing in his human life or his vampire existence had prepared him for living with a Valkyrie.

Myst had boundless energy, she was powerful, and she exuded an almost otherworldly sensuality that set his blood on fire. Each night he traced her to different locations to make love to her. He'd had her against the foot of a pyramid, gazed in awe as she rode him on a moonlit beach in Greece, licked her sex beneath a redwood until she begged for mercy. . . .

Throughout those nights, once he and Myst had worked the edge off their need, they talked for hours and he learned more about her and her kind. He'd given her the cross she'd admired at Oblak, but when the jewels glinted in their room's gaslight, she'd seemed to go into a trance. Finally, he'd covered it, and once she'd shaken herself, she'd admitted, "We all inherited Freya's acquisitiveness. Shining things, jewels and gems . . . We can't tear our gaze away without training for years and sudden glittering is sometimes irresistible."

Wroth had inwardly cursed that she had this vulnerability. He'd thought the Valkyrie were an almost perfect creature—no need to eat, immortal, strengthening with age—but he'd since learned that they were one of the few species of the Lore that could die of sorrow. And if one was weakened the others suffered since they were all connected with a "collective" power.

He couldn't always be there to protect her. Though he'd tried to use the chain as little as possible, he'd whispered to her as she slept that she would no longer have these weaknesses.

Wroth would have been content to hear only about her, but she'd been surprisingly curious about his past. He found himself revealing things he never had to anyone, yet feeling unburdened from it.

He'd told her of the pain he and Murdoch had felt to return home and see their other six siblings and their father dying of plague. Myst's eyes had watered as he'd spoken of the gut-wrenching decision to make them drink. Then came the agonizing vigil as they wondered if their family would be reborn, any of them. In the end, they'd lost their father and sisters, but regained their two brothers.

The night he himself had "died" seemed to fascinate her, and she repeatedly asked him to tell her the story of how he'd made demands of Kristoff. She never failed to tell him how proud she was of him. That comment had made him feel particularly uneasy. These days there wasn't much he was proud about. He avoided Kristoff, telling him little when they did meet. He was coercing his Bride to stay with him, and he suspected that if, at the end of the two weeks, she wanted to leave him, he'd break his vow to her in a heartbeat's time.

He sought any hint that might tell him how she felt and what she might decide. At times he was optimistic. When they fought mock battles with a game based on military strategy, she seemed to enjoy herself—and to like the fact that he always beat her. She wasn't a strategist, she'd explained to him. She was "front-line badassness" but she appreciated his talent. One time she had stood and sidled over to straddle him, placing his hands on her breasts. As she slid down his shaft, she whispered in his ear, "My wise warlord. You make my toes curl you're so good." He'd shuddered violently and had to fight not to come in an instant.

In fact she seemed to delight in every reminder that he'd fought and warred. She'd admired his sword, eyes widening at the considerable weight of it, only to narrow on him and grow silver with want. Her eyes had only to flicker silver and he went hard as iron.

And last night, as they lay spent in bed, he'd finally asked her, "What do you find attractive about me?" That could possibly compete against a demigod with a "mind-shattering kiss."

Without hesitation, she answered, "Your scars."

His brows drew together in surprise. "What? Why?"

"They're evidence of the pain you've survived. Pain survived builds strength." She traced down his stomach. "This is the one that killed you?"

"Yes."

"Then this one I admire the most." She brushed her lips so tenderly over it. "It brought you to me."

But his contentment was never whole. He'd never been in love, didn't believe he'd even slept with the same woman twice, yet now he wanted *everything* from this pagan immortal, was sick with wanting her. He wanted to strip her soul bare and make her give all of herself, all of what she'd been in the beginning before time twisted her.

His dreams reminded him of her past, preventing him from falling for her completely. Though he'd thankfully never seen her making love to another—and for some reason, he believed he never would—he drove himself mad with the mere idea of the lovers she'd taken into her body. He made himself crazed wondering how he compared to them. Each wicked thing she did to him that had him staring at the ceiling in an agony of pleasure and shock had him wondering later where she'd learned it.

How many had she had? She was two thousand years old. One bedmate a year? Two a year? One lover a month . . . ?

And how could he compete with *gods* for her? She was a creature so passionate and beautiful, it was clear she'd been made to be loved by them alone.

The dreams kept him from believing and falling into the life they could share—the life he wanted so badly he could taste it.

He dreaded sleep and took no succor from it, growing weary with each day though her blood built his muscle, making him physically stronger than he'd ever imagined. Each sunset, he treated her coldly, so she asked about his dreams. But he lied.

She would accept his reassurance, smiling over at him from her window seat. Her smile could bring down an army. *Probably had.*

How had he thought he was a match for it?

My apologies, Myst thought as she gazed down at Wroth, rolling her hips on him, but she was enjoying the hell out of her vampire.

His eyes were so fierce, his gorgeous, sculpted muscles rigid beneath her claws as she leaned forward to cup her breast to his mouth. He suckled and groaned around her nipple as he tensed to come, and when she exploded, he shot hotly inside her. She fell limp on top of him, loving it when he put his arms around her and clenched her into his chest as he shuddered for long moments afterward.

When he finally let her go with a kiss so he could dress and leave for Oblak, she said, "Okay. I'm down with being your dirty little secret out here—for now. But I can't just sit in this room for hours when you leave."

"What do you need, love?" he asked, piling her curls atop her head. He seemed fascinated by her hair, always touching it.

Wait, he'd called her *love?* Cool. "Do you know what an Xbox is? No? Well, your Bride has a teeny little addiction to it. . . ."

She wrote down the model of the console and the games she wanted as he showered and dressed. Just before he traced, she took his hands and gazed up at him solemnly. "Bring this back and you might as well have slayed a dragon for me."

As she waited, she painted her toenails—Valkyrie loved painting their nails since it was the only way they could semi-permanently alter their appearance—and reflected on how easily she'd settled in here.

In fact, there were only three things that prevented her from being truly comfortable in this situation. The first? Though they traveled most nights, he wouldn't take her to meet his friends and family and wouldn't let her see hers either. He'd explained that he wanted her undivided attention for these two weeks.

She suspected he was waiting until their relationship was cemented, which he believed would be in three days—the end of what she called the two-week vampire demo. Had it resulted in a sale? She knew it would mean pariah-hood in the Lore and having to give up her family. She could just imagine bringing Wroth to the coven. Her sisters would thank her for the surprise then pounce on him, swords and claws flying with glee.

As twin sister to Furie, Cara alone would fight him to the death simply for what he was. And though Wroth was incredibly powerful, Cara was quick, with thousands of years more experience and the boiling hatred of a separated twin. The two of them together would be like Godzilla versus Mothra, or some serious epic shite.

Her second concern was her worry for him. He often traced to Oblak, and each time she wondered if he would face some faction of the Lore intent on killing him just for being a vampire. She believed him when he told her of Kristoff's agenda and saw no conflict of interest with her covens, so call her an awful person, but she'd turned informant, teaching him how to protect himself.

Her third beef was that each sunset when they woke he was unbearably surly and curt with her. She feared he'd seen memories of her flirting or even making love—though Nïx had once told her that recipients of visions never saw things they couldn't recover from and usually only witnessed major, life-changing events. He'd assured her again and again that it was nothing, but Myst had suspicions. Yet she could tolerate his moods because he spent the rest of the night treating her like a queen.

Just when her toenails had dried, he returned with the slayed dragon and its attendant games and set them at her feet. He looked at her with his brows drawn like he'd missed her, and her heart did funky twisty things in her chest. The impulse came to jump him, so she did.

Only after he'd squeezed her up in his arms did she realize she'd run to get within them.

CHAPTER TEN

*W*roth shot up in bed, feeling nauseated, physically ill from his nightmares.

He'd been lashed by the usual dreams of her gloating at a gravesite, then the Roman stroking himself as she slowly dragged her skirt up her thighs. "I'll possess Myst the Coveted. . . ."

But details of the memories became more evident each time. This time he'd heard Myst's amused thoughts at his words—*No one possesses me, but in their fantasies. I'll kill you as easily as kiss you. . . .* "And I'll be yours, only yours," she purred, though she detested him.

Now he'd seen something new. A different, more recent memory. Myst was smoothing on hose, her foot daintily placed on his bed, as she made a decision to . . . *trick him?* To act as though she'd capitulated easily in order to get her chain back.

Play at love and act at surrender.

He gripped his forehead in his hand. Irrationally, he

waited for the soft touch of her hand on his back. She was his Bride, his *wife,* and she offered him no comfort.

Even had she truly had that urge, she couldn't, since he was still secretly commanding her to sleep throughout the day. So she wouldn't run away from him and leave him in torment again.

Kill you as easily as kiss you . . .

He'd thought they'd had a place to start from, to move forward from, but he'd been fooled by her beauty and abandon. She'd seduced him, made sure he "caught" her working her body that same night, knowing he would lose his mind at the sight.

He was as much a fool as the Roman, besotted with a fantasy that didn't exist. At least that long-dead Roman had suffered no delusions that she could care for him. He'd known that she was incapable of feeling and had wanted possession only.

Wroth had been falling for a fantasy, one that easily manipulated him.

She desired her freedom and she would use whatever means she had available to get it, leaving him as soon as she'd succeeded.

Fool.

When Myst woke, she burrowed down into the covers, feeling relaxed and content to her toes.

Today was D-day—delivery day for the chain—the end of the demo that she realized *had* resulted in a sale.

She snuggled into his pillow, loving his scent, and considered her new feelings. She'd feared her life as she'd known it had ended the minute he'd vowed to give her the chain back. It was a leap of faith on his part and she'd *responded* to it. Responded in kind. It was a bit ironic that she'd smugly planned to punk him only to get snared in her own machinations. She'd lasted only a few days playing easy till she *went* easy, her femme fatale plans culminating in the oh-sonefarious leap into his arms.

She grinned into the pillow. She'd take back her chain, but only because it looked so damned sassy on her.

When she rose and stretched, she found him watching her. Her grin widened, but he didn't return her smile, just glanced at her bare breasts and snapped, "Put on some clothes."

She drew her head back, frowning. "Are you angry with me?" He was usually brusque when they woke, but she could tell this was much worse. She was baffled by what could have happened since she'd gone to sleep, tucked against his chest, secure under his heavy arm. His eyes were somehow crazed and bleak at the same time, his face exhausted. Alarm began to build inside her.

"We have a lot to discuss tonight." He tossed her a robe. "Put it on and sit here."

She had no choice but to comply. He traced away and was back seconds later, holding the chain fisted in his whitened grip. "Tonight we're going to make some adjustments between us—or more accurately, in you."

Her eyes widened. "Wroth, what are you doing?" she asked slowly. "You vowed to give it back today."

"A woman like you should understand broken vows."

"What are you talking about? How can you do this to me now?" The evening she'd decided to stay.

His face was crueler than she'd ever seen it. "You mean after the last two weeks? Just because you wanted to be fucked and I complied doesn't mean I won't treat you as you deserve."

She put the back of her hand to her face as if she'd been struck. He didn't say "treat you as a whore," didn't call her that, but somehow he made her feel it. "As I deserve," she repeated dumbly.

He grasped her arm, squeezing it hard. "I can't live like this, Myst. *With* this." At her confused expression, he said, "I've seen your past. I know what you were, what you are."

"What I was?" Her frown deepened. She hadn't lived her life perfectly—there'd been missteps and misjudgments—but she'd done little to be *ashamed* of. Was the killing too much for him to handle? He'd been a freaking warlord! "If you find me lacking, know that I regret very few of my actions over my long life."

That seemed to enrage him. "No? What about playing at love and acting at surrender?"

"Wroth, that was—"

"Silence." He kissed her roughly, harshly, though she struggled against him before he pulled back. "I've realized you are heartless." His eyes appeared tortured, his entire body tight with tension. "But what if I just ordered you to be kinder, then made you forget all the men that came be-

fore me? Made you forget all that, forget your vicious sisters who kill without remorse?"

She gasped, eyes watering, but she couldn't speak after his command. Her hands clenched. She'd never wanted to scream more in her life, and yet her lips parted silently in shock when he said, "I believe I'll just order you to want me so fiercely that you can't think of anything or anyone else—"

A voice interrupted from downstairs. "General Wroth, you're needed at Oblak immediately."

"*What?*" he bellowed. She felt his eyes on her as she staggered to the window seat, tears beginning to fall. She curled up, leaning her forehead against the glass.

"Your brother's been badly injured."

He pointed at her. "Stay here," he bit out, then disappeared. She heard him downstairs, locking away her freedom again, then he was gone once more. *Stay here?* In the room or the manor? He'd been so thrown by the news that he hadn't elaborated.

So stumbling, clutching at the wall as energy funneled out of her, she finally made her way to his study. She pulled aside the cabinet, finding the safe behind it. When she reached for the lock, her hand veered off course as though pushed by an unseen force. She bit her lip and tried again, fighting to simply brush the metal.

Commanded not to touch it. Just like he would command her to forget who she was, that she even had a family. Lightning cracked outside in time with a sob. He'd been about to do it.

It was true then. Vampires couldn't be trusted—he'd seemed out of his mind with rage. Why had she gone against all she'd ever learned to be with him?

The years had been weighing on her and she'd been overwhelmed by the yearning to simply lean on someone, just for a while, to have a partner to watch her back and hold her when she needed it. Surely she'd convinced herself to accept him because he was strong and she had grown so weak. No longer.

There were ways she could get around his orders—nimble thinking, creative reasoning. As tears poured from her eyes and the lightning grew to constant furious bolts, she tore at the wall, at the very stone that housed it.

So he would use her? Like a toy. A mindless slave. *Adjustments?*

Toy, bait, whore . . . *Just because you wanted to be fucked,* he'd sneered.

Two millennia of people thinking they could use her. Always using her.

She'd take this safe with her teeth if she had to.

"You should see the other guy," Murdoch grated from his bed when Wroth traced into his room.

Wroth shuddered to see his brother's face torn and limbs broken like this even while knowing he couldn't die from anything short of a beheading or sunlight. He shook himself. "What has happened to you?" he asked, his voice a rasp.

"About to ask you the same. My God, Nikolai, you look worse than I do."

He thought about how he'd left Myst at the window, crying, staring out at the lightning storm that came from within her. It pained him so much to think of her hurting alone. . . ."We'll talk of my problems later. Who has done this to you?"

"Ivo has demons. Demons turned vampires. They are strong—you can't imagine it. He is looking for someone, but I don't think it's your Bride—they mentioned something about a 'halfling'."

"How many?"

"There were three in his party—other vampires as well. We took down two of the demons but one remains." He glanced behind him. "Where's your Bride?"

After a hesitation, he explained everything, seeking the same unburdening he felt when he spoke with Myst. His brother's expression grew stark.

Long moments of silence passed before he said incredulously, "Wroth, you took away the free will of a creature that has had it for two thousand years. A good wager says she's going to want it back."

"No, you don't understand. She's callous. Incapable of love. It eats at me, her deception, because it's the only thing that makes sense." More to himself, he muttered, "Why else would she want me?"

Murdoch weakly grabbed Wroth's wrist. "For all these years I've seen you continually choose the best, most rational course, even if it's the most difficult. I've been proud to follow your leadership because you've acted with courage and always—always—with rationality. I never thought I would have to inform you that your reason and judgment have failed you, Nikolai. If she's as bad as you say then you have to . . . I don't know, just help her change, but you can't *order* this. Get back to her. Explain your fears to her."

"I don't think I can. You saw her, Murdoch. Why would she so quickly acquiesce?"

"Why don't you just ask her?"

Because I don't want to show her again how craven I've become with wanting her.

"And about the other men—this isn't the sixteen hundreds anymore," Murdoch said. "This isn't even the same plane. She's immortal, not an eighteen-year-old blushing bride straight from a convent. She can't change these things, so if you want her, you have to adjust."

Wroth ran a hand over his face and snapped, "When did you get so bloody understanding?"

Murdoch shrugged. "I had someone explain a few rules of the Lore to me and learned we can't apply our human expectations to the beings within it."

"Who told you this?" When he didn't answer, Wroth didn't press, not with all the secrets he'd been keeping. "Will you be all right?" he asked.

"That's the thing about being immortal. It'll always look worse than it is."

Wroth attempted a grin and failed.

"Good luck, Nikolai."

Outside of the room, he spoke with those watching over Murdoch and emphasized what would happen to them should his brother worsen, then contemplated tracing back.

He was almost glad when Kristoff called a meeting about this newest threat, grateful for the time to cool off before he faced Myst again.

Kristoff didn't hesitate to ask, "Why didn't your wife tell you about the turned demons?"

"I don't know. I will ask her when I return." He wondered as well. Had she known? No, she'd been teaching him everything she knew—teaching him constantly.

Why would she do that if she only planned to leave him?

When he cringed, he realized Kristoff was still studying him.

"Something to add?"

He owed Kristoff his life and the life of his brothers. Three brothers and for Myst herself, he owed his king. He would withhold information on Myst's kind but relate the rest. "I've learned a good deal about the Lore from her and want to discuss it with you, but I left my wife feeling poorly. I'd like to get back to her."

"By all means," Kristoff said, his face unreadable. "But tomorrow we'll talk of this."

Wroth nodded, then traced back to Myst, frowning as a hazy idea surfaced in the turmoil of his mind. Had his brother's heart been beating earlier? But before he could contemplate this further, Wroth's attention was distracted by Myst's sleeping form. He gazed down at her, chest aching as usual. Sometimes he damned his beating heart because of the pain that seemed to follow it.

Murdoch was right. She couldn't change what she was, and he'd wronged her today. If only he could *think* more clearly where she was concerned instead of reacting viscerally. *Primitively.* Before, he'd never understood when men talked of madness and love in the same breath. Now he understood.

He only hoped that when he asked her to forgive him *his* weakness, she could.

After undressing, he climbed into bed with her. He pulled her close to him, running his hand down her arm, burying his face in her hair and smelling her soft, sweet scent. Finally at dawn, he passed out with exhaustion. When he dreamed, he opened his mind to her memories, to what had become his nightmares. They superseded all his other visions of battle and famine because these hurt him the most. *See her in a sordid light. Punish yourself.*

See them all.

CHAPTER ELEVEN

*T*he dream of the Roman appeared first. Wroth impatiently waited through the usual scene, seeking to see more. Did he truly want to? Could he ever turn back from this?

Too late, it was done. He knew that he'd unlocked the floodgates and that these dreams were going to play out, each spinning to their gruesome, perverted endings.

Myst slowly lifted her skirt up. Yet then Wroth felt something new—chills crawling up her spine as she peered down at the Roman with his wet lips and furious stroking.

She was ashamed at her disgust and closed her mind off it. She was the bait. She'd be whatever it took to *free her sister.*

"I'll possess Myst the Coveted . . ."

No one possesses me but in their fantasies. I'll kill you as easily as kiss you. . . . The Roman sought to make her his plaything just as he had Daniela for these past six months.

Suddenly Myst glanced up and Wroth saw through her eyes. Lucia had Daniela in her covered arms, the girl's body limp and burned over most of her icy skin. Daniela had been tortured, Myst realized, by this animal at her feet, by his very touch. The familiar rage erupted within her. Control it. . . . Just a moment longer. . . . "And I'll be yours, only yours," she somehow purred.

When Lucia signaled, Myst nodded, extracting her foot, his lips producing a loud sucking sound that made her cringe. She tapped the man's bulbous nose with her big toe. In a tone dripping with sexuality, she said, "You probably won't live through what I'm about to do"—her voice had gone to a breathy whisper belying the words and confusing the man—"but if you survive, learn and tell others that you should never"—a tap with the toe—"ever"—tap—"harm a Valkyrie."

Then she punted him across the room—

Another scene began—the one with the raiding party, the one he'd always dreaded seeing the most. The men were nearing; he could hear her feigning heavy breathing, a stumble. All a part of the game.

One tackled her hard into the snow. The others pinned her arms. She was pretending fear, weakly struggling. While others cheered, a burly Viking knelt between her legs and told her, "I hope you live longer than the last ones did."

Lightning streaked behind the man's head and the wind seemed to follow it—a few looked around uneasily with nervous laughter.

"The last ones' names were Angritte and her daughter Carin," Myst informed him. Carin, so young, simple in the mind, had for some reason immediately recognized Myst for what she was. *"Swan maiden,"* the girl had whispered, uttering one of the Valkyries' more beautiful names.

Both the careless mother and her innocent daughter had been killed, smothered under the weight of these men as they brutalized them. "I will live longer than them—and you." A change came over her, like a bloodlust, thoughts turned feral, the rage . . .

The frown on the attacker's face was the last expression he'd ever make. She rose up, easily shaking off the powerful men. She had loved Carin for her very innocence and joy, and these beasts had stolen these things from Myst, from the world, which was poorer from the loss. . . .

As lightning painted the sky, she mindlessly slashed her way through them. When all but one were felled, she told the one she allowed to live, "Any time you think to hunt down a woman or to force her, wonder if she's not like me. I've spared you, but my sisters would unman you with a flick of their claws, their wrath unimaginable." She wiped her arm over her face, found it was wet.

She crouched over the man and could see her reflection in his eyes. "There are thousands of us out there. Lining these coasts, waiting." Her eyes were silver, and blood marked the side of her face. He was frozen in terror. "And I'm the gentle one."

She turned from him, dusting off her hands and said to herself, "This is how rumors get started." But her swagger disappeared at the site of the rough gravestones atop the hill by the sea—Carin's beside her mother's. "You stupid human," she hissed at the mother's. "I've cursed you to your hell."

"Why did you disobey me? I told you to take Carin inland in the spring when they come down. *Stay far from the coasts,*" she said, her voice breaking on a sob as she flew to the girl's tombstone. She curled up against it, her face resting against the crude inscription. Then she hit it, her blood trickling along the new jagged fracture.

She stayed like that, unmoving for days, as villagers held a vigil at the base of the hill, offering up tributes fit for a goddess for her protection and benevolence. Wroth shuddered at the physical pain Myst didn't seem to feel—her hand frozen in blood to the stone, her muscles knotted, and skin raw from cold. On the third day, her sister Nïx found her and lifted her from the snow as easily as a pillow. Tears were ice on her face.

"Shhh, Myst," Nïx murmured. "We've already heard the tales of your revenge. They'll never harm another maid. In fact, I doubt that league of men will ever trouble this coast again."

"But . . . the girl," Myst whispered, awash in confusion, tears streaming anew, "is simply *gone.*" The last word was a sob.

"Yes, dearling," Nïx said. "Never to return."

Myst was weeping. "But . . . but it *hurts* when they die."

Nïx pressed her lips to Myst's forehead, murmuring, *"And they always do."*

Wroth's chest ached with Myst's sorrow as no physical wound had ever hurt him. She'd run from the men because the ones who would chase a "helpless" maiden were the ones who would die. Wroth wanted to stay with that memory, to make sure she recovered from this hellish pain, but another familiar dream began. Snow outside, packed so high it covered half of the window. The meeting around the hearth. "*. . . teach her to be all that was good and honorable about the Valkyrie . . .*"

Myst closed her eyes against a memory—the one he'd struggled to see—that she could never erase, never alleviate. She remembered and she vowed again that she would be worthy.

She was in the middle of her first field of battle, there as a chooser of the slain. She'd been sent young, barely fifteen, because she'd been born of a brave Pict who'd plunged a dagger into her own heart. Myst was supposed to be like that.

But she wasn't. Not yet. She was sick with terror.

One hundred thousand men, cut to pieces, blood like a river up to her ankles. "They were all brave," she said, peering around her, dizzily turning in circles as electricity rolled from her in waves. Sounding lost, she whispered, "How am I to choose? A beggar handing out coins . . ." She began trembling uncontrollably with fear.

He wanted to be there to protect her, comfort her.

Another memory. New to him. Could he withstand another?

Myst ran to him when he returned to Blachmount from some errand, and as he'd squeezed her up into his arms and kissed her, she'd thought, *I just ran to get in his arms. I just . . . Whoa. Whoa. Uhn-uh.*

Wroth remembered she'd clambered down from him, looking flushed and panicky, joking about the Xbox, saying she felt "a little like Bobby Brown" for introducing him to the addictive game.

Now he knew why she'd panicked. Myst, along with all her sisters, had been taught that she would know her true partner when he opened his arms and she realized she'd forever run to get within them.

Wroth woke to his own yelling, thrashing over, clutching for her. Everything he'd thought about her was wrong. His chest hurt with the loss and anguish she'd experienced. *"You're free. Myst . . ."*

The bed was empty.

He shot to his feet, scanning the room, finding a bloody note on the table by the bed, under the cross. *A heart for a heart . . .*

Dread settled over him, numbing his mind, even as panic was sharp, stabbing at his body like a blade. He half-staggered, half-traced into the study, eyes falling on the safe wall. To his horror, he saw no safe, but as he neared, growing more sickened, he found blood on the stone that had housed it, clawed away in a frenzy. She'd dug through it to get to her chain, to her freedom.

Wroth fell to his knees, head bowed as a guttural sound of pain erupted from his chest. At the first opportunity, he'd offered her torture, only to follow it by stealing her freedom from her.

And then . . .

A heart for a heart. She'd made his beat. Had he broken hers?

He'd lost her. And he'd deserved to.

CHAPTER TWELVE

*T*he coven met around the safe, all of them waiting for Regin to swing the Sword of Wóden to cut through the vampire's mojo-protected metal. Wóden's sword cut through anything. Well, anything but the chain, as Myst and Regin could attest to after one scary experiment that nearly made Myst a good deal shorter.

The sisters were still debating who would accept the responsibility of the chain because Myst was no longer allowed, not as long as Wroth lived. But no one wanted the thing, and killing Wroth seemed a bingo solution to them.

Regin raised the sword above her, and even the wraiths flying outside that they'd hired to guard Val Hall against intruders—like Wroth—seemed to slow their circling to catch a window. With a dramatic breath, Regin sliced through the safe as easily as powder, though sparks flew. When all was clear, Myst wearily reached forward to collect her torment.

She frowned to find a small, ornate box of wood inside as

well. All of her sisters seemed to realize at the same time that it was about the size of those velvet jewelry boxes—because the room went quiet, then they dove for it like a wedding bouquet. "Shiny, in the box, shiny," one of the younger sisters whimpered. Myst was closest and snagged it and even if she hadn't been able to she would've bitch-slapped anyone who made a run with it.

"Open it, then," Regin cried, out of breath.

Myst did.

And light seemed to blaze from it.

"Great Freya," someone breathed. "Diamond. Big. Glittery."

Another said, "That's not a rock, that's real estate. When did vampires start coming off with the bling? No. Really."

Myst closed her fingers over what had to be a perfect four-karat diamond, so she could look at the actual ring. It was inscribed with her name.

Suddenly feeling exhausted, she rose, dragging her feet to her room away from the excitement, though they booed her for taking away "My Precious." The chain was heavy and cold in her other hand. Nïx followed her up. She was a good listener and even though her lucidity came in erratic spurts, she'd been a boon to talk to.

Myst eyed her sister as she raised the ring. "You didn't look surprised about this." Nïx's pupils enlarged at it before Myst tucked it and the chain in her jewelry case. "You knew what was in the safe?"

"I'm not predeterminationally-abled for nothing," she said as she dug two bottles of fingernail polish and some cotton from her pocket. She hopped on the bed and set them up to paint each other's toenails, patting the bed for Myst to come sit. Myst had missed this little ritual, but she had no interest just now. Instead she crossed to the window and said, "Nïx, why didn't you come for me? You knew how to find me."

"You were fated to spend that time with Wroth."

Wroth. Who had found her so lacking that he'd needed to change her.

What had he seen that disgusted him so much? She'd wracked her brain for the last three days, but found nothing she'd be truly ashamed of, certainly nothing that would make a vampire *lose his freaking mind*. "He's out there right now." Myst stared out into the fog-shrouded yard. "Watching this house, waiting for a chance to take me again. But if I stay behind the wraiths, then I'm just as contained here as I was there."

"Without the weakness of the chain, you could fight him, yes?" Nïx asked. "I even imagine kicking some vampire tail might be good for you."

A few moments later, Regin popped her head in. "Cara and I are going out to canoodle ghouls. You in?"

Myst frowned, then turned to Nïx. "Any reason I shouldn't?"

She bit her lip, staring at the ceiling as if trying to recall a memory when it was just the opposite. "No, I think it would be just the thing."

Myst nodded slowly. "Yeah, I think I could use a little goo."

Regin beamed, then bounded across the landing to scream downstairs, "Myst is back online!"

Ready to fight, needing it, she quickly dressed as Nïx did

a buff-job on her neglected sword. Myst had no doubt Wroth would be out there watching her and that she would sense him every hour. *How long would he follow his "tarnished" Bride?* she wondered, but she knew the answer, had felt the wild emotion roiling within him. He'd follow forever.

Wroth crept among the shadows as Myst split up from Regin and Cara at a sprawling cemetery. Myst easily vaulted to the top of a mausoleum to observe the field below her, where ghouls snapped and clashed against each other or lazed in the dampness of the night.

He was spellbound, watching as she rested on the edge of the roof, perched down as a gargoyle might. Her eyes swirled silver and her claws curled into the clay tile. She was clearly eager for the kill but waited, studying them. This was the first time he'd seen her in days.

After Wroth had found her gone from Blachmount, he'd traced to her eerie home, but found it had just gotten eerier. Ghostly, howling creatures in ragged red cloth circled the manor like a tornado. He'd shrugged and traced to her room, but the things caught him. They had a grip he couldn't have imagined, and when he'd finally landed, his lesson had been learned. He rotated his arm, pleased he'd finally been able to force it back into its socket.

Those beings circled the house to protect it, and did so without cease and without fail, as he could well attest to. But the sentinel that protected Myst from threats like Ivo kept Wroth from her as well. Myst stayed behind them for night upon night, yet now he'd finally found her outside of their protection, no doubt waiting for her sisters to return so they could attack.

But dawn was coming soon and he needed to—

She leapt from the roof, drawing her sword from her back sheath as she dropped into the middle of the group of ghouls. There were at least fifty of them.

"What the fuck are you doing?" he bellowed, tracing to her side, unsheathing his own sword.

"This isn't happening," she said to herself. "You're not going to ruin my personal life *and* my fast-track career, Wroth."

"But in the middle?"

"I'm enraged enough to do this. You have no idea"—she struck out, slicing a ghoul from crotch to neck—"how much I need this."

"I do have an idea." A perfect one. He'd felt her rage and her need to fight from inside him. And yet he'd told her that as his wife she would never again fight.

"You had better leave, because once I finish with them, I won't stop there."

"I deserve your anger. I've wronged you and seek to make amends." He wasn't optimistic about his chances for that. She couldn't be all things to him already and then forgiving on top of that.

"You think?" When one ghoul's claw came close to his neck, he leapt back and she snapped, "Don't let them scratch you!"

"Concerned for me, Myst?" He didn't dare hope.

"Of course I don't want you to get scratched." She eyed him. "Vampires are easier to kill."

"If I help you will you speak with me?"

"Don't need your help." And she didn't. She was merrily felling them one after another with a skill that awed him, her sword flying so fast it was barely visible.

"Then you'll have to listen here," he grated, digging into the fight with her. "I'd had five years of torment. I'd had a hell of wanting you and feared you would leave me at the first opportunity. Then I had dreams of your memories." These ghouls were irritating him, especially when they got between him and Myst while he was trying to convince her about something so critical. He began killing them more quickly. "In each one you were evil . . . a seductress."

"Still am, Wroth." She kicked a ghoul in the belly, freeing her sword from his chest.

"No, you're not—"

"Duck!" Her sword whistled over his head to decapitate a ghoul behind him. "Yeah, well, as I recall, every sunset I asked you about your dreams and you brushed away my concerns."

He slew two with one sword thrust. "I know. I should have asked you, because all those excruciating scenes of you . . . doing things were all out of context." When the largest ghoul out there howled and attacked him, Wroth stabbed the thing in the face, dropping it. She raised her eyebrows as if impressed, then scowled, remembering herself.

"Myst, even then I was still falling for you."

That at least got her to pause. She blew a curl out of her eyes and just when he tensed to trace behind her, she took two hands and plunged her sword back along her side to kill the ghoul at her back.

Now he raised his eyebrows, but continued, "I was angry when I saw your plan to trick me, but I finally understand that you rightly wanted your freedom back. I know what and who you are now. I saw all the memories, clearly at last. Not out of context." Goddamn it, more ghouls? "Myst, can we not just speak about this? Away from here? Dawn nears and all I ask is for a chance to—"

"I gave you a chance. Freely. And you threw it away. You were about to brainwash me."

With one hand, he carved at a ghoul. "I couldn't have lived with myself for that. I was wrong in many ways. I took your freedom when you needed it, and I hurt you just when you'd given yourself to me." Never had he regretted his actions so much.

He could have *won* her. *A heart for a heart*.

"I wanted you so badly I resorted to anything I could and treated you ill when you didn't deserve it." He looked around. He'd been so intent on her, he'd scarcely noticed they'd cut such a swath that the others had run. "If you give me a chance, I will make it up to you."

"Oh, you got it, Wroth. Just let me go gift wrap my chain for you."

Wroth's eyes flickered black and his voice went low. "I'd destroy the thing if I saw it."

His reaction surprised her. "You'll certainly never get within arm's reach of it."

"Myst, I felt your feelings for me, felt you struggling against them. I know you care for me." Long moments passed as they stared into each other's eyes.

She was weak, undeserving of her family, she knew, especially when her heart had leapt at the sight of him. But she shook her head. "I can't. It's just too late. I have a lot to lose from this. I won't hurt my family by accepting you."

"Kristoff seeks peace. He would fight the Horde with you. There would be no conflict with them. And I would . . . make an effort with your sisters, Myst. I know how important they are to you now. Believe me, I know."

She tapped her chin. "So you can see why the idea of being forced to forget them made me cranky? Huh? And what if you saw more out of context? This would just happen again and again."

"I would not drink from you."

She rolled her eyes. "Yeah, just like I'm going to finally beat my Xbox addiction."

"I'm pleased you feel the same about that option. I've already vowed never to use the information to harm the Valkyrie in any way. And I would have to tell you everything I was thinking as if you could read my mind as well. We are wed. We *should* know each other's secrets. Myst, we are kindred."

That made her hesitate. She'd felt that way too. Kindred. *What the hell was she thinking? He'd been about to brainwash her.*

Making her voice firm, she said, "Wroth, I'm sorry, but I could never trust you—" Her words were cut off by a massive arm squeezing the breath from her throat. Not a ghoul. *A demon?* she thought wildly. *A turned demon?*

Wroth raised his sword, a savage, killing look in his eyes, but the arm tightened and he froze.

"I wouldn't do that if I were you," Ivo said as he sauntered to the front of his gang of vampires. "He'll snap her head right from her neck." Ivo's red gaze flickered over her. "Now Myst, I thought I told you to wait in my dungeon." To the demon, he said, "She's not the one."

He narrowed his eyes at Wroth. "So you're the turned human who took my castle from me. Grenades? Guns? I'll kill you just for bastardizing our war." He glanced from Wroth to Myst, then back again, smiling to see Wroth's body seeming to vibrate with tension. "I believe I have something he wants very badly indeed. I'll take his life in exchange."

The demon held her neck tight in his grip. She struggled against him until she could breathe, but he was unbelievably powerful. He was a turned demon, supposed to be a true myth. Apparently, the Horde had just upped their game. She'd known he'd been up to something. . . .

Wroth could trace away in a heartbeat. They couldn't get him, unless they had her. Wroth's eyes were assessing, and she could see him studying the situation.

"You walk into the sun, and I'll vow to the Lore that I'll free her. I'll hunt her again, but for this dawn I vow that she'll live. If you trace instead, I'll take her back to Helvita and dine on her perfect flesh every night for eternity."

"Fight me, coward," Wroth bit out, his eyes black with rage, his muscles tense and knotted with it.

"Why would I do that?" Ivo sounded confused. "Fight you for the cards I already hold?"

Wroth was so big and powerful and yet that strength was useless to him now because they wouldn't fight. She could feel his frustration roiling from his body in waves.

"You know we've got the power here. And you know my vow will compel me to release her."

She'd seen Wroth examining the situation, and she saw the exact moment that he determined his options. A calm seemed to wash over him.

"Her life or yours."

One tight nod. "Done." No hesitation. "It is done."

"Catch and release?" Myst sneered to Ivo as he and his gang traced with her back into the shade to ready for the dawn. Birdsong had begun. "Are you kidding me?" To Wroth, she said, "Are you eager to be ash?"

The sunlight hit the tops of the trees, descending inch by torturing inch. He stood sure and so brave, as if he was proud to give his life for hers.

The morning breeze blew his hair from his face. His eyes were riveted to hers.

The sunlight was inches away from him, almost reaching the moss of the great oaks that buckled the feet of the mausoleums. Now *she* felt frustration as she'd never known. "Wroth, don't be stupid."

In a low, steady tone, he said, "I love you, Myst."

Feeling erupted in her chest to answer his words. Yes, he'd wronged her, and yes, he was a vampire, but . . .

The light hit him. He did not close his eyes to the extreme brightness that would have hurt even her eyes.

And she knew it was because he wanted to see her longer.

Soon the intensity of the sun was too great; he fell to his knees, his hands curling in agonizing pain. He opened his eyes once more. Glowing, bare. A last look.

He's going to die.

They always do.

Just . . . gone.

"No." Saying the word out loud was like blasting a mountain to free an avalanche. An immortal like him didn't have to die. He could stay with her. "No, no, *no.*"

"*Milaya,* don't fight," he bit out. "It is done."

The demon holding her smelled of rotting flesh. The cowardly gang of vampires smirked at Wroth's death when Wroth was so much greater than they. How dare they?

She'd waited millennia to love—she'd waited for *him*—and they dared take him from her. From Myst the Coveted. She screamed long and loud with the shriek her kind was known for. The one that preceded death. The demon cursed and fought to snap her neck, but her muscles had lain in perfect concert and alignment to prevent it.

Wroth struggled toward her, trying to get to her even as he burned as though from the inside. Battling to save her as he *died.*

He was hers.

She freed her arms and raised them up. Lightning leapt to enter her grasp and filled her body. That they would *dare* . . .

The two holding her were blown from her, percussive thunder exploding them from within. Her hand shot down to collect one's sword just as he was cast into the light.

She struck out, slashing and clawing at the others with the rare gift of direct lightning from the sleeping ones pouring strength into her. She cut through the number, barely flinching when her arm was broken and the butt of a sword cracked her cheekbone. *Don't look through that eye, switch hands.* She cut a swath to Ivo, who alone remained.

"And here I thought you were merely the pretty one." With a mock bow, the coward traced.

Arm shattered, face beaten to a pulp, she flew to Wroth. She vainly attempted to cover his body, dragging him into the cool shade even as she bit her wrist open for him to drink. He was unconscious, his body twisting in pain, his skin looking like lava burned within him.

"Seems like we missed the party," Regin said as she and Cara strolled over to Myst. "Why does Myst get to kill all the vampires? No. Really. This was just supposed to be ghouls."

"Myst, what are you doing? We heard your scream and thought it was something *important*," Cara said. She waved a dismissive hand at Wroth's writhing form, clearly unable to comprehend why Myst was frantically dragging him with one arm while shoving her gashed wrist at his lips. "The being dies. Leave him."

Regin added, "Oh, for Freya's sake, Myst. He's a vampire. Let him fricassee."

Myst shrieked and snapped her teeth at her sisters. Then she screamed two words she'd never uttered in her entire life—

"Help me."

CHAPTER THIRTEEN

Wroth woke to wetness on his chest.

Her silky hair tumbled over his arm. When he opened his eyes he realized she was crying over him. Impossible. "Myst?" he rasped.

Her head shot up and she gave him a watery smile that quickly faded. She slapped him, a hard, cracking blow. Then she leapt on him, nuzzling, squeezing, as if she couldn't get close enough to him, as if she wanted *in* him.

"Don't you ever do anything so stupid again." She slapped at his chest, which he was surprised to find was healed.

He flexed and tensed his muscles throughout. He was bandaged in places, but he had all his limbs. This was good. Now if he could just get his wife to cease slapping him. "If you do not stop, *milaya,* we will have words."

So she turned to kissing him again with whispers in his ear and tears dropping to his face, each one like a gift. "You've been out for five nights. And you wouldn't *wake the hell up.*"

"Where are we?"

"In Val Hall."

He stiffened.

"No, you're safe." She leaned back and raised an eyebrow. "Do you think I would just let my sisters fall on you like a carcass?"

He winced at the image. "Can't wait to meet them all. How did you get away?"

"Ivo traced, but Cara and Regin are on his trail."

"I'm just glad I was there to save you," Wroth said solemnly, making her grin. "Did you kill the turned demon?"

"The lightning and I did."

He remembered then. She'd been hit directly, hair whipping, eyes silver, the most awing sight he'd ever witnessed. "I *saw* you get struck." His voice went low. "You smiled."

"It feels good. It's very rare to get a direct hit—"

Outside, something, some male, howled with fury. Wroth tensed to trace her away.

"Oh, don't worry. Just another crazy day at the manor." She waved away his tension. "A Lykae nabbed little Emmaline and took her back to Scotland—thinks she's his werewolf queen or something."

"Werewolf queen?"

"Uh-huh. So Lucia trapped the Lykae's brother for leverage, but apparently he's proving most uncooperative. Anyway, if you knew Em you'd see how ridiculous the idea is. She's terrified of her own shadow, much less a roaring Lykae's unique . . . appetites."

He'd have to ask her about that later. "She's the halfling—the one that's part vampire." When her brows drew together he rushed to assure her, "I will never tell Kristoff about her, but I suspect that Ivo's searching for her."

"They know. They'd already sent a retrieval party after her, and once they bring her back, she'll be safe here. The wraiths will shut out any threat." One flew by the window at that moment cackling to punctuate her statement.

He raised his eyebrows and when she grinned, he cupped her face with a bandaged hand. "I love you."

"I know."

"Could you . . . could you feel the same way? Before you answer, I want you to know that I meant what I said. I am sorry for forcing you to stay and for losing my head. I will always be shamed by my actions."

"Wroth, I wanted to stay with you after, oh—*about a day!* I'd planned to play you, but realized early that I was falling in love with you."

He hadn't heard her correctly. Yes, she'd been upset over his injuries, but that didn't mean she *loved* him. "You're saying you love me too?"

She nibbled her lip and nodded. "I'd always had a crush on you, you know."

When he frowned, she said, "I used to adore hearing tales about you. And was saddened when we'd heard you'd died. Then to meet you in person?" She blushed a little. "I found that you lived up to my fantasy of you."

He was bewildered to hear this from his fierce, stunningly beautiful wife. In a gravelly voice, he spoke an utter understatement, "That gives my ego a bit of a boost coming from you."

Her lips curled. "Among other things, the uncommon gift of a direct strike of lightning, *and* the fact that you were the only man able to free me from my chain, *and* the fact that you were so sodding eager to give up your life for mine—though mind you, if you try that again, I'm going to kill you—have all convinced me that we should be together."

"Always, Myst. I'd do it easily." When she was about to protest, he asked, "What about your family? I will try if they will."

"For all the reasons I just listed, a couple of my sisters have decided they'll try to overcome their repugnance of you."

He scowled at that. "Big-minded of them."

"Yet they want nothing to do with Kristoff or any among your order. You're the exception because they felt like they knew you as a human and because of what has happened between us. But if, say, your brother showed up here, they'd . . . it would be . . . bad."

"I understand."

"If you can make a genuine effort, I believe they will all come to accept you in time."

He wanted to be clear on this. "Accept you as my wife and me as your husband?" He wanted everything from her. Not just a few decades. He wanted eternity. And as long as she was in a giving mood . . .

She nodded, a smile playing about her pink lips. "We still have a lot to muddle through, mind you. Our families and our factions, and who controls the remote, and living logistics—because Blachmount needs TLC *and* lightning rods in a bad way . . . But I suppose I have to take possession of you, since I've already taken possession of my engagement ring."

He grinned. "You liked that, did you?"

"I couldn't take my eyes off of it," she said with a saucy smile.

He clasped her to him and pulled her close, knowing she craved being wrapped tight and secure in his arms as much as he needed her soft and trusting within them. "I can't quite believe this. Even after everything?" If she could give him another chance, Wroth thought they could do anything together.

"Yes. But . . ." She stroked the smooth backs of her claws down his arm. "You'll have to spend eternity making it up to me."

He released her to lever himself above her, cupping the back of her neck. His gaze flickered over her face, then met the eyes of his wife as she smiled up at him. Feeling love for her so strong it hurt him, his voice ragged with it, he rasped, *"Milaya,* it is done."

If you enjoyed Kresley Cole's
"The Warlord Wants Forever"
in *Playing Easy to Get*

Don't miss

A Hunger Like No Other

KRESLEY COLE

Coming April 2006 in paperback
from
Pocket Star Books

Here's a preview of
A Hunger Like No Other

PROLOGUE

Sometimes the fire that licks the skin from his bones dies down.

It is *his* fire. In a recess of his mind still capable of rational thought, he believes this. His fire because he's fed it for centuries with his destroyed body and decaying mind.

Long ago—and who knew how much time has toiled past—the Vampire Horde trapped him in these catacombs deep beneath Paris. He stands chained against a rock, pinned at two places on each limb and one around his neck. Before him—an opening into hell that spews fire.

Here he waits and suffers, offered to a column of fire that may weaken, but is neverending—neverending just like his life. His existence is to burn to death repeatedly only to have his dogged immortality revive him again.

Detailed fantasies of retribution have gotten him this far; nursing the rage in his heart is all he has.

Until her.

Over the centuries he could sometimes hear uncanny new things in the streets above, occasionally smell Paris changing seasons. But then he scented her, his mate, the one woman made for him alone.

The one woman he'd searched for without cease for a thousand years—up until the day of his capture.

The flames have ebbed. At this moment, she lingers somewhere above. It is enough. One arm strains against its bonds until the thick metal cuts into his skin. Blood drips, then pours. Every muscle in his weakened body works in concert, attempting to do what he's never been able to for an eternity before. For her, he can do this. He must. . . . His yell turns to a choking cough as he rips two bonds free.

He doesn't have time to disbelieve what he's accomplished. She is so close, he can almost feel her. *Need her.* Another arm wrenched free.

With both hands he clenches the metal biting into his neck, vaguely remembering the day the thick, long pin had been hammered into place. He knows its two ends are embedded at least three feet down. His strength is waning, but nothing will stop him when she's so close. In a rush of rock and dust, the metal comes loose, the recoil making him fling it across the cavernous space.

He rips at the bond wrapped tight around his thigh. He frees that and the one at his ankle, then begins on the last two of his other leg. Already envisioning his escape, not even glancing down, he pulls. Nothing. Brows drawn in confusion, he tries again. Straining, groaning with desperation. Nothing.

Her scent is fading—*there is no time.* He pitilessly regards his trapped leg. Imagining how he can bury himself in her and forget the pain, he reaches above his knee with shaking hands.

Yearning for that oblivion within her, he attempts to crack the bone. His weakness ensures this takes a half-dozen tries.

His claws slice his skin and muscle, but the nerve running the length of his femur is taut like a piano wire. When he even nears it, unimaginable pain stabs up its length and explodes in his upper body, making his vision go black.

Too weak. Bleeding too freely. The fire would build again soon. The vampires returned periodically. Would he lose her just when he's found her?

"*Never*," he grates. He surrenders himself up to the beast inside him, the beast that will take its freedom with its teeth, drink water from the gutters and scavenge refuse to survive. He sees the frenzied amputation as though watching a misery from a distance.

Crawling from his torture, abandoning his leg, he pulls himself into the shadows of the dank catacombs until he spies a passageway. Ever watchful of his enemies, he creeps through the bones littering the floor to reach it. He has no idea how far he has to go to escape, but he finds his way—and the strength—by following her scent. He regrets the pain he will give her. She will be so connected to him, she'll feel his suffering and horror as her own.

It can't be helped. He is escaping. Doing his part. Can she save him from his memories when his skin still burns?

He finally inches his way to the surface, then into a darkened alley. But her scent has faltered.

Fate has given her to him when he needs her most and God help him—*and this city*—if he can't find her. His brutality had been legendary, and he will unleash it without measure for her.

He fights to sit up against a wall. Clawing tracks into the brick street, he struggles to calm his ragged breaths so he can scent her once more.

Need her. Bury myself in her. Waited so long. . . .

Her scent is gone.

His eyes go wet and he shudders violently at the loss. An anguished roar makes the city tremble.

One week later . . .

On an island in the Seine, against the nighttime backdrop of an ageless cathedral, the denizens of Paris came out to play. Emmaline Troy wound around jugglers, fire eaters, and chanteurs de rue. She meandered through the tribes of black-clad Goths that swarmed Notre Dame like it was the Gothic mother ship calling them home. And still she attracted attention.

The human males she passed turned their heads slowly to regard her, frown in place, sensing something, but unsure. Probably some genetic memory from long ago that signaled her as their wildest fantasy or their darkest nightmare.

Emma was neither.

She was a co-ed—or recent Tulane grad—alone in Paris and hungry. Wearied from another failed search for blood, she sank onto a rustic bench beneath a chestnut tree, eyes riveted to a waitress pouring espresso at a stand. If only blood poured so easily, Emma thought. Yes, if it came warm and rich from an unending tap, then her stomach wouldn't be clenched in hunger at the mere idea.

Starving in Paris. And friendless. Was there ever such a

predicament? Couples strolling hand in hand along the gravel walk seemed to mock her loneliness. Was it just her or did lovers look more adoringly at each other in this city? Especially in the springtime. *Die, bastards.*

She sighed. It wasn't their fault that they were bastards who should die.

She'd been spurred to enter this fray by the prospect of her echoing hotel room and the idea that she might find another blood pusher in the City of Light. Her former hook-up had gone south—literally—fleeing Paris for Ibiza. He'd given little explanation for abandoning his job, saying only that with the "arrival of the risen king" some "serious epic shit" was brewing in "gay Paree." Whatever that meant.

As a vampire, she was a member of the Lore, that stratum of beings who've convinced humans they exist only in imagination. Yet though the Lore was thick here, Emma had been unable to replace her pusher. Any creatures she could scout out to ask fled her solely because she was a vampire. They scurried without knowing that she wasn't even a full-blooded one, nor that Emma was a wuss who'd never bitten another living being. As her fierce adoptive aunts loved to tell everyone, "Emma cries her pink tears if she dusts a moth's wings."

Emma had accomplished nothing on this trip that she'd insisted on. Her quest to uncover information about her deceased parents—her Valkyrie mother and her unknown vampire father—was a failure. A failure that would culminate in a call to her aunts to get them to retrieve her. Because she couldn't feed herself. Pitiful. She sighed. She'd be razzed about this for another seventy years—

She heard a crash, and before she even had time to feel bad for the waitress getting docked, another crash and then another followed. She tilted her head in curiosity just as a table umbrella across the walk shot fifteen feet up to be batted high in the sky, fluttering all the way to the Seine. A cruise boat honked and Gallic curses erupted.

Half-lit by the walk's torch lights, a towering man turned over café tables, artists' easels, and book stands selling century-old pornography. Tourists screamed and fled from the wake of destruction. Emma shot to her feet with a gasp, looping her satchel over her shoulder.

He was cutting a path directly to her. His size and his unnaturally fluid movements made her wonder if he could possibly be human. His hair was thick and long, concealing half his face, and several days' growth of beard shadowed his jaw.

He pointed a shaking hand at her. "*You*," he growled.

She jerked glances over both of her shoulders looking for the unfortunate *you* he was addressing. Her. Holy shite, this madman had settled on her. He turned his palm up and beckoned her to come to him—as if he was confident she would.

"Uh, I–I don't know you," she squeaked, trying to back up, but her legs immediately met the bench.

He continued stalking her, ignoring the tables between them, tossing them like toys instead of varying his direct pursuit of her. Furious intent burned in his pale blue eyes. She could sense his rage more sharply as he neared, unsettling her because her kind was considered the predator in the night—never the prey. And because at heart, she was a coward.

"*Come*," he bit out the word as though with difficulty and motioned for her again.

Eyes wide, she shook her head, then leapt backward over the bench, twisting in the air. She landed forward and began speeding down the quay. She was weak, more than two days without blood, but terror made her quick as she crossed the Archevêché Bridge to exit the island.

Three . . . four blocks covered. She chanced a look behind her. Didn't see him. Had she lost him? Sudden blaring music from her purse made her cry out. Who—in the hell—had programmed the Crazy Frog ring tone into her cell phone? Her eyes narrowed. Aunt Regin. The world's most immature immortal, who looked like a siren and behaved like a frat pledge.

In their coven, cell phones were for dire emergency only. Ringers would disturb their hunting in the back alleys of New Orleans, and even a vibration would be enough to trigger a twitching ear in a low creature. Forced to flip it open. Speak of the devil. Regin the Radiant.

"Little busy right now," Emma snapped, taking another peek over her shoulder.

"Drop your things. Don't take time to pack. Annika wants you at the executive airport immediately. *You're in danger.*"

"Duh." Click. That wasn't a warning—that was a narration. She'd ask the details once she was on the plane. As if she'd needed a reason to return home. Just the mention of danger and she would scamper back to her coven, to her Valkyrie aunts who would kill anything that threatened her and who would keep malice at bay.

As she tried to remember her way to the airport she'd landed in, the rain started to fall, warm and light at first—April lovers still laughing as they ran under awnings—but swiftly turning to pounding cold. She came to a crowded avenue, feeling safer as she wound through traffic. She dodged cars with their wipers and horns going full-force. She didn't see her pursuer.

With only the satchel slung around her neck, she traveled quickly, miles passing beneath her feet before she spied an open park and then the airfield just beyond it. She could see the diffused air around the jet engines as they warmed, could see the shades on every window already pulled tight. Almost there.

Emma convinced herself she'd lost him, because she *was* fast. She was also adept at convincing herself of things that might not be—good at pretending. She could pretend she took classes at night by choice and that blushing didn't make her thirsty—

A vicious growl sounded. Her eyes widened, but she didn't turn back, just sprinted across the field. She felt claws sink into her ankle a second before she was dragged to the muddy ground and thrown to her back. A hand covered her mouth though she'd been trained not to scream. "Never run from one such as me." Her attacker didn't sound human. "You will no' get away. *And we like it.*" His voice was guttural like a beast's, breaking, yet his accent was . . . Scottish?

As she peered up at him through the rain, he examined her with eyes that were golden in color one moment, then flickering that eerie blue the next. No, not human.

Up close, she could see his features were even, masculine. A

rong chin and jaw complemented the chiseled planes. He
s beautiful, so much so that she thought he had to be a fallen
el. Possible. How could *she* rule out anything?

The hand that had been covering her mouth roughly
rasped her chin. He narrowed his eyes, focusing on her lips—
n her barely noticeable fangs. "*No,*" he choked out the word.
No' possible. . . ." He yanked her head side to side, running
is face down her neck, smelling her, then growled in fury,
God damn you."

She shook her head, uncomprehending. "Please." She
nked against the rain, pleading with her eyes. "Y-you have
e wrong woman."

"Think I'd know you," he bit out as though speech was dif-
ult. "Make sure if you insist." He raised a hand . . . to touch
r? strike her? She fought, hissing desperately.

A calloused palm grasped the back of her neck, his other
and clenching her wrists. As he held her like this, he bent
down to her neck. Her body jerked from the feel of his tongue
against her skin. His mouth was hot in the chill, wet air, making her shudder until her muscles knotted. He groaned while
kissing her, his hand squeezing her wrists hard. Below her
skirt, drops of rain tracked down her thighs, shocking her with
cold.

"Don't do this! *Please . . .*" When her last word was a whimper, he seemed to come out of a trance, his brows drawing together as his eyes met hers, but he didn't release her hands.

He flicked his claw down her blouse and sliced it and the
flimsy bra beneath open, then slowly brushed the halves past
her breasts. She fought but it was useless against his strength.

He studied her with a greedy gaze as rain splattered do
stinging her naked breasts. She was shivering uncontrolla

She knew he could take her or tear open her unprote
belly and kill her. Yet he ripped open his own shirt, then pl
his huge palms against her back to draw her into his chest
groaned when their skin touched and electricity seem
flash through her. Lightning split the sky.

He rumbled foreign words against her ear. She felt
were . . . *tender* words—making her think she'd lost her n
She went limp while he shuddered against her, his lips so
in the pouring rain as he ran them down her neck, across
face, even brushing them over her eyelids. There he k
clutching her; there she lay boneless and dazed as she wat
the lightning streak above them.

His hand cradled the back of her head as he moved he
face him. He seemed torn as he watched her with some fie
emotion—she'd never been looked at so . . . consuming
Confusion overwhelmed her. Attack or let her go. *Let me go.*
tear slipped down her face, warmth streaking down amid the
drops of rain.

The look disappeared. "*Blood for tears?*" he roared, clearly
revolted by her pink tears. He turned away, blindly swatting at
her shirt to close it. "Take me to your home, vampire."

"I-I don't live here," she said in a strangled tone, staggered
by what had just occurred and by the fact that he knew what
she was.

"Take me to where you stay," he ordered, finally facing her
as he stood.

"No," she amazed herself by saying.

He, too, looked surprised. "Because you doona want me to walk? Good. I'll take you here on the grass on your hands and angles"—he lifted her easily until she was kneeling—"till well the sun rises." He must have seen her resignation because he hauled her to her feet and pushed at her to get her moving. "Who stays with you?"

"My husband, she wanted to snap. The linebacker who's going to kick your ass. Yet she would never have the nerve to provoke him. "I am alone."

"Your man lets you travel by yourself?" When she didn't answer, he said with a sneer, "You've a careless male for yourself then. His loss."

She stumbled in a pothole and he gently steadied her, then seemed angry with himself that he'd helped her. But when he heard them in front of a car, he threw her out of the way, leaping back at the sound of the horn. He swiped at the side of the car, his claws crumpling the metal like tinfoil, sending it reeling. When the car finally stopped, the engine block dropped to the street with a thud. The driver threw open the car door, dived for the street, then darted away.

Mouth open in shock, she frantically scrambled backward, realizing her captor looked as though he'd . . . *never seen a car.*

He crossed to her, looming over her, his black trench coat trailing in his wake. In a low, deadly tone, he grated, "I only hope you run from me again. . . ."